The Butchers

Brian Lane came to writing via fine art, experimental music and theatre. His longstanding preoccupation with the consequences of violent death led to the theatre production of his own *Red Roses for Lorca*. After working for the United Nations in Geneva and Vienna, he returned to Britain to found the Murder Club, compiling the eight-volume series, *The Murder Club Regional Guides to Great Britain*. Brian Lane lives in London.

The Butchers

A Casebook of Macabre Crimes and Forensic Detection

Brian Lane

This edition first published in 1998 by
Virgin Publishing Ltd
332 Ladbroke Grove
London W10 5AH

First published in 1991 by W H Allen & Co Plc

A catalogue record for this book is available from the British Library.

ISBN 0 86369 600 7

Typeset by Phoenix Photosetting, Chatham, Kent
Printed and bound in Great Britain by
Cox & Wyman Ltd, Reading, Berkshire

Contents

Illustrations

John George Haigh
John White Webster and Dr Parkman
Miss Emily Kaye, victim of the Crumbles murder
Margaret and Peter Hogg
Mrs Catherine Hayes, cutting off her husband's head, and being burned alive at the stake
Contemporary sketches from the Second Brighton Trunk Murder
The corpse of Miss Violette Kaye
The corpse of Mr Charles Bessarabo
Dr Hawley Harvey Crippen
Mrs Cora Crippen
The arrest and trial of Dr Crippen
Contemporary sketches of events after the crime of Louis Voisin
Detective Macé confronts Pierre Voirbo
Marcel Petiot in court
The head of Mary Jane Rogerson

Acknowledgements

No book can ever be said to be the work of just one author. From conception to bound volume we are indebted to countless individuals and institutions for their practical guidance, information and encouragement.

In the case of *The Butchers,* thanks are due once again to the British Library Reading Room, where the bulk of the book was assembled, and to the unfailing courtesy and expertise of its staff. I was lucky to have the resources of the international membership of *The Murder Club*, whose creative approach to the crime of homicide is a continual revelation; in particular to Wilf Gregg whose encyclopedic knowledge and vast library have never been more than a phone call away.

For the kindness and generosity that has been extended by scores of museums and libraries, and to all those people who knew about things and were willing to share, I hope this book may represent my modest gratitude. To the many people who allowed me access to their picture collections and gave permission to use their material, my thanks, and to any whose copyright I have failed to trace, my apologies in advance.

That *The Butchers* should have appeared at all is due in no small part to the patience and perseverance of my editors at Virgin, Gill Gibbins and Paul Forty; to them must go the final thanks for moulding the concept into the book that you are reading now.

Brian Lane
London
April 1992

Introduction

THE PERFECT MURDER

We have all used the phrase; we all know what we mean. But to try to describe the 'rules' of perfection in murder, to ask what it *is*, means confronting a bewildering series of answers, none going beyond, at best, a half-truth; at worst a misinterpretation.

'It is the kind of murder every killer hopes to commit.' A good start, if not terribly helpful.

'The perfect murder is one in which the killer gets away with it.' Better; but get away with it how?

He may simply not have been caught. Take the case of Richard Bingham, seventh Earl of Lucan, known to his friends as 'Lucky'. Lucan disappeared on 7 November 1974, leaving behind, in the west London home of his estranged wife, the body of their children's nanny. At an inquest, the coroner's jury returned a verdict of 'murder by Lord Lucan'.* Although since then there have been reported sightings from every corner of the globe, Lucan remains a fugitive – he is widely considered to have 'got away with murder'. We encounter 'The Lucan Jinx' again on page 198.

Another category of killer, closer to 'perfection' than that represented by Richard Bingham, is that of the murderers whose identities are quite well known to the police but who, for lack of concrete proof, are never charged. Take the 'unsolved' Witchcraft Killing at Lower Quinton.

---

*This was the last time in England that a coroner was permitted to name a murderer.

When 74-year-old Charles Walton failed to return home from his hedge-trimming work at Alfred Potter's farm, daughter Edith and a friend went in search. Quite suddenly, out of the darkness their flashlight picked out the figure of a man: old Charlie had been impaled by a hay-fork, the two prongs driven with such force through his neck that they had penetrated six inches into the earth. On his cheeks, throat and body the sign of the cross had been etched with his own slashhook – the way the Warwickshire witches used to do it! It was the thankless task of Robert Fabian, one of Scotland Yard's best-known detectives, to investigate. Charlie Walton, it was said, had lent money to Farmer Potter; quite a lot of money. And Charlie was asking for it back! Motive for murder? Robert Fabian thought so, and said as much in his autobiography published some years later; but there was no *proof* that would convince a jury.

Then there are the 'perfect' murders where the killer goes on for years, adding to his catalogue of crime without a whisper of suspicion; killers like 'Ted' Bundy.

A well-educated, good-looking man, Bundy's charm and wit made him an attractive companion, and he experienced no difficulty in his relations with women – except the need to kill them. In 1972 he completed his college programme by receiving a BSc in psychology, and was later successful in gaining entrance to the University of Utah to study law – it was subsequently noted that when he moved to Salt Lake the mysterious spate of killings of young women in Washington State stopped and a new wave of disappearances began in Salt Lake. Eventually Bundy was arrested and imprisoned for kidnapping an eighteen-year-old named Carol DaRonch. Which was

when officers investigating the murder of Caryn
Campbell began to take an interest in him, proving
eventually that Bundy had been at the location of
Caryn's death on the day she was killed. An extra-
dition order was issued, and Bundy removed to Colo-
rado to face a charge of murder. In June 1977, while
awaiting trial, he escaped and carried out a further
series of robberies, rapes and murders in the Florida
area. It was February 1978 before Bundy was finally
recaptured – by officers investigating a minor traffic
violation. Under interrogation, Bundy admitted that
the number of his killings had reached more than 100.
At his subsequent trial, Ted Bundy was sentenced to
death. On 24 January 1989, he was executed.

Still others kill many times and are *never* identified,
despite intensive police inquiries. During a nine-
month period in 1969, an unknown assassin killed five
people and wounded two more in the State of California. The murders were followed by letters to two
San Francisco newspapers which were so detailed that
they could only have been written by the killer: all had
been signed with a Zodiac cross on a circle, giving the
killer his pseudonym 'Zodiac'. Although there were
no further killings, the San Francisco Police Department received another letter from Zodiac in 1974
threatening 'something nasty' and claiming a total of
37 murders. Zodiac has never been heard from again
and the crimes remain unsolved.

But this fails to reach true perfection. In none of
these cases can the killer rest easy – no matter how
clever, no matter how lucky, there is always somebody out there looking for him. A body has been
found, a murder has been committed; a killer is at
large.

Quite how many 'perfect murders' are committed

we will never know; that is the secret of success. In all but a tiny number of cases it is the body that gives the game away. A body discarded where it fell 'in suspicious circumstances' – a case for investigation. For murder to be perfect there must, in effect, have been no murder. *No Corpse.**

This book records the misdeeds of those men and women who strove for this kind of perfection, who sought to dispose of their victims so completely as to leave no trace. That they are chronicled here at all is witness to their failure – but some came very close indeed, for nowhere has the assassin displayed his diabolical ingenuity better than in the unwelcome labour of disposing of his victim's earthly remains. For no matter how it is done, concealing the presence of a large, awkwardly shaped object, full of liquid and liable to smell, is a messy, time-consuming business.

ACID BATHS

It really should come as no surprise that the disposal of the tell-tale evidence of murder by means of acid is a merciful rarity. After all, it does suggest a shade more than simple premeditation; almost, one might think, a large-scale tactical operation. Few people – even those of a murderous temperament – have 30 gallons of sulphuric to hand to cope with emergencies; and where on earth do you store an acid bath?

Of course, John Haigh (page 31) had one answer – he styled himself 'engineer', purchased acid for his 'work', and rented 'workshops' to which it could be

---

*Very different from no *corpus delicti*, as we shall see on page 45.

delivered without suspicion, and where the inconvenient, but unavoidable, mess and smell of degrading body tissue would attract little attention.

A cellar is useful. All sorts of things can go on 'down there' without provoking domestic disharmony or neighbourly intervention. It certainly worked for French lawyer Georges Sarret (page 50), a dyed-in-the-wool rascal of the type that *would* have a few carboys of vitriol in case the situation demanded. And it would have been surprising had Herman Mudgett (alias H. H. Holmes) *not* found some subterranean corner of his Chicago death-house to accommodate the acid tank so necessary to facilitate the disposal of the surplus flesh and bone created by his prodigious taste for homicide (see page 25).

Having solved the daunting logistical difficulties, there must be a comforting certainty about the destructive effects of acid – remember that Haigh had already successfully disposed of five victims in this way before he was caught out, and then, heaven knows, if he had been just a bit less arrogant . . . Sarret was betrayed not by bodies, but by his very much alive confederates.

The commonly available acids are: hydrochloric (HCl), called spirits of salts; nitric (HNO_3), or aqua fortis; and sulphuric (H_2SO_4), oil of vitriol. Of these, the most corrosive is sulphuric acid, favoured by Messrs Haigh and Sarret. A colourless, oily liquid, the concentrate is a powerful dehydrating agent which extracts water from body tissue, leaving a soft fatty residue which is easily flushed away. The intense heat generated by this chemical process effects the eventual destruction of the bones. This heat production was an important factor proved during the investigation of the Haigh case by Dr Turfit, deputy director of Scotland Yard's Forensic Laboratory. Dr Turfit found that a human foot, amputated from the body, completely dissolved in about four hours; however, a sheep's femur, stripped of flesh, took four days.

It is tempting, but incorrect, to see 'acid-bath' murders as a trifle old-fashioned, the stuff of the 'classics'. Erwin Spengler, though, would surely have considered himself a thoroughly modern young man – if a thoroughly wicked one as well. And there was certainly nothing 'historic' about the apartment on Lake Constance, where Germany borders Switzerland, and which wealthy 74-year-old Katharina Kornagel called home. Called home, that was, until 6 December 1987, which was the last time that she had been seen by anybody but her chauffeur, 33-year-old Erwin Spengler. To all enquiries he replied simply that Frau Kornagel was visiting Bremen. On 18 January, Spengler decided to box clever and report his employer's disappearance to the police. Detectives searching the flat could find evidence enough of a fierce struggle, but no lead as to where the victim might be. The forensic team seconded from the State Criminal Investigation Office were able to be a little more helpful, identifying a multitude of human bloodstains on walls and floor, and a gory trail leading to the bathroom where more blood and traces of hydrochloric acid were found. The conclusion was clear: Katharina Kornagel had been subjected to a brutal and bloody murder, and her corpse reduced to a pourable liquid with acid. Despite the fact that there was no body (nor for that matter very much in the way of direct evidence against him) Spengler was found guilty of a thoroughly modern murder. On reflection, though, it had been a thoroughly old-fashioned motive – if greed can be thought to be governed by 'fashion'.

BURNING

One could well invoke all manner of fanciful symbolism when dealing with the destruction of the body by fire. Almost all of the ancient civilisations at one stage in their history viewed burning as the only dignified and honourable means of disposal. (Indeed the Romans reserved burial for suicides and murderers!) Although cremation has only comparatively recently been legalised in Britain, it has for millennia been favoured among the Eastern nations who frequently contrive the most elaborate forms of public cremation.

More appropriate in our present context might be the raging fires of Hell, where the flesh of the damned burns for eternity. But it is a disappointing fact that murderers tend to choose fire for more prosaic reasons – its generous simplicity:economy:effectiveness ratio being foremost. There is no denying that fire, well handled, can consume as voraciously as any acid bath; even in the hands of a bungler, burning can severely lengthen the odds against positive identification.

The dead are most commonly identified visually, by a close friend or relative. Only in cases of extreme trauma, where visual identification is either impossible or likely to cause distress, is the expertise of forensic medicine required. Even so, medical identification, by whatever means, needs to be based on a comparison of ante-mortem records with post-mortem remains. In cases of severe burning, the 'oral structures' have proved to be the most scientifically reliable means of identification for a number of reasons: (1) Human dentition tends to outlast all other body tissue after death; (2) Dental repairs, restorations, and prostheses (false teeth) are particularly resistant to chemical and physical degradation, including intense heat; (3) Given the infinite number of permutations of aspects of dentition, any configuration is, for practical purposes, unique; (4) In current practice, radiographic (x-ray) examination is capable of revealing even fuller data on structural features of teeth and jaws.

It must be emphasised, however, that for successful positive identification via dental patterns, both ante- and post-mortem records must be available. With a complete ante-mortem chart it may be possible to make an identification from as little as a single tooth, or fragment of a denture.

In two of our cases it has been forensic dentistry that provided this necessary identification to trap a killer. The first, Professor John White Webster (page 55), is celebrated not only for being the first Harvard professor to be convicted of murder (and the last), but also for being the first person to be convicted on dental evidence in an American court. In the second case, it was the meticulous record-keeping by a local dentist that enabled police to put the name 'Rachel Dobkin' to a decomposing, charred corpse found after the Blitz of London, and to send her husband, Harry, to the gallows for murder (page 230).

The cases of Alfred Arthur Rouse (page 97) and Kurt Tetzner (page 105) are prominent because it was not their victim that they wanted to dispose of, but themselves. The former because his present life had become too cumbersome, the latter to defraud an insurance company. Both failed. Rouse because he panicked, Tetzner because his case came up against one of Germany's leading forensic pathologists who proved that it could not have been Tetzner in his burnt-out car.

There is an interesting modern parallel to Rouse and Tetzner in the case of Clive Freeman. Freeman was a

Rhodesian national who had fled to London in 1987 after that country gained its independence as the Republic of Zimbabwe. A born loser, and dying from cancer, Freeman decided that he would make one last bid for 'big money'. He insured himself for £300,000 and then lured a vagrant alcoholic to his broken-down south London flat with the promise of whisky. There he suffocated the man and set fire to the building, subsequently making his getaway to Australia to await the insurance company's cheque. Having failed all his life, Clive Freeman was not about to surprise anybody now; due to a combination of bad luck and stupidity the body of his victim had burned beyond recognition – except for his fingers, which revealed the fingerprints of Alexander Harvey, on file at Scotland Yard from some previous misdemeanour. As Suspect Number One, Freeman was arrested, extradited, tried and convicted at the Old Bailey, and sentenced to life imprisonment.

CANNIBALISM

There is extensive evidence to confirm that people have eaten human flesh at various times throughout mankind's history and over a wide area of the world. In the main, cannibalism has had a religious significance, though other reasons have included the basic provision of sustenance, and a ritual means of absorbing another individual's outstanding features by ingestion. Sometimes the eating of human flesh accompanied victory celebrations after a battle, and in some cultures the consumption of recently deceased elders was held to transfer acquired wisdom to the family.

The eating of flesh associated with homicide is most commonly encountered as a complication of sado-sexual perversion, though there is some indication that cannibalism has been used as a symbolic and practical means of disposing of the victim's body – Ed Gein (page 120) characterises the former, while Anna Zimmermann (see below) might stand representative of the latter. Of course, in the cases of Fritz Haarmann (page 125) and Georg Grossmann (page 123), the sale of human flesh as a means of disposing of the evidence gave a profit motive to inherent perversion that is in distinct contrast to the uncomplicated greed of fictional archetypes like Sweeney Todd and Mrs Lovett.

The standard response of any civilised society to cannibalism is one of incredulity, of horror; in short, we need no reminding that eating people is wrong. It is comforting to believe that cannibalism – if it exists at all – is confined to those remote and inaccessible areas of the globe where half-naked savages in grass skirts with bones through their noses dance around cauldrons. Nevertheless there is reason enough to believe that behind this comic-book world inhabited by missionary-eaters, there lurk atavistic memories and attachments to an heretical practice that began before history – long before the Spanish conquerors of the Caribbean transliterated the name of the anthropophagous inhabitants from Carib through Calib to Canib, and so cannibals. As far back as half a million years and more, to Africa, cradle continent of modern man, and the days when Peking Man and his descendants saw human flesh, brain and bone marrow as suitable nourishment in times when the wild beasts of forest and plain were scarce.

But in 1987 the world was reminded that the cannibal feast had not died out with *pithecanthropus erectus*. In March of that year the dethroned Emperor of Central Africa, Jean-Bedel Bokassa, was put on trial charged with mass murder and cannibalism committed during his thirteen-year rule. Witnesses testified to finding human corpses, some with missing limbs, in the deep-freeze at the self-appointed ruler's palace. Bokassa's cook wept in court as he recalled the former dictator taking him to the kitchen one evening and ordering 'a very special meal' to be prepared from a human body stored in the freezer. It was clear that all that had changed in half a million years was the convenience of refrigeration.

Cannibalism as a complication of homicide is thankfully comparatively rare, occurring as it generally does as a sexual perversion associated to that at the root of the killing.

A characteristic case began in Paris in 1981, when two girls summoned the police to a spot in the Bois de Boulogne where they had seen a diminutive oriental attempt to push two absurdly large suitcases into the Lac Inferieur. When he saw them coming, he had scampered off as fast as his tiny legs would carry him, abandoning his luggage. Reassembled, the contents of the plastic bags inside the suitcases were identified as 25-year-old Dutch student Renee Hartevelt. It was through the taxi driver who had transported the small man and his cases to the park that the police came to visit No. 10 rue Erlanger, where they found and arrested Issei Sagawa, a 32-year-old Japanese student, with his gun, his bloodstained carpet, and a refrigerator full of human flesh. Sagawa, unmoved, unrepentant and under arrest, told how he had shot fellow-student Renee Hartevelt after she had rejected his sexual advances; how he had stripped the body naked and had intercourse. Then began the slow process of dismembering the corpse, pausing alternately to photograph his handiwork and to nibble on strips of raw human flesh. Finally Sagawa selected some cutlets to refrigerate for later and the rest of the body ended up in the Bois de Boulogne. With the kind of back-door chicanery that only money can buy, Issei Sagawa spent only three years in hospital in France before being returned to Japan where he was declared sane and released. It was not only the cynics who noticed how the Paris cannibal had been released from France at the same time as two large international companies – Kurita Water Industries of Japan and Elf Aquitaine of France – had signed a very lucrative business deal. Coincidentally, Sagawa's father was the president of Kurita Water Industries. Following his discharge in September 1985, Sagawa claimed that the eating of Renee Hartevelt's flesh had been 'an expression of love', the culmination of a life-long desire to eat the flesh of a young woman. More disturbing still, he could not rule out the possibility that he might 'fall in love' again.

Although the total consumption of a human body by a murderer in order to dispose of the evidence is somewhat impractical, it has at least provided a partial solution in many cases where the inclination to cannibalism already existed. Like the case of Frau Anna Zimmermann.

When Josef Wirtz went missing from home and job in Moenchengladbach at the beginning of June 1984, it was his landlord that reported the disappearance – not out of any great concern for Wirtz's welfare, but from a sincere desire to recover his rent and relet the flat. When the routine circulation of his description failed to yield any result, the file on Wirtz was added to the missing persons register. There it remained until 7 July, when a young woman stumbled, quite literally, on Josef Wirtz's head – what the maggots had left of it – in the shrubbery of an ornamental garden. In plastic rubbish sacks nearby was the rest of the dismembered body – or rather the skeleton, for according to the pathologist's report the flesh had been carefully stripped off with a sharp knife, much as one would fillet an animal for meat. Frequently, where insect activity and putrefaction have rendered a head unrecognisable, identification can be made with certainty from dental records, and this was achieved in the Wirtz case. Meanwhile, detectives had been interviewing the proprietor of a video-hire shop in whose plastic carrier bags the body had been transported to the garden – a shop with a library of rental films top-heavy with sex, sadism and horror in all their combinations. It seemed at least possible that there was a connection between the shop's horror fans and the murder of Josef Wirtz. A check through the list of registered customers led inevitably to Walter Krone, an habitual cannibal who had already served a seven-year prison sentence for eating flesh from a young woman who had been killed in a road accident. Astonishingly, Krone was totally innocent; which meant that there must be other cannibals at large in the town of Moenchengladbach! A re-run through the list of local video-nasty aficionados now turned up 26-year-old Anna Zimmermann, horror-freak, cannibal and, it turned out, the mistress of Josef Wirtz, portions of whose body were still in Frau Zimmermann's deep-freeze awaiting culinary attention; a matter on which she was modestly unforthcoming. Not so her estranged husband Wilhelm. Having himself escaped the marital home before contributing to a casserole or roast, he had nevertheless returned to help his wife dispose of Wirtz – after drugging and drowning him in the bath, Anna took knife and electric saw to Wirtz's body, managing to store nearly four dozen plastic boxes of cutlets and assorted offal in the home freezer for use over the coming months, thus solving the problem of disposal in a most nourishing and economical way.

THE MEAT VENDORS

By comparison, how much more practical is the trade in human flesh to customers blissfully innocent of their initiation into cannibalism, and living proof that human meat is as toothsome and nourishing as that of any other of nature's creatures. Indeed, Fritz Haarmann and his compatriot Georg Grossmann discovered that marketing their victims provided a long-term profit-spinner.

The culinary expertise of Kate Webster was modest, though the same cannot be said for her personality or crime. Quite how the cautious, genteel Mrs Thomas came to employ an habitual thief and ex-convict as her personal maid is a mystery; but in 1879 Kate Webster, then 30 years of age, was taken into service. We are not sure what provoked Kate to batter her elderly employer to death with a coal-axe – probably a simple case of robbery – but we know that when the deed was done, the awful Kate proceeded to hack apart the corpse with carving knife and meat saw. The resulting cuts were boiled down in the kitchen copper, and after being neatly parcelled were disposed of, some in the river, some on the fire. The fat, however, had been skimmed off, bottled, and sold to the local public house as dripping.

Truth is, decidedly, stranger and often much more horrid than any fiction. Bon appetit.

DISMEMBERMENT

All books with any credit go through many changes on their journey from concept to finished volume, *The Butchers* not least. It was the original plan to chronicle only those killers who had embellished their crime with dismemberment for the purpose of defeating identification. It began with the case of Catherine Hayes (page 133), held to have set the 'fashion' in dismemberment. When Mrs Hayes hacked the head from her murdered husband's body and cast it into the Thames, there existed no other means of making positive identification of a corpse than visual recognition; and through the unusual expedient of being prominently displayed on a pole in St Margaret's churchyard, John Hayes' head was, by chance, so recognised.

In the 250-odd years since Catherine Hayes was the talk of London, such advances have been made in the science of forensic pathology that it is almost impossible for human beings – whole or in parts – to remain unidentified for very long. An appendix to the book was therefore planned to supplement the case histories. Following a general overview of the forensic sciences, an attempt is made to co-ordinate some brief explanations of the methods involved in investigating the identity of dead, decomposed, and skeletal remains.

However, in compiling the case-list, it became increasingly clear that many other issues were involved than simple dismemberment. Indeed, a glance at the table on pages 26–7 will reveal that dismemberment is most often only the prelude to some more permanent method of disposal. And so the book became an examination of methods of disposal, most, but not all, involving dismemberment; for a dead body, even in its smaller versions, is a cumbersome, weighty problem to conceal, and piecemeal dissemination provides at least a partial solution.

The competence with which such an operation (so to speak) is carried out clearly depends on the acquired professional skills of the individual. Buck Ruxton approached the task with the calm confidence of a qualified surgeon, not only reducing two live human beings to a shambles of 70 mutilated lumps of flesh and bone, but being sufficiently astute and medically aware to remove those parts like the tips of the fingers, facial features and teeth, which are important in identification. The solution of the Ruxton case remains one of the foremost achievements of forensic medicine.

Louis Voisin (page 156), while no medic, was able to carry out a fairly adequate disassembly of Madame Gerard using the techniques necessary to his calling as a butcher and slaughterman.

Others, like Patrick Mahon (page 70), simply plunged in with hacksaw and kitchen knife and hoped for the best.

Dismemberment while the victim is still alive is horrific even in the context of a barbaric crime. But lest it be thought that the devil has all the good tunes it is a sobering recollection that, in centuries past, the nearest thing to this brutal variation on murder was a brutal variation on State execution. The cruelties of judicial punishment are worthy of a study on their own, and cannot be served by a mere note, but a work concerned with dismemberment would be incomplete without mention of the dread excesses of hanging, drawing and quartering.

As a punishment, this was not to be wasted on

common ruffians and delinquents, but reserved as retribution for that most heinous of crimes – high treason. The process was lengthy and complex, suiting the gravity of the crime, with the added advantage of elevating the event to a major public spectacle. Allowing for tokens of individual creative talent on the part of the executioner, the procedure was as follows.

1. The traitor was 'drawn' to the gallows from his place of incarceration. At first this was achieved with great economy of effort by simply tying the prisoner to the tail of a horse and dragging him along the ground; and with the optional aggravation of having sharp stones scattered on the road, this proved a great favourite with the crowds that customarily lined the route. However, the method proved less satisfactory when, as in the majority of cases, the leading actor in this spectacle was dead long before the more imaginative scenes could be played out. Thus the refinement was developed of drawing on an ox-hide, and later a hurdle, which in its turn was replaced by a sledge.

2. The prisoner was hanged by the neck from a gallows and cut down while still alive. This was not difficult, as even a 'standard' hanging was little better than slow strangulation at the end of a rope, frequently allowing the felon to linger for hours on the edge of death.

3. The 'privy members', or 'private parts', were cut off, and the bowels hacked out and thrown into a fire before the victim's eyes.

4. The head was severed from the body by the executioner who was expected to hold it aloft, addressing the crowd with such words as, 'Behold the head of a traitor.'

5. What remained of the corpse was butchered into four quarters and customarily displayed above the city

gates or, in the case of London, London Bridge. In his *History of the Life of Thomas Ellwood written by his own hand*, Ellwood, a Quaker imprisoned in Newgate at the beginning of Charles II's reign, described the barbaric preparation of the relics for display:

> When we came first into Newgate, there lay the quartered bodies of three men who had been executed some days before for a real or pretended plot; and the reason why their quarters lay so long there was, the relations were all that while petitioning to have leave to bury them, which at length, with much ado, was obtained for the quarters but not for the heads, which were ordered to be set up in some part of the City. I saw the heads when they were brought up to be boiled. The hangman fetched them in a dirty dust basket, out of some by-place, and setting them down among the felons, he and they made sport with them. They took them by the hair, flouting, jeering and laughing at them, and then giving them some ill names, boxed them on the ears and cheeks. Which done, the hangman put them into his kettle, and parboiled them with bay-salt and cumin seeds that keep them from putrefaction, and this to keep off the fowls from seizing on them. The whole sight (as well as that of the bloody qarters first, and this of the heads afterwards) was both frightful and loathsome, and begat an abhorrence in my nature.

FED TO THE PIGS

Stanislaw Sykut was last seen returning to the Cefn Hendre farm, Cwmdu, which he worked in part-

nership with fellow Pole Michael Onufrejczyc, on 14
December 1953. By January 1954 his disappearance
was generating enough local gossip for the police to
begin investigations into his whereabouts.

Onufrejczyc claimed that there had been a dis-
agreement, and that he had bought Sykut out of the
partnership. His obstructive manner and demonstra-
ble lies, however, increased suspicion of the farmer,
and an examination of the farmhouse was carried out
by the police Forensic Science Laboratory. The
investigating team identified as blood more than two
thousand tiny stains on the walls of the kitchen and
hallway, and found a large dark stain on the surface of
the kitchen dresser. Onufrejczyc's reluctant explanation that he had been skinning rabbits collapsed
when the laboratory confirmed that the blood-spots
were of human origin and the stain on the dresser was a
bloody hand-print. Michael Onufrejczyc was still protesting his innocence when he was sentenced to death
for murder.

But what had happened to the body of Stanislaw
Sykut? In his own account of 'The Butcher of
Cwmdu', ex-Detective Superintendent David
Thomas made this suggestion: 'My own opinion,
which I put forward at the time of the investigation
and which I still hold to, is that the chopped-up pieces
of Sykut's body were probably fed to a herd of rave-
nous pigs which roamed the farm. It would have been
a simple matter for Onufrejczyc to have boiled the
parts of the dismembered body with the pigs' mash in
the days immediately following 14 December, and
before Sykut was missed . . . Onufrejczyc always
seemed confident that the body would never be found.
What better confidence did he need than to know his
pigs had eaten the evidence?'

A fate bizarre enough to be unique? Not a bit of it!
The undiscriminating palate of the pig is legendary,
and has featured in several memorable murder cases.
One of the outstanding features of the Onufrejczyc
case was this lack of a corpse. It is a misunderstanding
of the law that leads many people even today to believe
that a charge of murder cannot be brought without a
body (see the case of John George Haigh). In fact there
was another famous murder-without-a-body trial in
1970, when Arthur and Nizamodeen Hosein were
convicted of the murder of Mrs Muriel McKay (page
217). Like the unfortunate Pole before her, Mrs
McKay is widely supposed to have ended up as a meal
for the pigs.

QUICKLIME

In popular fiction 'quicklime' has always had emotive
associations connected with the secret disposal and
disintegration of corpses – not only, it might be added,
of the victims of murder, but also of the victims of the
hangman's noose. No reader could fail to be haunted
by these chilling words from Oscar Wilde's *The Ballad
of Reading Gaol**:

> And all the while the burning lime
>   Eats flesh and bone away,
> It eats the brittle bone by night,
>   And the soft flesh by day,
> It eats the flesh and bones by turns
>   But it eats the heart alway.

**The Ballad of Reading Gaol*, Oscar Wilde; based on the execution
of Thomas Wooldridge in Reading Gaol for the murder of his wife
in 1896.

The reality is rather less dramatic, however, and in most cases quite the contrary result occurs; that is, the chemical reaction tends to preserve the remains by arresting putrefaction.

Lime of the type favoured by murderers falls into three categories:

1. *Quicklime*. Produced by strongly heating limestone to form calcium oxide: has the appearance of irregular white lumps.
2. *Slaked lime*. Calcium hydroxide, a dry white powder produced by adding water to quicklime.
3. *Chlorinated lime*. Product of the action of chlorine gas on slaked lime; at one time widely used as a disinfectant.

When a body is buried in quicklime and the lime is quickly slaked with water, the chemical reaction produces intense heat. However, when slaking occurs by the lime slowly abstracting liquid from the body, only a superficial burning will occur (less effective still if the body is clothed or wrapped), and the main effect will in fact be to prevent putrefaction by desiccating the tissue.

Nevertheless, a sufficient quantity of good quality slaked lime, given time, could significantly hasten decomposition. Evidence in the well-known 'Manning Case' of 1849 certainly indicates that the five bushels in which Frederick and Maria buried the unfortunate Patrick O'Connor worked 'so rapidly that its [the corpse's] identity was only established by the remarkable and less perishable feature of an extremely prominent chin and a set of false teeth'.

Dr Crippen (page 227) was rather less successful with a smaller amount of quicklime in the cellar at 39

Hilldrop Crescent, though it was to his advantage in arresting decomposition, as the lime would have largely prevented the tell-tale odour of putrefaction. On the other side of the Channel, French mass murderer Dr Marcel Petiot (page 235) believed in ordering quicklime in the same bulk in which he killed his victims. Considering the grisly lumps of human flesh in various stages of desiccation that were salvaged from his several lime-pits, Petiot's protestation that it was to kill cockroaches seemed like a macabre joke.

For Harry Dobkin (page 230), the use of quicklime appeared to be incidental to his overall plan for the disposal of Mrs Dobkin, and like the Mannings a century before him, Dobkin's success was confounded by his victim's teeth.

TRUNK MURDERS

There is something irresistibly quaint about the concept of putting a body in a trunk; an association, no doubt, with the days of more leisurely transportation, of steam trains and ocean liners. Who *sells* trunks now? – even if you could find a left-luggage office to deposit them in. Of course, apart from the decidedly anti-social aspects of leaving dead bodies around, whole or in kit form, in trunks, it must rate as one of the least successful means of disposal – a temporary measure at best, to give the killer a head start . . . for corpses begin to go off very quickly in the warm confines of a piece of luggage.

Which makes it the more puzzling that Winnie Ruth Judd should have decided to chaperone the trunks containing her two victims on their long journey round America. The 'Phoenix Trunk Murders', as they have come to be known, took place in an apartment in the Arizona capital on the night of 16 October 1931. The flat had been occupied by Hedwig Samuelson and 27-year-old Agnes LeRoi, and on the night in question a former flat-mate and colleague at the local clinic, Winnie Judd, had been with them. A quarrel seems to have arisen over men-friends which erupted into physical violence, and Hedwig had, in true saloon-bar style, pulled out a gun and shot Winnie in the hand. Winnie grabbed the gun and – in self-defence, she later claimed – shot both girls dead. Agnes LeRoi fitted comfortably into one large trunk, but Miss Samuelson needed to be reduced to her constituent parts before being packed into a smaller piece of luggage.

On 18 October, Winnie Judd, together with the two trunks, embarked on a westbound train for the Southern Pacific station of Los Angeles. By the time Mrs Judd, accompanied now by a young man whom she identified as businessman Carl Harris, was ready to claim her baggage, one of the trunks had begun to leak a sticky, foul-smelling liquid. Requested to open the trunks, Winnie and Carl left the office on the pretence of getting the keys and never returned. It was the baggageman who prised open the luggage, launching a nationwide hunt for double-killer Winnie Ruth Judd (by now nicknamed 'The Tiger Woman'). Following a plea from her doctor husband, Winnie turned herself in and at her trial was found guilty and sentenced to death. At a retrial just ten days before the execution date, Mrs Judd was judged insane and committed to the Arizona State Hospital, whence she was paroled in 1971.

Four years previously, on the other side of the Atlantic, John Robinson was creating a similarly unappetising smell in the left-luggage office of

London's Charing Cross railway station. On 6 May 1927, the clerk had taken charge of a large black trunk deposited by a respectable 'military-looking' gentleman who had arrived at the station by taxi. When the all-pervading odour that began to emanate from the luggage became so offensive as to arouse suspicion, the police were summoned to investigate its contents – several brown paper parcels, neatly wrapped, and containing the parts of a female corpse. It was the taxi driver whose fare had deposited the trunk that led investigating officers to the pick-up point at 86 Rochester Row (ironically just opposite the police station). A pair of knickers in the trunk led by a circuitous route to Minnie Bonati, the estranged wife of an Italian waiter; by which time Sir Bernard Spilsbury had reassembled the body of a short, plump 35-year-old woman who had been asphyxiated. When Robinson was apprehended he not surprisingly denied any knowledge of Minnie Bonati or the trunk. It was the discovery of a blood-stained match at his office at 86 Rochester Row that finally broke Robinson's confidence. He now admitted to the police that Mrs Bonati had propositioned him at Victoria station, and back at the office had become abusive and demanded money; they struggled, and she had fallen and hit her head on a coal bucket. In panic Robinson fled the building not to return until the following morning when he found Minnie still where she had fallen. He made no attempt to deny the dismemberment – he had cut up the corpse with a chef's knife, purchased in the same shop in Victoria Street as the one used by Patrick Mahon (page 70) to cut up Emily Kaye three years before. Nor did he make any attempt to deny dumping the remains at Charing Cross Station. But he denied absolutely killing Mrs Bonati. Unfortunately for Robinson, Sir

Bernard Spilsbury had already proved conclusively that the victim had been suffocated *after* being struck on the head. John Robinson was hanged at Pentonville Prison on 12 August 1927.

Although there is no longer a large left-luggage office at Charing Cross railway station, the spiritual heirs of the famous Charing Cross Trunk can still be encountered in the form of the humble suitcase – an olive-green example of which was dumped by Suchnam Singh Sandhu (see page 203) on a train to Wolverhampton, containing the remains of his daughter.

CONCLUSION

All that having been said, homicide remains a very inexact activity, and nowhere is this more apparent than in the disposal of the corpse. There were, it must be admitted, those like Acid-Bath Haigh who knew exactly what they were doing – who had practised and planned carefully. For others, however, disposal became a matter of trial and error, and it comes as no surprise to find many of our brief selection of killers using more than one of the methods which we have defined. For many, dismemberment was just the beginning of their problems.

Spare a thought also, in conclusion, for those men and women who enjoyed variety for variety's sake. Who entered enthusiastically into the spirit of experiment and innovation. Pioneers like H. H. Holmes . . .

Bigamist, swindler and mass murderer, the final total of Holmes' killings will never be known. His real name was Hermann Webster Mudgett, and following a brief spell practising as a doctor in New York,

Name/Case	BESSARABO, Hera	BOWDEN, John, et al.	BOYCE, Nicholas	BRIGHTON TRUNK 1	BRIGHTON TRUNK 2	CAMB, James	CRIPPEN, Dr H. H.	DAVID, John	DOBKIN, Harry	DUDLEY/MAYNARD	ELMES, Ernest	FISH, Albert	GARDELLE, Theodore	GEIN, Ed	GROSSMANN, Georg K.	GUNNESS, Belle
Headless corpse							●		●							
'No body' trial						●										
Trunks	●			●	●											
Burial							●		●							●
Submersion							●		●							
Quicklime							●		●							
Fed to pigs								●								
Making sausages															●	
Selling meat															●	
Cannibalism												●		●	●	
Burning									●		●		●			
Acid bath																
Dismemberment while alive	●															
Dismemberment	●	●	●			●		●	●		●	●	●	●	●	●

HAARMANN, Fritz
HAIGH, John George
HAYES, Catherine
HOGG, Peter
HOSEIN, A. and N.
HUME, Donald

KISS, Bela

LANDRU, Henri

MAHON, Patrick
M'KAY, James

NILSEN, Dennis

PETIOT, Dr Marcel

ROUSE, Alfred A.
RUXTON, Dr Buck

SANDHU, Suchnam S.
SARRET, Georges
SHARK-ARM CASE

TETZNER, Kurt

VOIRBO, Pierre
VOISIN, Louis

WEBSTER, John W.

Holmes moved to Chicago and entered employment in a drug company, which he took over when the manageress mysteriously disappeared. In fact, a lot of people whose paths crossed Mudgett's disappeared mysteriously – notably a succession of bigamous wives and mistresses.

In 1882 Holmes gave up the drug business and moved in to manage the bizarre hotel that he had had built after the style of a medieval castle. The conclusion of an extensive series of murders and insurance frauds was that H. H. H. came to the attention of the Chicago police authorities, who in turn focused attention on 'Holmes' Castle' which they found to have served a second purpose as torture chamber and house of execution. They found air-tight rooms into which gas could be pumped, a kiln large enough to take a human body, vats of acid, and rooms equipped with surgical dissection instruments and the paraphernalia of torture. At the trial, one prosecution witness described being employed by Holmes to strip the flesh from three bodies – at the rate of $36 per corpse.

Sentenced to death, Holmes wrote his memoirs, listing only a modest 27 murders; on 7 May 1896, he was himself executed.

One

'So will I melt into a bath
To wash them in my blood'

Robert Southwell
The Burning Babe

JOHN GEORGE HAIGH
(England, 1949)

A Woman's Intuition

'Tell me, frankly, what are the chances of anyone being released from Broadmoor?'

We are in a police station, during a murder investigation – one of the most gruesome stories of multiple death in the history of British crime; murders whose horror would shock the world; murders for which the only motive was abject greed.

'If I tell you the truth you would not believe it, it is too fantastic for belief. Mrs Durand-Deacon no longer exists. She has disappeared completely, and no trace of her can ever be found again. I have destroyed her with acid. You will find the sludge that remains at Leopold Road. Every trace has gone. How can you prove murder if there is no body?'

John George Haigh and the police officer who sits across the table from him, Inspector Albert Webb, are no strangers. Nor is it Haigh's first visit to Chelsea police station. A week earlier, on Sunday, 20 February 1949, shortly after midday a dapper little man with a bristling 'Hitler' moustache accompanied by a smartly dressed woman in her later years approached the duty desk at Lucan Road station. Mr Haigh and his companion, Mrs Constance Lane, expressed their growing concern over the apparent disappearance into thin air of a fellow resident of the nearby Onslow Court Hotel. Her name was Mrs Durand-Deacon – Mrs

Olive Henrietta Helen Olivia Robarts Durand-
Deacon, sixty-nine, wealthy, and, in the quaint termi-
nology of the day, 'well preserved for her age'.

She had last been seen on the morning of 18 February going out to keep a rendezvous with Mr Haigh.
Dear Mr Haigh was taking her down to his factory in
Crawley, Sussex, to discuss a new business venture
she had dreamed up of manufacturing false fingernails.
Haigh hastily sought to correct Mrs Lane's unwelcome revelation by stating that Mrs Durand-Deacon
had, in fact, not turned up for their appointment.

Next day, when detectives called on Haigh at the
Onslow Court Hotel to further their enquiries into the
disappearance of his fellow-resident, John Haigh,
happy to 'tell you all I know about it', proceeded to
issue forth a rambling statement of which the essence
was that he had absolutely no idea of the whereabouts
of Mrs Durand-Deacon.

Three days later Haigh was again interviewed at his
hotel, the singular difference on this occasion being the
presence of a woman police officer. Now whether we
believe in what is patronisingly called 'woman's
intuition', or whether we give her credit for simply
being, in another expression of the time, 'a damned
good copper', Woman Police-Sergeant Alexandra
Lambourne smelled a rat – a mannerly, silver-
tongued, smoothly pressed rat, perhaps, but WPS
Lambourne smelled a rat. Her report of the interview
that day concluded: 'Apart from the fact that I do not
like the man Haigh, with his mannerisms, I have a
sense that he is "wrong", and there may be a case
behind the whole business.'

And indeed there was. On the following day, Scotland Yard's Criminal Record Office was able to tell a
lot more about John Haigh than he had been prepared

to say for himself. Not least that he had been imprisoned on three separate occasions, each time for fraudulently obtaining money.

By this time officers of the West Sussex Police had been alerted to the 'Crawley connection', and had interviewed Mr Edward Jones, managing director of Hurstlea Products Limited, of which Haigh claimed to be a director. The claim was bogus of course – as so much of John Haigh's facade was but he did have one interesting connection with Hurstlea. Haigh used the firm's storeroom in Leopold Road for what he called his 'experimental work'. It was Jones's impression that he was engaged on a 'conversion job' there. He could hardly have been closer to the truth.

The storeroom turned out to be a sturdy, two-storey brick-built structure situated in Giles Yard, off Leopold Road, surrounded by a high fence. On 26 February it began to be apparent just what sort of 'experimental work' Haigh was engaged on. That Saturday morning Detective-Sergeant Pat Heslin, in company with Mr Jones, entered Haigh's 'factory'.

Inside, Heslin noted the presence of several carboys labelled 'Sulphuric Acid', a stirrup pump, gas mask, rubber gloves, and a rubber apron spattered with blood. In a leather hatbox the detective found a recently fired Webley .38 revolver and the receipt from a Reigate cleaners for a black Persian lamb coat.

Seven-thirty p.m., Monday, 28 February 1949. Inspector Albert Webb and Superintendent Barratt have just brought Haigh back to the police station where only a week previously he had reported his victim's disappearance; he is about to confess to her murder. The fourth occupant of the interview room, Inspector Shelley Symes, is meeting Haigh for the first time.

It was obvious from their conversation that the officers knew about the fur coat; in fact that little touch of luxury which once lent elegance to Mrs Durand-Deacon's portly frame had long since been recovered from the Reigate Cottage Cleaners. The lady's jewellery had been recovered from Messrs Bull of Horsham, where Haigh had left it for valuation.

Barely ruffled, Haigh sat gently pufffing at a cigarette. 'I can see you know what you're talking about. I admit the coat belonged to Mrs Durand-Deacon, and that I sold her jewellery.'

'How did you come by the property; and where is Mrs Durand-Deacon?'

There was a pause; three pairs of eyes on John Haigh. 'It's a long story. It's one of blackmail, and I shall have to implicate many others.'

Quite what preposterous story Haigh would have told given half a chance we will never know, because at this point some pressing business summoned Symes and Barratt from the interview room. Questioning was, for the moment, suspended.

'Tell me, frankly, what are the chances of anyone being released from Broadmoor?'

Haigh is alone now with Albert Webb. The rat cornered; desperate for a line of defence against a charge of murder, a defence which might allow him to escape the fearful consequences of his obvious crime.

'I can't discuss that sort of thing with you.'

'If I tell you the truth, you would not believe it; it is too fantastic for belief.'

'You are not obliged to say anything . . .' began Webb.

'I understand all that,' interrupted Haigh impatiently. 'I will tell you all about it. Mrs Durand-Deacon no longer exists. She has disappeared completely and no trace of her can ever be found again. I have destroyed her with acid. You will find the sludge that remains at Leopold Road. Every trace has gone. How can you prove murder if there is no body?'

Quite clearly the time had come when Inspector Webb must summon his superiors, and tell them about Haigh and the acid bath.

Once Haigh had been formally cautioned, Inspector Symes began taking down the statement which, apart from a brief interval for tea and cheese sandwiches, took two-and-a-half hours to transcribe.

CHELSEA POLICE STATION
'B' DIVISION

28 February 1949

STATEMENT of JOHN GEORGE HAIGH, age 39 years, an Independent Engineer of the ONSLOW COURT HOTEL, QUEENS GATE, SW7, who saith:—

I have been cautioned that I am not obliged to say anything unless I wish to do so but whatever I say will be taken down in writing and may be given in evidence.

(Signed) J.G. Haigh

I have already made some statements to you about the disappearance of Mrs Durand-Deacon. I have been worried about the matter and fenced in the hope that you would not find out about it. The truth is, however, that we left the hotel together and went to Crawley together in my car. She was inveigled into going to Crawley with me in view of her interest in artificial fingernails. Having taken her into the storeroom at Leopold Road I shot her in the back of the head whilst she was examining some paper for use as fingernails. Then I went out to the car and fetched in a drinking glass and made an incision, I think with a penknife, in the side of the throat and collected a glass of blood, which I then drank. Following that I removed the coat she was wearing, a Persian lamb, and the jewellery, rings, necklace, earrings and cruciform, and put her in a forty-five gallon tank. I then filled the tank up with sulphuric acid by means of a stirrup pump from a carboy. I then left it to react. I should have said that in between putting her in the tank and pumping in the acid, I went round to the 'Ancient Priors' for a cup of tea. Having left the tank to react, I brought the jewellery and the revolver into the car and left the coat on the bench. I went to the 'George' for dinner and I remember I was late, about 'ninish'. I then came back to town, and returned to the hotel about halfpast ten. I put the revolver back into the square hatbox.

The following morning I had breakfast and, as I have already said, discussed the disappearance of Mrs Durand-Deacon with the waitress and Mrs Lane. I eventually went back to Crawley, via Putney, where I sold her watch en route at a jeweller's shop in the High Street for ten pounds. I took this watch from her at the same time as the other jewellery. At Crawley I called in to see how the reaction in the tank had gone on. It was not satisfactorily completed so I went on to Horsham, having picked up the coat and put it in the back of the car. I called at Bull's, the jewellers, for a valuation of the jewellery but Mr Bull was not in. I returned to town and on the way dropped in the coat at the 'Cottage Cleaners' at Reigate. On Monday I returned to Crawley to find the reaction almost complete, but a piece of fat and bone was still floating on the sludge. I emptied off the sludge with a bucket and tipped it on the ground opposite the shed, and pumped a further quantity of acid into the tank to decompose the remaining fat and bone. I then left that to work until the following day. From there I went to Horsham again and had the jewellery valued, ostensibly for probate. It was valued at just over £130. I called back at the West Street factory and eventually returned to town.

I returned to Horsham on Tuesday and sold the jewellery for what was offered at a purchase price of £100. Unfortunately the jewellers had not got that amount of money and could only give me £60. I called back for the £40 the next day. On Tuesday, I returned to Crawley and found decomposition complete and emptied the tank off. I would add that on Monday I found that the only thing that the acid had not attacked was the plastic handbag, and I tipped this out with the sludge. On the Tuesday when I completely emptied the tank I left it in the yard.

I owed Mr Jones, who I have said is co-director of Hurstlea Products, fifty pounds, and I paid him the £36 on the Tuesday from the money I got from the jewellers. The revolver which the police found at Crawley in the storeroom is the one I used to shoot Mrs Durand-Deacon, and I took it down there in the hatbox on the Saturday morning. Before I put the handbag in the tank I took from it the cash – about thirty shillings, her fountain pen, and kept these and tipped the rest into the tank with the bag. The fountain pen is still in my room. She also had a bunch of keys attached to the inside pocket of the coat by a chain and large safety pin. I discarded the chains of the cruciform and the keys in the bottom of the hedge in the lane going down to Bracken Cottage, where I went to stay with friends on the Wednesday. The keys themselves I inserted separately into the ground and also the cruci-form . . .

Haigh finished making his final statement in the early hours of 1 March and was immediately placed under arrest. But terrible as the murder of Mrs Durand-Deacon was, it was only part of the story; only a very small part really. For John George Haigh had claimed five further victims – 'The subjects,' as he put it, 'of another story'.

Not surprisingly, the police turned their attention once again to the storeroom and its small patch of yard in Crawley. The investigation team was now led by Scotland Yard's Detective Chief Inspector Guy Mahon, supported by Dr Keith Simpson of London University, pathologist to the Home Office.

On that chilly morning of 1 March Simpson focused first on the storeroom, in particular on the finely spat-tered bloodstains on the whitewashed wall just above the bench. This is consistent with Haigh's claim that Mrs Durand-Deacon had been examining some red cellophane on the bench at the time he shot her. But facts like this have to be *proved* – even if there is a con-fession. It has to be shown that the blood is human; and it has to be analysed for comparison with the known group of the victim.

Dr Simpson then directed his attention to the scrubby, overgrown yard outside Haigh's 'Murder Factory' following the zig-zag scratches in the earth where the killer had trundled the heavy drum across to empty it, to the spot where Haigh claimed he had dumped the 'sludge', the last mortal remains of the late Olive Durand-Deacon.

But the impetuous Haigh had failed to take account

of two very important factors – the skill and tenacity of
Dr Keith Simpson, and the fact that some substances
take longer to corrode in acid than others. How was
Haigh to know that gallstones don't dissolve in acid –
or for that matter that his victim even suffered from
such a disorder? How was he to know that the acrylic
resin from which Mrs Durand-Deacon's false teeth
were fashioned required a further two weeks before
they would succumb to the corrosive attack of vitriol.
The victim's red plastic handbag and its few sad contents were barely harmed by their contact with the
acid. Olive Durand-Deacon may have disappeared,
but by no means without trace!

From this section of the yard, Dr Simpson ordered
three inches of the topsoil carefully removed within an
area measuring 24 square feet. 475 pounds of it –
'dirty, partly yellow greasy, partly charred oily
residue, soaked into pebbly earth' were taken to the
Metropolitan Police Laboratory at New Scotland
Yard and patiently sifted.

It was Simpson's painstaking analysis of the ground
at Giles Yard and the topsoil taken from it to the
laboratory that identified the 'body' of Mrs Durand-
Deacon 'beyond reasonable doubt':

Three gallstones – Simpson had not been out in the
yard for more than a few minutes before his sharp eyes
picked out the first of the clues that were to identify
John Haigh's last victim: 'The ground outside the store
room was rough, with many small pebbles lying on
the earth. Almost immediately, and I suppose rather
impressively, I picked one up and examined it through
a lens. It was about the size of a cherry and looked very
much like the other stones, except that *it had polished
facets.* "I think that's a gallstone" I said.' And so it proved; gallstones – compacted bile-sand – are covered

with a fatty substance that resists corrosion by acid. Simpson was always rather hurt by the suggestion that his discovery was just 'lucky', and subsequently claimed that he had told Chief Inspector Mahon: 'I was looking for it. Women of Mrs Durand-Deacon's age and habits – sixty-nine and fairly plump – are prone to gallstones.'

Left-foot bones – The second find was of equal importance in establishing an identity: 'Embedded in a thick charred greasy substance I saw several masses of eroded bone. When X-rayed, the largest of these proved to be the greater part of a left foot.'

Superintendent Cuthbert of the Metropolitan Police Laboratory later made a cast of this foot, and found it fitted perfectly into one of the dead woman's shoes.

Fragments of eroded bone – Eighteen pieces in all, of which Simpson, after laborious work with microscope and X-ray, was able to identify eleven with the human anatomy. Furthermore, a groove in part of the pelvic bone called the 'hip girdle' proved that it came from a woman's body, and osteoarthritis was present in certain joints.

Bodyfat – Such is the effect of sulphuric acid on animal body tissue that 28 pounds of a yellow greasy substance was all that remained of Mrs Durand-Deacon's body after she had been melted down.

Set of dentures – It was Haigh's biggest mistake to miscalculate the time required for acid to break down the acrylic resin from which false teeth were made. With the speed characteristic of a Scotland Yard murder hunt, Miss Helen Mayo, a dentist, had been located; she positively identified the dentures as having been made for her patient, Mrs Olive Durand-Deacon.

Handbag and contents – As well as Mrs Durand-Deacon's bodily possessions, her plastic handbag was also found intact, with those of its contents that had resisted the acid: a notebook, diary, part of a lipstick holder, a small pencil, a metal travelling pen, and a face-powder compact.

By comparison with the dramatic course of the investigation, Haigh's trial was something of an anti-climax. On Monday morning, 18 July 1949, the prisoner faced Mr Justice Humphreys across the panelled courtroom of the historic Lewes Assizes in Sussex.

As Haigh sat in the dock, apparently disdainful of the whole proceedings pencilling in a newspaper crossword puzzle, Attorney-General Sir Hartley Shawcross KC, MP, most senior of His Majesty's law officers, opened the Crown's case against John George Haigh, during the course of which he would call no fewer than 33 witnesses.

Sensing the futility of any useful contradiction of this formidable wall of prosecution evidence, Sir David Maxwell Fyfe KC, MP, to whose undoubted skill and integrity the flimsy tissue of Haigh's defence had been entrusted, chose to cross-examine on only three brief occasions.

Haigh did not enter the witness box to give evidence on his own behalf, relying instead solely on the expert medical testimony of Dr Henry Yellowlees, Consultant in Mental Diseases at St Thomas's Hospital, London. It was for Dr Yellowlees to convince the jury that Haigh was possessed of a paranoid constitution, resulting in paranoid insanity. Haigh's early home life and religious upbringing were invoked – responsible, the doctor claimed, for sowing in his brain those demons of madness that were to result in multiple murder – and worse.

Bringing a touch of the bizarre to this august occasion, Dr Yellowlees relayed to a hushed court John Haigh's recurring nightmare of blood:

'[He saw before him] an entire forest of crucifixes which gradually turned into trees, the branches of which appeared to be dripping with dew or rain. This was then seen to be blood. One tree, gradually assuming the shape of a man, would collect blood in a bowl. As this happened he saw the tree getting paler in colour and he felt himself losing strength. Then the man in the dream, when the cup is full, approaches, offers the cup to him and invites him to drink. At first Haigh is unable to move before the man and the man recedes, he cannot get to him and the dream ends.

Sir David Maxwell Fyfe: In the statement he made he has given a history, which we have heard, that in each case, as he put it, he 'tapped' the victim and drank some blood. What do you feel as to the truth or otherwise of that statement?

Dr Yellowlees: I think it pretty certain that he tasted it; I do not know whether he drank it or not. From a medical point of view I do not think it is important, for the reason that this question of blood runs through all his fantasies from childhood like a motif and is the core of the paranoiac structure that I believe he has created, and it does not matter very much to a paranoiac whether he does things in fancy or in fact.

In cross-examination, it was the task of Sir Hartley Shawcross to establish the crucial point which would determine whether Haigh could be considered to possess the only standard of insanity acceptable to an English court of law – whether at the time of committing the act of murder he either did not know what he was doing or, if he did, that he did not know it was wrong.

Sir Hartley Shawcross: I am asking you to look at the facts and tell the jury whether there is any doubt that he must have known that, according to English law, he was preparing to do, and subsequently had done, something which was wrong?

Dr Yellowlees: I will say 'Yes' to that if you say 'punishable by law' instead of 'wrong'.

Sir Hartley Shawcross: Punishable by law and, there-fore, wrong by the law of this country?

Dr Yellowlees: Yes, I think he knew that.

'Does he think', interrupted the judge curtly, 'that he will not be punished?'

Dr Yellowlees: He says: 'I am in the position of Jesus Christ before Pontius Pilate, and the only thing I have to say is that you have no power against me unless it is given to you from above.'

Mr Justice Humphreys: I do not know what that may mean.

Little more than 24 hours after it had begun hearing evidence, the jury retired to consider its verdict. The decision could not have been a difficult one, for in just seventeen minutes – barely enough time to elect a fore-man and smoke a cigarette – the panel found John Haigh guilty, as charged, of the capital murder of Mrs Olive Durand-Deacon; they found Haigh not mad, not just bad, but thoroughly evil.

From beneath the Black Cap – since the days of the Tudors that most potent symbol of the awful power of the law – Mr Justice Humphreys intoned, as if from some unfathomable depth, the dread sentence of death.

Whatever Haigh's inner emotions at hearing his sen-tence, he seemed to all the world quite unruffled – rather as if he had lost a couple of quid on the horses but wasn't letting it get him down. It is said that as he was taken down to the warders' common-room beneath the court, the judge's chaplain sent a court official down to ask Haigh if he would appreciate a little spiritual comfort. When the messenger arrived, Haigh was sitting with his feet up on a table calmly puffing on a cigarette and swigging from a mug of tea.

'The padre has asked me if you would like him to come down to see you.'

'I don't see much point in it, old boy, do you?'

At nine o'clock on the morning of Monday, 10 August 1949, John George Haigh kept his appointment with executioner Pierrepoint. For Henry Pierrepoint, too, it was a special day, and, in one of the few eccentricities allowed to a hangman, accorded Haigh a rare distinction reserved for only the elite among his clients – the 'special strap'. With some pride, the hangman recalled:

'When the time came for me to carry out the execution of Haigh I took a special strap in with me to bind his wrists. It is a strap made of pliant pale calf-leather, no different in design from the straps I normally used, supplied by the Home Office in the box of execution apparatus, but it is personal to me. I have used it only about a dozen times. Whenever I used it I made a red ink entry in my private diary. This is the only indication I have ever given that I had more than formal interest in this particular execution.'

The vampire's teeth drawn, John Haigh's mortal remains were consigned to the most exclusive cemetery in the land: that patch of scrub deep within the walls of Wandsworth prison. Buried eight feet below the weed-grown surface of the 'Potters' Field', Haigh's body was laid in a special coffin bored with holes and filled with water to speed putrefaction of the flesh – not as swift as sulphuric acid, but just as certain.

POSTSCRIPT

It was during the time that Haigh spent as a guest of His Majesty King George VI on Dartmoor that he began to plan a future for himself in the sub-culture of the thoroughly unscrupulous. 'Go after women,' he pompously advised his fellow-prisoners. 'Rich old women who like a bit of flattery. There's your market if you're after big money.'

Arrogant little cleverjack that he was, John Haigh thought he had it all worked out; in fact he repeated so often his conviction that a murder could not be proved without a body that he was given the nickname 'Old Corpus Delicti'. If he had been a little less confident, done a little more homework, Haigh might have steered away from his collision course with justice, and in the process saved his own life. For John George was labouring under the by no means uncommon misunderstanding that in *corpus delicti, 'corpus'* meant, literally, a 'corpse'. In reality, this legal concept describes the 'body' not of a victim, but of the crime itself – the *essence* of the crime that has to be established in order to bring a successful prosecution. It is necessary only to prove that a specific person has been killed, and that death was the consequence of unlawful violence.

Had Haigh been paying more attention to the details of his master plan, he might have absorbed the knowledge that, less than eighteen months before he was arrested on the charge of killing Mrs Durand-Deacon, a ship's steward named James Camb (see page 251) had laboured under the same misapprehension. In

October 1947, he raped and murdered actress Gay Gibson aboard a ship, and although Camb disposed of his luckless victim through one of the liner's portholes and the body was never found, forensic evidence established not only the fact and cause of death, but pointed the finger convincingly at James Camb. In March 1948 he was tried, convicted and sentenced to death.

There have been a number of subsequent instances of successful prosecutions being brought where no body was ever discovered: for example, the brothers Arthur and Nizamodeen Hosein, who were eventually imprisoned for the abduction and murder of Mrs Muriel McKay (see page 217) And as recently as 1987, Kingsley Rotardier, a 46-year-old model and composer, was committed for trial at the Old Bailey charged with the murder of David Hamilton, his homosexual lover. It was claimed that Hamilton's body, which was never found, had been cut into small pieces and incinerated.

THE 'OTHER STORY'

But what of those 'other subjects', that 'other story' to which Haigh had so enigmatically referred while in custody? For herein lies the true horror of John Haigh's crimes; the dapper little chap with the engaging manners did not start with the murder of Mrs Durand-Deacon. It was on 28 February 1949, shortly after his confession to the Durand-Deacon murder, that Haigh made a second extraordinary statement, confessing to no fewer than five further killings that had ended in a bath of acid:

The Ration Books and clothing coupon books and other documents in the names of McSwan and Henderson [which police had found in his room at the Onslow Court Hotel] are the subject of another story. This is covered very briefly by the fact that in 1944 I disposed of William Donald McSwan in a similar way to the above [Mrs Durand-Deacon] in the basement of 79 Gloucester Road, S.W.7., and of Donald McSwan and Amy McSwan in 1946 at the same address. In 1948 Dr Archibald Henderson and his wife Roasalie Henderson also in a similar manner at Leopold Road, Crawley.

Going back to the McSwans, William Donald, the son, whose address at that particular time I can't remember, met me at the Goat public house, Kensington High Street, and from there we went to No. 79 Gloucester Road, where in the basement which I had rented, I hit him on the head with a cosh, withdrew a glass of blood from his throat as before and drank it. He was dead within five minutes or so. I put him in a forty-gallon tank and disposed of him with acid as before in the case of Mrs Durand-Deacon, disposing of the sludge down a manhole in the basement. I took his watch and odds and ends, including an Identity Card, before putting him in the tank. I had known this McSwan and his mother and father for some time and on seeing his mother and father explained that he had gone off to avoid his 'Call up'. I wrote a number of letters in due course to his mother and father purporting to come from him and posted in, I think, Glasgow and Edinburgh, explaining various details of the disposition of properties, which were to follow. In the following year I took separately to the same basement the father Donald and the mother Amy, disposing of them in exactly the same way as the son. The files of

the McSwans are at my hotel and will give details of
the properties which I disposed of after their deaths. I
have since got additional Ration Books by producing
their Identity Cards in the usual way.

I met the Hendersons by answering an advertisement offering for sale their property at 22 Ladbroke Square. I did not purchase. They sold it and
moved to 16 Dawes Road, Fulham. This runs in a
period from November 1947 to February 1948. In
February 1948, the Hendersons were staying at Kings-
gate Castle, Kent. I visited them there and went with
them to Brighton, where they stayed at the
Metropole. From here I took Dr Henderson to
Crawley and disposed of him in the same store room at
Leopold Road by shooting him in the head with his
own revolver, which I had taken from his property at
Dawes Road. I put him in a tank of acid as in the other
cases. This was in the morning and I went back to
Brighton and brought up Mrs Henderson on the pre-
text that her husband was ill. I shot her in the store
room and put her in another tank and disposed of her
with acid. In each of the last four cases I had my glass of
blood as before. In the case of Dr Henderson I
removed his gold cigarette case, his gold pocket watch
and chain and from his wife her wedding ring and dia-
mond ring and disposed of all this to Bull's at
Horsham for about £300. I paid their bill at the Hotel
Metropole, collected their luggage and their red setter
and took the luggage to Dawes Road. The dog I kept
for a period at the Onslow Court Hotel and later at
Gatwick Hall until I had to send him to Professor
Sorsby's Kennels in the country on account of his
night blindness. By means of letters purporting to
come from the Hendersons I kept the relatives quiet,
by sending the letters to Mrs Henderson's brother

Arnold Burlin, who lives in Manchester. His address
is in the Index book in my room. No. 16 Dawes Road,
I acquired by forged deeds of transfer and sold it to the
present owner, J.B. Clarke. The McSwan properties
were also acquired in a similar way and disposed of and
the particulars are in the file at the Hotel.

I have read this statement and it is true.
(Signed) John George Haigh

MAITRE GEORGES SARRET
(France, 1925–4)

The French Connection

When John Haigh embarked on his career as an acid-bath murderer it is unlikely that he was even aware of the precedent set by Maître Georges Sarret; at the time of the crimes in France, Haigh was still working his way up the rogues' ladder, getting by on what he made from selling cars that didn't belong to him.

Sarret had been born Giorgio Sarrejani in the Adriatic port of Trieste in the years when it was ruled by Austria, moving with his parents when he was just three years old to Marseilles, where the boy enjoyed a good French education and the youth took up the journalist's quill. At the age of 40, Sarret must have wearied of a life of doorstepping because he undertook the study of law and, although he was called to the bar, never practised as a barrister, preferring instead to establish a somewhat dubious reputation as a 'business consultant'. It was during this period that he 'advised' the Bavarian-born Schmidt sisters, Katherine and Philomene, that French nationality and future comfort could best be secured by marriages to appropriately elderly and infirm Frenchmen. Philomene's septuagenarian obligingly died within months, the blow to his widow being significantly cushioned by a substantial insurance settlement.

Next Katherine, who was by now doubling as Sarret's mistress, contrived to marry a man who was terminally ill with cancer, and arranged for a defrocked priest, now moneylender, named Chambon to pose as her husband for the purpose of taking out a 100,000 francs life insurance (insurers being understandably reluctant to issue policies to those at death's door). In time death occurred naturally, and Sarret, Chambon and the Schmidts divided the spoils.

Chambon, being possessed of an instinctively greedy and naturally criminous character, sought to increase his portion with a little blackmail against his partners. Which was a pity for Chambon, because on 19 August 1925, at the Villa Ermitage★ outside Aix, they shot him. They also despatched Chambon's mistress, Madame Ballandreaux, who had been privy to the scene. The two bodies were then laid in a bath and covered with twenty-five gallons of sulphuric acid.

On another occasion, the terrible trio insured Katherine Schmidt for a large sum of money and together they found a consumptive girl who, when she had been poisoned, was buried with a death certificate in the name of Katherine Schmidt. This time it was Philomene's turn to claim the insurance.

Swindlers extraordinaire, Sarret, Schmidt et Cie, remained active and at liberty for the next six years. It was not until the spring of 1931 that the insurance frauds were brought to an abrupt end with the arrest of Georges Sarret and his unceremonious incarceration in Chave prison, Marseilles. The Schmidts followed close behind, protesting the while that *they* had nothing to do with acid baths.

★Students of coincidence may care to note that Henri Landru, the 'French Bluebeard', disposed of no fewer than seven victims at the Villa Ermitage outside Gambais.

When the case came to trial at the Aix-en-Provence assizes in October 1933, preliminary proceedings had already lasted for two years, and the accused faced an impressive list of charges including four counts of murder. So great was public outrage, that soldiers with fixed bayonets supplemented the usual strong force of gendarmes guarding the approaches to the court, and admission was refused to all but authorised persons.

From the witness box, Sarret maintained that it had been Chambon who shot Madame Ballandreaux and that he, Sarret, had accidentally shot Chambon while trying to disarm him. With a notable lack of chivalry, the lawyer claimed that it was only because the Schmidts had refused to let him call the police that he was obliged to dissolve the two victims' bodies in acid.

On 31 October 1933, Georges Sarret was sentenced to death on the guillotine and felt the blade drop at Marseilles on 10 April 1934. Katherine and Philomene Schmidt were each sentenced to ten years' imprisonment in Montpellier followed by ten years' banishment.

Two

'Terror of darkness!
O, thou king of flames!'

George Chapman
Bussy d'Ambois

JOHN WHITE WEBSTER
(USA, 1849–50)

The Undoing of Sky-rocket Jack

When it came to disposing of bodies, John White Webster was more than averagely well advantaged; indeed, it required almost superhuman bungling not to have, in a phrase, got away with murder.

Webster held the elevated position of Professor of Chemistry and Mineralogy at Harvard, America's oldest and most distinguished university. He was a Doctor of Medicine, whose academic territory embraced a dissecting room and private laboratory containing an assay-furnace by which means he might easily have reduced the burdensome body of his victim so completely as to leave no trace. Yet, with all these endowments, Professor Webster overlooked the one trivial fact that would be his downfall – his victim wore false teeth!

An over-indulged child, John Webster grew accustomed early to the largesse bestowed by a wealthy family, and carried with him into maturity an insatiable appetite for rich living. Inconveniently for him, the rewards of a chemistry professor – even at so exalted an establishment as Harvard – were more munificent in terms of position and esteem than in negotiable currency, and his annual salary of 1200 dollars fell far short of what Webster was inclined to spend on entertaining. Thus, endowed with greater generosity than good sense, this hapless academic soon fell heavily into debt.

The man to whom he turned in his time of need was Dr George Parkman, member of a wealthy Boston family, who had given up the practice of medicine in favour of the more lucrative pursuit of property development. It happened that the two were also old friends, having graduated from Harvard together. In 1842 Webster borrowed 400 dollars. Five years later, having repaid little of the original loan, he again approached Parkman, and 500 dollars was exchanged for a mortgage on Webster's furniture, books and mineral collection.

With a tragic inevitability, the Professor fell yet further into debt, and now stood in danger of losing his worldly possessions to his creditor. The solution seemed simple, as it had to a thousand debtors before him – borrow some more money.

John Webster's grasp on common sense has already been challenged, but his next move defies belief. From Mr Robert Shaw he extracted a loan of 1200 dollars, and as security offered his mineral collection (the one that had already been pledged to Dr Parkman as security for *his* loan).

Robert Shaw was George Parkman's brother-in-law, and the latter was distinctly unimpressed to learn of the transaction. In fact, one could say he was furious, and from that day pursued Webster with a single-minded determination to secure the repayment of his debt. It is said that he went so far as to attend Webster's lectures in order to sit in the middle of the front row and intimidate him.

On Friday, 23 November 1849, Webster made an appointment to meet Dr Parkman at the Harvard Medical College where he had his laboratory. It was an appointment from which Parkman never returned.

On the following day a search was organised, and

many thousands of reward notices distributed. Although he was routinely questioned at the Medical College, there was never any suggestion of suspicion against Professor Webster; indeed he was by all accounts a thoroughly good-natured and obliging fellow, popularly known to his students as 'Sky-rocket Jack' on account of his fondness for fireworks, and seems to have been universally trusted.

Except, that is, by one man – college janitor Ephraim Littlefield. It transpired that he had been around the building one day when Parkman told Webster: 'Something must be done!', and he noticed the decidedly aggressive atmosphere that enveloped the conversation. On the day of Parkman's disappearance, Ephraim Littlefield had seen the doctor arrive for his appointment with Webster. Some time in the middle of the afternoon, while about his caretakerly routine, Littlefield went to clear up Professor Webster's laboratory, the door of which he found inexplicably locked, though Webster could be heard scurrying about behind it. The door of the professor's lecture room was also locked and bolted; as they were when he checked again at six o'clock in the evening; and at ten that night.

'Suspicion', the Bard of Avon cautioned, 'shall be stuck full of eyes,' and on Sunday evening the janitor confided to Mrs Littlefield that he intended to watch the professor very closely.

On Monday Webster was still to be heard at work behind locked doors; and on Tuesday too. By Wednesday Ephraim Littlefield had grown frustrated with trying to peep through keyholes and could be seen lying full-length upon the floor in an attempt to look under the laboratory door; though it should be said that he found the sight of the professor's boots moving about the room neither satisfying nor instructive.

That afternoon, Littlefield felt a fierce heat from the wall of the staircase which backed on to the still locked laboratory – heat from a furnace never used before. As soon as Webster had left the building, Littlefield, breaking all the rules of gentlemanly etiquette, crawled through a small back window into Webster's lair. The furnace was still hot, but beyond that there was nothing to justify further suspicion. Janitor Littlefield was a tenacious man, and one over whose eyes he would allow none to pull wool; he had remembered a private lavatory in the laboratory. Not surprised to find the privy door locked he began, with hatchet and chisel, to dig through from the vault beneath. It was a labour hard and slow, but not without reward when he held a light to the hole he had opened and beheld a man's dismembered pelvis and legs.

No doubt with a sense of pride and self-satisfaction mixed with his horror, Ephraim Littlefield lost no time in relaying his intrepid exploits, and their awful conclusion, to the police. With his detective work already enthusiastically carried out for him, it only remained for senior officer Clapp to arrest Webster and lodge him temporarily in the Leverett Street prison.

His confidence now in tatters, John Webster began to whimper: 'You might tell me something about it. Where did they find him? How came they to suspect me? Oh, my children! What will they do? What will they think of me?' With this, the distraught man pressed something into his mouth and was in the instant seized with violent spasms. But even in his own suicide Webster proved a muddler; for while the capsule contained enough strychnine to inflict on him severe discomfort, it fell far short of a fatal dose.

While Webster was enacting this pathetic spectacle in Leverett Street, his laboratory at Harvard was being subjected to a meticulous search. In a tea chest a severed left thigh was discovered, in company with a thorax and a hunting knife. The dissection exhibited some anatomical skill, and the thorax showed signs of having been treated with potash. As a chemist, Professor Webster would have been well aware that this substance, heated long enough, would ultimately reduce body tissue and even bone to liquid. Unfortunately he had no receptacle large enough for the whole body, requiring it to be done piecemeal.

Among the ashes of the furnace fragments of bone were found, and the heat-fused remains of a set of false teeth. These were the only positive means of identifying George Parkman, which was helpfully confirmed by Dr Nathan Cooley Keep, the dentist who had fashioned the dentures for the late Dr Parkman in October 1846. Students of the history of crime might note that this was the first time that dental identification evidence was presented to an American court.

17 March 1850 found John White Webster before the Supreme Court of Massachusetts, where he faced an overwhelming, but fair, prosecution. Which is a lot more than could be said for the defence. A situation which had already become a losing battle was being severely handicapped by the bewildering variety of alternative defences advanced on Webster's behalf – that Dr Parkman wasn't even dead; that he had been slain by Ephraim Littlefield; that the doctor had been murdered elsewhere and his body dumped in the college to frame Webster; and that Webster had, indeed, been the instrument of George Parkman's

death, but in circumstances amounting only to manslaughter. Even John Webster, in a formal statement to the court, complained bitterly about the quality of his defence.

The jury was clearly puzzled enough to spend the three hours between eight and eleven o'clock in the evening debating the merits of the prisoner's several defences; prepared, according to the trust invested in them, to extend to him the benefit of any doubt they may have had as to his guilt. It turned out that there were no such doubts, and all that was required in conclusion was the sentencing of John Webster by Massachusetts Chief Justice the Hon. Lemuel Shaw:

'And now nothing remains but the solemn duty of pronouncing the sentence which the law affixes to the crime of murder, of which you stand convicted, which sentence is: that you, John White Webster, be removed from this place, and detained in close custody in the prison of this county, and thence taken, at such time as the executive Government of this Commonwealth may, by their warrant appoint, to the place of execution, and here be hung by the neck until you are dead. And may God, of His infinite goodness, have mercy on your soul.'

At the conclusion of this morbid speech, Webster broke down and wept freely.

In the end, John Webster confessed to the murder of Dr Parkman, and perhaps the relief of shedding this burden allowed him to face a higher judgement with more fortitude. On 30 August 1850, Harvard, for the first and last time, lost a professor to the public executioner.

HENRI DESIRE LANDRU
(France, 1915–22)

The Red Man of Gambais

It was the end of the Great War, that folly of conflicts whose four relentless years of avoidable suffering had left the people of Europe numb – numb with exhaustion, numb with grief, numb with anger. It was a time during which Death had lurked in every heart, had left few families untouched. In France, the citizens were sick of death.

But they were not so sick that they could not make exceptions – for when sex, drama and humour conspire with death there are few who can resist the cocktail. France was not so tired of corpses that it could turn its back on 'The Landru Case'.

Henri Landru's early life was almost a cliché. How many times have we heard it said of a notorious criminal that he came of 'poor but respectable parents'? Well, he did, and they were. Born in Paris on 12 April 1869, young Henri had a predictably undistinguished childhood, standard education at the Roman Catholic Ecole des Frères in the rue Bretonvilliers, an inevitable flirtation with the church (like John George Haigh of acid-bath fame he was an enthusiastic chorister, lending his voice to the choir of St-Louis-en-Ile, near Notre Dame). As a conscript with the 87th Infantry Regiment at St Quentin, Landru had risen to the rank of *sergent-fourrier*, or assistant to the quartermaster-sergeant, after which he settled down

to make the best of his marriage to Mademoiselle
Marie Catherine-Remy, a laundress whom he had
seduced and made pregnant. The modest living with
which he supported his family Landru earned dealing
in second-hand furniture and cars. On the surface,
Henri Landru was not unlike most of his neighbours.

It was deeper down that the differences lay. The
more romantic might have said that Henri Désire
Landru had a 'black soul', a heart hardened by the
disease of avarice. This inability to keep his hands off
other people's property first came to official notice in
1904, and on 21 July of that year Landru received his
first prison sentence for swindling. Four more prison
terms followed closely each upon his release from the
last. The final stretch – four years – he earned on 26
July 1914 – just days before Germany declared war on
France, which should have meant that Henri Landru
would be out of mischief for the duration of hostilities,
but the bird had already flown, and his conviction *in
absentia* was never pursued; France was facing a
greater problem than one small-time embezzler.

Landru now found himself in a situation which
compared with his fondest concept of paradise. The
present conflict, he could not help noticing, was filling
Paris with a population of widows – nervous,
unaccustomed to making decisions without the benefit of advice from husbands or other male members of
the family, and terrified by the spectre of a lonely old
age. Enter Henri Landru. His short stature, bald head
and long black beard did not ideally suit him to the role
of the smooth seducer, but a plausible tongue and an
apparent sincerity at least made him a credible suitor.
Anyway, that was to be the opinion of nearly three
hundred women during the next few years.

The war was certainly working to Henri Landru's

advantage so far, but with the inevitability of all good things coming to an end, someone was bound to see through the swindle – someone unprepared to allow their modest treasures to be swallowed up by the voracious Monsieur Landru. In fact we know of eleven, and in April 1919 Landru was arrested on charges connected with their disappearance.

The formula had not required a great intellect to concoct – in fact in retrospect it seems rather crude. Take Madame Celestine Buisson. A widow with a young son, Madame had read in the classified columns of the newspaper a matrimonial advertisement inserted by a 'Monsieur Fremyet':

Widower with two children, aged forty-three, with comfortable income, affectionate, serious, and moving in good society, desires to meet widow with a view to matrimony.

Her child deposited with his doting aunt, Mademoiselle Lacoste, Mme Buisson joined 'Monsieur Fremyet' on a trip from which she never returned nor was heard from again. Things might have gone smoothly if the child had not died; but it did, and desperate to inform the mother, Mlle Lacoste recalled her sister confiding the address to which she sallied forth with her new lover – the Villa Ermitage, at Gambais, near the Forest of Rambouillet. She wrote to the local mayor to enquire of her relative:

Since September 1917, I have been unable to contact Mme Celestine Buisson, my sister. She came to live in your village with her fiancé, Monsieur Fremyet. I have written to them both several times without ever receiving a reply . . . I wonder whether the address I am using is incorrect or incomplete. Could you inform me of the correct address . . .

The letter she received in reply informed her that the present tenant of the Villa Ermitage was a Monsieur Dupont; he could find no record of a M. Fremyet ever being its tenant. The mayor also observed that the relatives of a Madame Anna Collomb had made a similar enquiry about the villa recently.

The police, hard pressed no doubt by the extra duties imposed by a war, could not find M. Dupont, or M. Fremyet, or Diard, or any one of the numerous aliases that had just a single identity – Henri Landru.

The disappearance of Mme Buisson was representative of Landru's *modus operandi*, but it was also unique. Landru had no reason to guess it at the time, but she was, from the grave, to prove his Nemesis. Or rather, her sister was.

It was all a remarkable coincidence, really: that Mlle Lacoste happened to be walking down the rue de Rivoli at the same time as the man she knew as Monsieur Fremyet, her sister's lover. The date was 12 April 1919. When he went into a porcelain shop, the 'Lions de Faïence', Mademoiselle followed at a discreet distance, and when the man had transacted his business managed to persuade the tradesman to give her his customer's address.

When the police knocked at the door of number 76, rue de Rochechouart, they were received by Monsieur and Madame Lucien Guillet; except that the short, stocky man with the bald head and black beard was Henri Landru, and Madame Guillet was in reality his mistress, Fernande Segret, shop assistant and part-time actress. Landru was immediately taken into custody.

The police were quite sure that their prisoner was a murderer – probably a multiple murderer – but they were having a desperate time proving it. Of the deceits, the heart-breaking swindles and downright theft, there was no shortage of evidence; nor was there any shortage of missing persons. What the good men of the Sûreté lacked were corpses. Then they looked more closely at the property taken from Henri Landru on his arrest; at the unremarkable-looking little black notebook which was to prove very remarkable indeed. On one page was a list of names: 'A. Cuchet, G. Cuchet. Bresil. Crozatier. Havre. Ct. Buisson. A. Collomb. Andrée Babelay. M. Louis Jaume. A. Pascal. M. Thr. Mercadier.'

Now we know – as did the police – that Mesdames Buisson and Collomb were missing; they also knew that Madame Cuchet and her son André had disappeared. It proved a long job putting identities to Landru's 'hit' list, but eventually the police had their eleven names, their eleven suspected victims. Meanwhile, another team of officers had been addressing the problem of the lack of bodies, and had meticulously searched and re-searched the house at Gambais; had dug and re-dug its garden and grounds. Interviews with local villagers revealed occasions when there had been smoke and the foul smell of burning meat coming from the villa, and eventually pieces of charred bone and teeth were found on a refuse tip next to an outhouse; the kitchen boiler yielded a further cache of calcined human bone mixed with half-burnt coals. In all, experts identified forty-seven teeth or pieces of teeth and about four pounds' weight of bones, mostly from skulls, hands and feet; in other words, those parts of the body most likely to be of use in identification. Among the ashes were also found some more resistant metal objects later identified as various types of fastening for women's clothes.

In all, it was two and a half years before Henri Landru came to trial, during which time his frequent appearances before magistrates had made him one of the most popular entertainments in Paris, his impudent answers to questions and comic asides exciting much merriment both inside and out of court. Under various affectionate nicknames – Old Bluebeard, The Ladykiller, The Red Man of Gambais – Landru was entering popular mythology via songs, cartoons, jokes and music-hall theatricals.

On 7 November 1921, Landru stood before the presiding judge, Conseiller Gilbert, at the Versailles Assizes. As had been expected, the prisoner lived up to his burlesque reputation and provided a pleasing spectacle for the fashionable audiences that packed the court. But in trying too hard to live up to that reputation, Henri Landru forgot the people who really mattered – the jury. Humorous as his replies were, Landru was simply not defending himself; he was allowing a clever prosecutor in the person of the Avocat General, Maître Godefroy, to make out a powerful case against him without the least contradiction. In answer to a question on the subject of the fatal notebook, Landru replied sarcastically: 'Perhaps the police would have preferred to find on page one an entry in these words "I the undersigned confess that I have murdered the ten women whose names are herein set out".' To the fact that all ten had disappeared, he observed: 'Are there no others who have also disappeared without anyone being accused of their death?'

Henri Landru was beginning to look and sound like

a smart-alec, like a man who uses the gift of the gab to get himself out of difficult situations – a schemer. The sort of man who would charm defenceless women out of their possessions and – why not say it? – their very lives.

On 30 November 1921 that was exactly the conclusion reached by the jury. After a deliberation of just two hours, the foreman announced a verdict of guilty on all charges with no extenuating circumstances; death on the guillotine.

For his loyal audience Henri Landru had no more quips, no more cute turns of phrase. The only reaction he allowed himself was to turn to his long-suffering counsel and thank him: 'If I could have been saved, you would have done it.'

It was three more months before Landru drew his last breath. In the meantime he refused absolutely to confess his crimes, and he refused to hear Mass. On 25 February 1922, Henri Landru's last day on this earth, he declined the stiff drink he was offered and to the official who asked if he would care now to confess, Landru replied that he found the question very insulting at a time like this. His last request, to wash his feet, was refused.

In the cold 4 a.m. dawn on the cobbles in front of Versailles prison, the group of observers awaited the arrival of executioner Anatole Deibler, called by tradition 'Monsieur de Paris'. Among them was writer Webb Miller, who gave this account of the last seconds in the life of 'The Bluebeard of Paris':

The jailers hastily pushed Landru face downward under the lunette, a half-moon-shaped wooden block which clamped his neck beneath the suspended knife. In a split second the knife flicked down, and his head fell with a thud into the basket. As an assistant lifted the hinged board and rolled the headless body into the big wicker basket, a hideous spurt of blood gushed out.

POSTSCRIPT

The world had to wait 46 years for what was described by the newspapers that published it in 1963 as 'Landru's true confession'.

It had been scribbled, it was said, on the back of a framed drawing made by Landru while in the death cell, and given to M. Navieres du Treuil, one of his lawyers, just before the killer's fatal appointment with Monsieur de Paris. When the frame was removed for cleaning by Navieres du Treuil's daughter, a message was revealed which was variously translated by the *Daily Express*: 'I did it. I burned their bodies in my kitchen oven,' and the *News of the World*: 'The trial witnesses are fools. I killed the women inside the house.'

There was a second, bizarre postscript to the Landru case. In 1965 one of France's leading authors, Françoise Sagan, scripted a film of the arch-criminal's life which was released under the title *Landru*.

To the amazement of everybody, Fernande Segret, Landru's 'fiancée' at the time of his arrest, arrived out of the blue, like a ghost from the past. She was there to sue the film's production company for 200,000 francs for misrepresenting her.

Mlle Segret, after a brief period of celebrity on the music-hall stage during Landru's trial, left France to work as a governess in the Lebanon. When she returned 40 years later, 'the fiancée that got away' installed herself in an old people's home at Flers-de-l'One, in the apple-growing region of Normandy. Fernande Segret was eventually awarded damages of 10,000 francs by the court, but if it had been a financially rewarding resurrection, the case had also brought with it a renewal of public interest in 'Bluebeard's mistress'. So ugly did the consequent publicity become that Mlle Segret, unable to face the pointing fingers and wagging tongues, threw herself into the moat of the castle of Flers-de-l'One and drowned; her last note read: 'I still love him [Landru], but I am suffering too greatly. I am going to kill myself.'

PATRICK MAHON
(England, 1924)

Murder on the Crumbles *

By the time Patrick Mahon had selected the Crumbles as the location for his appalling vandalism on Emily Kaye's body in April 1924, this desolate stretch of shingle beach which runs between Eastbourne and Pevensey had already acquired an unenviable reputation. On 20 August 1920, the body of a young woman was discovered hastily buried in the shingle; her head had been murderously battered with a brick. In December of the same year Jack Field and William Gray, two unemployed ruffians, stood in the dock at the Lewes Assizes to hear sentence of death passed upon them for the crime. It is in the same historic County Hall at Lewes that Patrick Mahon stands four years later; in the same dock. His sentence will be passed by the same judge – Mr Justice Avory. Avory; a small, thin-featured man who had amply earned his soubriquet 'The Hanging Judge'. A man responsible during his years on the bench for sending to the gallows a rogues' gallery of infamous killers.

There is coincidence, too, in the choice of prosecuting and defending counsels, respectively Sir Henry Curtis-Bennett KC and Mr J. D. Cassels KC.

*An abridged version of this case-history appeared in *The Murder Club Guide to South-East England*, Harrap, 1988.

Both had been cast in the identical role four years previously. And there was another member of the cast who was appearing four years on. He had played a minor part in the case against Field and Gray; this time it was to be a starring role: Sir Bernard Spilsbury, Pathologist to the Home Office. It had been Spilsbury's task to identify the body of Emily Kaye, what was left of it, from the scraps that Mahon had left; remains, Spilsbury confessed, which were the most gruesome he had ever seen, and this from a man whose career had inured him to most horrors.

The scene has been set; the supporting cast introduced. It is time to meet the central character, time to retrace the steps that led Patrick Mahon to the dock of the Lewes Assize Court, led to his being placed at the top of the list of Britain's wickedest men.

Born into a large middle-class Liverpool–Irish family in 1890, Patrick Herbert Mahon gave little indication in his early years of the monster that was to develop. He proved to be a moderately good scholar, a keen and talented footballer, and a regular participant in both the sacred and social aspects of the local Catholic church; one could also discern the blossoming good looks and easy charm that were fated to make him almost as irresistible to women as they became to him.

It was while he was at school that he met the future Mrs Mahon, and enjoyed the confidence and affection of the companion whom he was to betray so badly, so many times, in the succeeding years. In 1910, when she was only eighteen, they married. In 1911 Mahon swindled his employers of £123 by forging cheques, and with the ill-gotten wealth began the first of a series of extra-marital affairs which were to characterise and ultimately compromise his future. When he was eventually tracked down in the Isle of Man and returned home it was to be treated rather better than he deserved; the court took a lenient approach to his case and bound him over, and the ever-loving Mrs Mahon forgave him.

But for all that, a pattern seems to have been set; for despite the gesture of confidence extended to him by a Wiltshire dairy company in giving him a job, it was not long before Patrick Mahon had his fingers in his new master's till, to the tune of £60. This time the Assizes at Dorchester were less accommodating, and Mahon was sent down for one year.

But Mrs Mahon was characteristically understanding, and at the end of his twelve-month stretch the couple started again in the town of Calne. It may be no more than a coincidence that Mahon's arrival in town was accompanied by an outbreak of unsolved burglaries. It is certain, though, that he was quickly developing a taste for horse-racing, and was frequently to be seen on the course in the capacity of a bookmaker's clerk. However, such dishonesties as there were – not discounting a string of love affairs – attracted nothing by way of retribution. It was not until 1916 that Patrick Mahon stepped back into the legal limelight.

It was in the early part of that year that the branch of the National Provident Bank situated in Sunningdale was entered late at night and for no honest purpose. Indeed, a servant girl who was disturbed by the intruder and rose from her bed to investigate was rewarded with a severe beating about the head with a hammer. The attacker, the intruder, was Patrick Mahon. Now, whatever explanation one cares to allow – stupidity, arrogance, sheer lust – Mahon's subsequent behaviour was, to say the least, extraordinary; for when the poor girl recovered consciousness she found herself embraced in Mahon's arms being kissed; being asked to forgive the previous crude introduction. Not surprisingly, identification proved no problem at his trial, and Patrick Herbert Mahon was handed down a five-year sentence.

By the time he returned to the forgiving arms of his wife she had managed, by dint of hard work and resourcefulness, to rise to the responsible position of company secretary to the firm of Consols Automatic Aerators Ltd at Sunbury, now a part of Greater London. In fact her integrity was held in such regard that, when she interceded on behalf of her errant husband, Patrick was taken on as a travelling representative. It was a job at which he did surprisingly well, though perhaps it was having been provided with a legitimate reason for leaving his wife 'on business' that helped sustain his interest. Certainly he never passed up the opportunity to socialise with members of the opposite sex; sometimes, as we shall soon learn, in grotesque circumstances.

It was as the direct result of his job with Consols Automatic that Mahon met the unfortunate Emily Beilby Kaye. Emily was a not unattractive woman, though at the age of 37 she remained unmarried and living at a London residential hostel for girls in Guildford Street, Bloomsbury. Perhaps she had tired of the single state; perhaps she was beginning to glimpse the spectre of a lonely old age. Whatever prompted her, she needed no great coercion to enter into an affair of the heart with Consols' new sales manager. The almost unseemly speed with which the romance developed may well have disconcerted Mahon; it is certain that the intensity with which Miss Kaye was prepared to give her passionate all was not fully reciprocated.

It was not long before Mahon was frankly worried; worried that he might be becoming a victim to a will stronger – or more desperate, or both – than his own; worried about how he could escape. Worried most of all because (though he denied it at his trial) he had made Emily Kaye pregnant, and she was now demanding that they go away together abroad.

It was at this stage, in the early days of April 1924, that Emily Kaye suggested – in fact insisted on – what she called a 'love experiment'. She had long held that Patrick's resistance could be overcome if only they had an extended period alone together to allow their affections free rein, to allow their love to flower. Besides, he could hardly refuse now; not since her fortuitous discovery.

The discovery came about quite by accident when Emily was clearing out a drawer and (product of the wildest coincidence) found the drawer lined with the very newspaper that reported Mahon's trial at Guildford all those years before. It would be unlikely if this piece of knowledge – with its implicit threat of exposure – did not play a large part in Mahon's capitulation; in his agreeing to rent a bungalow on the lonely Crumbles. It may also have been the final straw that resulted in so awful an end for Emily Kaye.

Unaware of the scheme that must by now have taken hold of Mahon's mind, Emily decided to press him further; press him to elope with her to South Africa. She had already bought herself an engagement ring and announced the forthcoming voyage to her friends and relatives; and it was probably with that wild and distant view of the future that Emily Kaye travelled on ahead of her paramour to Eastbourne; to the bungalow known as Officer's House, formerly the residence of the commander of the coastguard station on that part of the beach. At any rate, she had cashed in the last of her shares before leaving London (the remainder of her nest-egg had already found its way in large part into Mahon's pocket).

Mahon travelled down on 12 April from his home at Pagoda Avenue, Richmond, where he had told his wife he was going out 'on business'. Unsurprisingly (but in the light of what was to transpire, indicative of what was hatching in his mind) Mahon picked up a young lady named Duncan on his way and arranged to meet her for supper the following Wednesday. His only other diversion was to purchase a chef's knife and a tenon saw at a shop near London's Victoria Station.

The 'love experiment' seems to have started in an optimistic enough atmosphere; Emily met Mahon at the station and they travelled thence by taxi to Officer's House. Emily, still entertaining high hopes of persuading Patrick out to South Africa, outlined the plan in a letter she wrote to a friend, dated Eastbourne, 14 April. On the following day, Tuesday, 15 April, the couple travelled back up to London, Mahon having strict instructions to get himself a passport; this he resolutely avoided doing, and the row that his refusal instigated was to gather momentum on the return train journey to the bungalow. Once 'home', Emily insisted that Mahon write a letter to his friends informing them of his intention to depart for Africa; Mahon, equally insistent, refused.

Now we only have Mahon's version of what happened next – poor Emily was not to survive the impassioned scene – and this is how he recounted that version to the court in his examination by Mr J. D. Cassels:

Mr Cassels: You say she got very excited, I think?

Mr Justice Avory: Very angry.

Mahon: Very angry and excited.

Cassels: Tell us what was done then.

Mahon: I realised from her manner that a crisis was coming; she seemed hysterical and overwrought.

Avory: This is all description; a sort of narrative. We want to know what happened, not what you thought and what you imagined, but what happened.

Mahon: I said to Miss Kaye, 'Peter [a pet name], I am going to bed' . . . Miss Kaye said something, I could not catch what she did say, but as I turned by the bedroom door she flung the [coal] axe which was on the table. I barely had time to avoid it, and it struck me on the right shoulder, here; it glanced off my shoulder and hit the framework of the door . . . I was astounded by the suddenness, by the attack altogether, and in a second Miss Kaye followed up the throw. She leaped across the room, clutching at my face . . . I did my best to keep her off. We closed and struggled backwards and forwards. I realised in a minute that I was dealing with a woman almost mad, mad with anger. I became absolutely uneasy with fear and fright.

Avory: You did?

Mahon: I did, my Lord, and with almost a last despairing throw I pushed Miss Kaye off and we both fell over the easy chair to the left of the fireplace. Miss Kaye's head hit the [coal] cauldron and I fell with her . . . I think I must have fainted with the fear and with the shock. I do not remember when I became conscious of what was happening or had happened. Miss Kaye was lying by the coal scuttle and blood had flowed from her head where she was lying on the floor . . . Miss Kaye was motionless . . . I pinched her and spoke to her and did what I could to rouse her, and she never moved or answered . . . [I remember] getting up and dashing water into Miss Kaye's face and calling her by name, and she did not answer. I think I must have gone half mad, I think I must have come out into the garden and crazy, I think, with fright and fear. I remember coming back to the bungalow later and Miss Kaye was still lying there . . . It would be hours later, I think; it would be neither towards day-break or day-break.

Avory: When you came back she was still lying there?

Mahon: Still lying there.

Cassels: And dead?

Mahon: And dead.

Could it possibly have been as Mahon had testified? Could it have been a horrific accident, the obvious gravity of which sent him into a delirium of panic? Or did Patrick Mahon cold-bloodedly put into execution a plan which he had been contemplating for weeks; for which he had already purchased the means of decimating the body?

It is almost certain that the jury, in opting for the latter supposition, were bearing in mind Mahon's movements immediately after the death of Emily Kaye. Remember, he had made an appointment to meet Miss Duncan on the following day; and it is an appointment which he honoured, taking the lady for dinner in London, at the Victoria Street Restaurant. This might have been excused as a move calculated to allay suspicion; but if that is true, what explanation can be given for his next move? Could there have been any justification for inviting Miss Duncan down to the bungalow to spend the Easter weekend with him; any possible justification for inviting her to share the bed in which Emily Kaye had joined him three nights previously? Sharing a bed in the room next to which was deposited a travelling trunk containing Emily's already decapitated corpse. Because that is exactly what he did. Until Easter Monday when they caught the late train back to London.

It is not necessary to go into details of how Mahon returned the following day to Eastbourne; how he hacked his way through Emily Kaye's body in an attempt to dispose of it; the testimony of Sir Bernard Spilsbury reproduced below is eloquent enough to describe the scene of carnage that it was his misfortune to examine.

But return now to Surrey, to Richmond, to Pagoda Avenue; and to Mrs Mahon, the wife who had proved a constant refuge. A wife who, unhappily for Mahon, was at last beginning to see through him. For some time she had been suspicious of Patrick's activities in the direction of other women; that, and a fear that he may have returned to his shady bookmaking activities on the racecourse, had led her to start spying on him; had led her to retain the services of a private investigator – by name, Mr John Beard, by experience a former detective-inspector with the railway police. It is interesting to base this next stage of Patrick Mahon's inexorable fall from grace on the recollections of ex-Superintendent Percy Savage of the CID, the man who was to lead the Crumbles investigation; the hand of retribution that was to settle on Mahon's most deserving shoulder.

Mrs Mahon had been searching the pockets of her husband's clothes when she turned out a left-luggage ticket for a bag that had been deposited at Waterloo railway station. After consulting with Mr Beard, the two of them went to redeem the bag which though locked revealed to Beard's exploring fingers a large knife and a quantity of bloodstained cloth. His years of detective experience served him well now. Beard handed back the bag to the attendant, receiving in return the ticket, which he sent Mrs Mahon home with to return to the place whence it had been lifted. He next telephoned Scotland Yard, and spoke to Chief Inspector Savage, voiced his suspicions, and finally accompanied the senior officer to Waterloo where Savage managed to remove a small sample of the stained cloth from the bag for analysis – analysis which was to prove the presence of human blood. Sending detective-sergeants Frew and Thompson to wait for Mahon at Waterloo station, Percy Savage returned to Scotland Yard to wait. At 6.15 the following morning Patrick Mahon redeemed his bag, and an instant later was flanked by two policemen:

'We are police officers. Is that your bag?'

'I believe it is.'

Told he would have to accompany his captors to the police station, Mahon replied indignantly, 'Rubbish!' He was then escorted there with no more ado. Savage's memory of Mahon at that first meeting was that 'Mahon, who was in the waiting room, stood up and received me with a pleasant smile. He was a man above the average height, and was dressed in a well-made dark brown lounge suit, a brown tie, and brown shoes. His brown soft hat, tanned gloves, and folded umbrella lay on the table. "Chief Inspector Savage? I've heard about you," he said, greeting me in the most friendly manner, "But this is the first time we have met".'

In a private room Mahon was confronted with the contents of the locked bag – a torn pair of silk bloomers, two pieces of new white silk, a blue silk scarf – all stained with blood and grease – and a large cook's knife; also a canvas racket bag with the initials 'E.B.K.' and some disinfectant powder. Mahon watched in silence.

'How do you account for the possession of these things?'

'I am fond of dogs, and I suppose I have carried meat home for the dogs in it.'

'Dog's meat? But this is human blood.' Mahon was silent.

'You don't wrap dog's meat in silk. Your explanation does not satisfy me.'

'Dog's meat, dog's meat,' repeated Mahon. 'Dog's meat,' again. Then, 'You seem to know all about it.'

By the early hours of the following morning Mahon had made his statement; had begun his irreversible journey to the scaffold.

All this evidence has been given to a packed court at Lewes. Mahon's defence – that Miss Emily Kaye had met her death by accidentally banging her head – collapsed; not least because that vital part of her anatomy had been completely destroyed, thus rendering the cause of death unascertainable. The suspicions aroused by the complete disappearance of the uterus of this obviously pregnant woman – a fact of which Mahon had denied being aware – did little to help his case. And Patrick Mahon himself, in the witness box, made a very poor showing.

At two o'clock on Saturday, 19 July 1924 the foreman of the jury settled Mahon's fate; minutes later Mr Justice Avory addressed the prisoner:

'Patrick Herbert Mahon, the jury have arrived at the only proper conclusion on the evidence which was laid before them. They have arrived at that conclusion without knowing anything of your past life, to which you yourself made reference in your statements to the police, which references have, in mercy to you, been excluded from the consideration of the jury; they did not know that you had already suffered a term of penal servitude for a crime of violence. There can be no question that you deliberately designed the death of this woman . . .

[*Mahon:* I did not.]

'. . . For that crime you must suffer the penalty imposed by the law. The sentence of the court upon you is that you be taken from this place to a lawful prison, and then to a place of execution, and that you be there hanged by the neck until you be dead, and that your body be afterwards buried within the precincts of the prison wherein you shall have been last confined before your execution. And may the Lord have mercy upon your soul.'

On 9 September Patrick Mahon faced the hangman in the execution shed at Wandsworth Prison; as had Jack Field and William Gray four years previously.

A significant part of the prosecution case concerned the technical requirement to identify the human remains found at Officer's House as those of Emily Kaye, and it had been Sir Bernard Spilsbury's brief to establish that identity. The passage in the trial transcript recording the examination of Sir Bernard by Curtis-Bennett shows just how difficult and unenviable a task it had been.

Curtis-Bennett: Your names are Bernard Henry Spilsbury?

Spilsbury: Yes.

Curtis-Bennett: You are a lecturer on special pathology at St Bartholomew's Hospital, London, and you are Honorary Pathologist to the Home Office?

Spilsbury: Yes.

Curtis-Bennett: On 4 May last did you visit the

Officer's House at Langley Bungalows in company with Chief Inspector Savage and other officers?

Spilsbury: I did.

Curtis-Bennett: Did you make an examination of all the rooms there?

Spilsbury: Yes.

Curtis-Bennett: Perhaps you would tell us in your own language what you found?

Spilsbury: In the bedroom marked No. 3 on the plan I saw a saw described as a tenon saw; it was rusty and greasy and had a piece of flesh adhering to it. I also saw a number of articles of female clothing and a tea-cloth, which were blood-stained, and most of them were greasy and had some soot or coal dust on them.

Curtis-Bennett: I think they were collected?

Spilsbury: Yes, they were.

Curtis-Bennett: In the dining-room did you see the cauldron coal-scuttle?

Spilsbury: I did.

Curtis-Bennett: Did you notice anything upon that scuttle?

Spilsbury: There were two tiny spots which I thought were blood, and I noticed that one leg of the coal-scuttle was badly bent.

Curtis-Bennett: Was there a saucer upon the floor?

Spilsbury: There was.

Curtis-Bennett: Was that close to the fireplace?

Spilsbury: Close to the fireplace. That contained solid fat.

Curtis-Bennett: Was there also a large two-gallon saucepan?

Spilsbury: There was.

Curtis-Bennett: What was the condition of the inside of that?

Spilsbury: It was about half-full of a reddish fluid with a layer of thick grease at the top, and at the bottom of that I found a piece of boiled flesh with some skin adhering to it.

Curtis-Bennett: In connection with that saucepan, whereabouts was the coal cauldron?

Spilsbury: It was on the right side of the fireplace.

Curtis-Bennett: The saucepan in the fireplace?

Spilsbury: The saucepan in the fireplace.

Curtis-Bennett: Was the fender splashed at all?

Spilsbury: Yes, splashed with grease.

Curtis-Bennett: I think in the fireplace there were ashes, were there not?

Spilsbury: Yes.

Curtis-Bennett: Perhaps you will deal with that later on?

Spilsbury: Yes, I will. There were no other blood stains to be seen in that room.

Curtis-Bennett: The dining-room?

Spilsbury: No.

Curtis-Bennett: Was the scullery next?

Spilsbury: Yes, I saw the dustpan which contained the ashes, which I afterwards examined.

Curtis-Bennett: You will perhaps deal with all the bones later on?

Spilsbury: Yes.

Curtis-Bennett: Was there anything else you found?

Spilsbury: Yes, there was a saucepan with a deposit of grease in the bottom; a galvanised iron bath containing a little greasy fluid, and an enamelled bowl smeared with grease on the inside.

Curtis-Bennett: Inspector Savage has told us he had the hat-box and the trunk removed on 3 May to the scullery.

Spilsbury: I found them there, yes.

Curtis-Bennett: Did you examine first of all the hat-box?

Spilsbury: I did.

Curtis-Bennett: What did you find in that?

Spilsbury: I found articles of clothing together with a large number of pieces of flesh, thirty-seven in all.

Mr Justice Avory: Thirty-seven separate pieces?

Spilsbury: Thirty-seven separate pieces. One piece had been cut from the back of the right shoulder and included the shoulder-blade, and part of the collar bone, and part of the bone of the upper arm. Both of these bones had been sawn across. The second piece consisted of skin, fat and muscle from the region of the navel.

Curtis-Bennett: And the other thirty-five?

Spilsbury: The other thirty-five consisted of skin, and many of them also muscle.

Curtis-Bennett: Upon five of the pieces of flesh what did you find?

Spilsbury: On five pieces I found hair resembling that from the private parts – pubic hair.

Curtis-Bennett: Fair or dark?

Spilsbury: It was fair.

Curtis-Bennett: Did all the pieces of flesh that you found in the hat-box appear to have been boiled; were they in fact boiled?

Spilsbury: All had been probably boiled. May I add that of course they were all human.

Curtis-Bennett: In the trunk, Exhibit 8, what did you find?

Spilsbury: I found four large pieces of a human body. One of the left half of the lower part of the body resembling the pelvis, with muscle and skin attached to it, and the upper part of the thigh bone, including also the lower part of the spine.

Curtis-Bennett: Had the spine been sawn across?

Spilsbury: Yes, all the bones practically had been sawn across.

Curtis-Bennett: Is there anything you want to tell us about that?

Spilsbury: Only a small fragment of the wall of the vagina, the female congenital passage, was attached to it.

Curtis-Bennett: Now the second piece.

Spilsbury: The second piece formed the lower part of the right half of the trunk and having a portion of the thigh bone attached to it. The third piece consisted of the right half of the chest together with the spinal column from the level of the sixth vertical bone from the neck to a point at which the pelvis had been sawn off. The breast bone was attached to this piece, and portions of most of the left ribs.

Curtis-Bennett: Was the right breast present on that piece?

Spilsbury: Yes, it was.

Curtis-Bennett: Is there anything you want to tell us about that?

Spilsbury: When I pressed it milky fluid escaped from the nipple.

Mr Justice Avory: You had better say at once what that indicates.

Spilsbury: May I deal with the other piece first, my Lord?

Mr Justice Avory: Yes.

Spilsbury: The fourth piece formed the left side of the chest and on the back of this piece I found an area two inches long over the shoulder blade which had a recent bruise. The left breast was attached to this fragment also, and had a similar appearance.

Curtis-Bennett: Where was the bruise?

Spilsbury: On the back of the left shoulder blade.

Curtis-Bennett: The left breast presented the same appearance?

Spilsbury: The same appearance as the right one.

Curtis-Bennett: Did these four pieces fit together accurately?

Spilsbury: Yes.

Curtis-Bennett: And fitted together they would form practically the whole trunk of a woman?

Spilsbury: Almost the whole.

Curtis-Bennett: With portions of the limbs attached which you have spoken of?

Spilsbury: Yes.

Curtis-Bennett: Had they been boiled or not?

Spilsbury: No, they had not.

Curtis-Bennett: Did you make any further examination of the breasts?

Spilsbury: Yes, I did. Both by cutting into them and by microscopical examination afterwards.

Curtis-Bennett: As the result of that examination are you able to express an opinion as to the condition of the woman before she died?

Spilsbury: Yes, I am; from the condition of the breasts I am of the opinion that at the time of her death she was pregnant, and in the early stages of pregnancy.

Curtis-Bennett: In the same trunk was there a large biscuit tin with a lid upon it?

Spilsbury: Yes. May I deal with something else first?

Curtis-Bennett: Please do.

Spilsbury: There were portions of certain organs attached to the trunk. A portion of the right lung adhering to the right half of the chest wall, and portions of some of the other organs of the abdomen were still attaching, and pieces of liver, a small piece of spleen, and one kidney, not otherwise accounted for when I examined the contents.

Curtis-Bennett: There were certain organs attached to those four pieces?

Spilsbury: Portions, and there was also rather fine hair

about eight to nine inches long adhering to one of those pieces.

Curtis-Bennett: That I think you kept and it was exhibited?

Spilsbury: Yes.

Curtis-Bennett: From your microscopical and other examinations of the breast you express the opinion that this woman was in fact pregnant at the time of her death?

Spilsbury: Yes.

Curtis-Bennett: Have you been able to find at all anywhere the uterus?

Spilsbury: No.

Mr Justice Avory: You mean no portion of it?

Spilsbury: Only the lower end, which I found in the contents of the tin box to which I am about to refer. The bulk of the uterus was entirely absent.

Curtis-Bennett: Give us the contents of the tin box.

Spilsbury: In a large square biscuit tin I found human organs of the chest and of the abdomen in nine separate pieces. Shall I detail all the pieces separately? One long piece was a portion of the large intestine eight inches long.

Curtis-Bennett: The second?

Spilsbury: The second a piece of small bowel together with the lower end or the neck of the womb or uterus.

Curtis-Bennett: Had that been cut clean across?

Spilsbury: Yes.

Mr Justice Avory: The uterus had been separated from its neck by a clean cut?

Spilsbury: Through the neck itself.

Curtis-Bennett: In the one ovary which you found did you notice anything?

Spilsbury: Yes, when I cut into the ovary I found a large yellow body which is characteristic of a condition of pregnancy. This is also confirmed by microscopical examination.

Curtis-Bennett: I do not know that you need to give us in detail the other pieces unless there is anything you want particularly to refer to?

Spilsbury: I do not think there is.

Curtis-Bennett: On examination of all those organs which you found in the tin box was there any condition of disease about any of them?

Spilsbury: No active disease at all. There were evidences of a previous attack of pleurisy on the right side of the chest from the adhesions which were present.

Curtis-Bennett: Would that or not have anything to do with the cause of death?

Spilsbury: Nothing at all.

Curtis-Bennett: Did you also examine the fragments of burnt bone which had been recovered from the sitting-room and dining-room grates?

Spilsbury: I did.

Curtis-Bennett: And from the ashes in the dustpan in the scullery?

Spilsbury: Yes.

Curtis-Bennett: Did you yourself search through those ashes?

Spilsbury: Yes, I did.

Curtis-Bennett: Did you altogether find between 900 and 1000 fragments of bone?

Spilsbury: I did.

Curtis-Bennett: Could the flesh which you saw have been cut off with the knife, Exhibit 58, the cook's knife?

Spilsbury: Yes.

Curtis-Bennett: And the bones, could they have been sawn through by the saw which has been produced?

Spilsbury: Yes, they could.

Curtis-Bennett: I should like you to give us what your opinion is as a result of your examination altogether of the flesh and bones and organs which you examined.

Spilsbury: May I, before I do so, add one further small matter, that as a result of the examination of the fragments of bone *I am now satisfied that the skull and the bones of the upper part of the neck were not present in those fragments*, nor have I identified any fragments of bone from the lower left limb beyond the point at which it had been severed from the trunk.

Curtis-Bennett: Are you quite positive there is no sign of any skull bone?

Spilsbury: Yes.

Curtis-Bennett: Or neck bone?

Spilsbury: Or neck bone.

Curtis-Bennett: Can you tell us what your opinion is after your examination?

Mr Justice Avory: As to what?

Curtis-Bennett: As to first of all was this the body of a woman, what size woman, and so on?

Spilsbury: All the material which I have examined, portions of the trunk, the organs, pieces of boiled flesh, and those fragments of bone which I have been able to identify are all of them human, and correspond with the parts of a single body – there are no duplicates at all. The four pieces of chest and abdominal wall fit accurately to form one trunk, and the organs in the tin box, together with the fragments of organs attached to the four pieces of the trunk, form a complete set of human organs, with the exception of certain missing portions, of which the uterus and one ovary are the most important. The body was that of an adult female of big build and fair hair. She was pregnant, in my opinion, at the time of her death, and at an early period, probably between one and three months . . .

No disease was found to account for natural death, and no condition which would account for unnatural death.

Mr Justice Avory: I do not follow what that means.

Curtis-Bennett: Just explain that.

Spilsbury: In the parts of the body which I examined the only injury which I found was the bruise at the back of the left shoulder. *The head and neck being missing* there was no evidence of death by some unnatural cause.

Curtis-Bennett: You say there is an absence of any cause of death in the parts which you have examined?

Spilsbury: Yes.

Curtis-Bennett: What does that indicate to you?

Spilsbury: That the cause of death . . .

Mr Justice Avory: One moment! That is rather a question for the jury.

But what of the missing head? What importance was the jury to attach to that? Was it, as Mahon claimed in his defence, simply the first piece, randomly chosen, to receive the total obliteration treatment planned for the whole body? Or was it disposed of so carefully and quickly in order to conceal the real cause of death? Not the accidental blow on the head being proposed, but a massive bludgeoning with an axe; a blow delivered with such manic force that it shattered the weapon's shaft.

Under cross-examination by Sir Henry Curtis-Bennett, Mahon describes the treatment of the head:

Curtis-Bennett: Do you still say you burned the head?

Mahon: I not only say I burned the head, but I did burn the head.

Curtis-Bennett: In which room did you burn the head?

Mahon: In the sitting-room.

Curtis-Bennett: The front sitting-room?

Mahon: This sitting-room here. [Indicating on the model]

Curtis-Bennett: How long did you say it took?

Mahon: I cannot say, six hours probably.

Curtis-Bennett: Are you not clear upon the matter at all?

Mahon: I am clear that I burned the head.

Curtis-Bennett: Are you not clear about the time? This was a terrible thing you were doing. Did you not realise how long it took?

Mahon: If you knew the circumstances in which the head was burned (I can only say burned), I could not even stay in the room while it was burning.★

Curtis-Bennett: I want to test this story of yours a little. You say it took six hours?

Mahon: I think about six hours.

Curtis-Bennett: Did you say to Sergeant Frew: 'I

★This enigmatic reference was clear at least to Mr Cassels, for in Brixton Prison awaiting trial, Mahon had related the following story: On the day on which he had disposed of the head of Emily Kaye, the sky was grey and heavy with rain clouds; as Mahon stoked up the fire and put the head into the flames, the storm suddenly broke with a fearful crash of thunder and streaks of lightning. As if this had been a signal, the dead eyes of the burning head flickered open – sending Mahon shrieking out of the cottage on to the rainlashed beach, where he cowered, terrified, in the midst of the squall. It must have seemed like Nemesis that, at the very moment when Mahon stood in the dock denying the dreadful act of murder, there burst another storm, over Lewes, the thunder catching Mahon in mid-sentence and sending him, shrinking back, speechless at the memory of the dead eyes. For this anecdote we are indebted to the late Edgar Wallace to whom it was told, and who retold it in the Introduction to his edited version of the trial transcript (*Notable British Trials*, William Hodge and Co.).

burned the head in an ordinary fire. It was finished in three hours. The poker went through the head when I poked it.' Do you remember saying that?

Mahon: No, I do not remember saying that.

Curtis-Bennett: And what was left you put in the dustbin. Is that what you say?

Mahon: No, what I actually did with the remains of the head was to take the bones out of the fire grate and break them up and put them in the dust-tray, not the dustbin.

Curtis-Bennett: 'The next day I broke the skull and put the pieces in the dustbin?'

Mahon: I meant the dustbin in the scullery.

Curtis-Bennett: That, we know, has been examined, and we have the results of that.

Mahon: I did not leave them there.

Curtis-Bennett: Where did you put them?

Mahon: I broke them up very small and threw them away.

Curtis-Bennett: You did not do that with the bones of any other part, did you?

Mahon: Bones of the other parts were thrown away.

Curtis-Bennett: You have heard Sir Bernard Spilsbury's evidence. Were not they left either in the ashes in the different rooms or in the dust-tray in the scullery, the other bones?

Mahon: That was simply because I had not been down to the bungalow for a week.

Curtis-Bennett: Where did you throw the bones of this most important part of the body, the skull?

Mahon: I threw them about over the garden wall. They were tremendously small bones.

Curtis-Bennett: Where were they thrown?

Mahon: They were thrown on the shingle around the house.

Curtis-Bennett: What did you break them with?

Mahon: I broke them with my hands like this; after they came out of the fire they would break just like that.

Curtis-Bennett: I suggest to you that would be impossible?

Mahon: Your suggestion is entirely wrong, Sir Henry.

Curtis-Bennett: I may have leave to recall Sir Bernard about it.

Mahon: That is a thing which I know.

Curtis-Bennett: You broke them with your hands?

Mahon: I broke them with my hands.

Mr Justice Avory: Very small pieces, you say?

Mahon: Very small pieces.

Curtis-Bennett: Did you break up any of the bones of the other parts of the body and throw them over the wall?

Mahon: No. What other bones there were were burned.

Curtis-Bennett: And left?

Mahon: Left simply because I had not finished.

Curtis-Bennett: Did you not burn some other parts of the body when you burned the head, the same day?

Mahon: I think I burned one of the feet, or the two feet.

Curtis-Bennett: Did you break up those bones?

Mahon: No.

Curtis-Bennett: Only the bones of the skull?

Mahon: Only the bones of the skull.

Curtis-Bennett: And that was done on the 22nd April, on the Tuesday, was it not?

Mahon: On the 22nd, yes; I burned the head on the 22nd.

Curtis-Bennett: You burned the head and the legs and the feet in the same grate?

Mahon: I do not think I burned them all together; it is obviously impossible.

Curtis-Bennett: No, but on the same day?

Mahon: I did not mean that I burned them all on the same day.

Curtis-Bennett: Just listen. 'On that day [22 April] I opened the trunk and burned the head in the sitting-room grate. I came back to town either late Tuesday night or early Wednesday morning.' Did it not mean you burned them on the same day?

Mahon: Yes.

Curtis-Bennett: And yet although you had burned these other parts of the body, the feet and legs, the only part you destroyed altogether by throwing it away were the bones of the skull?

Mahon: I destroyed parts of the legs altogether by throwing the bones away.

Curtis-Bennett: Did you?

Mahon: Of course I did.

Curtis-Bennett: By throwing the bones away?

Mahon: By throwing the bones away.

Curtis-Bennett: Where?

Mahon: Out of the train.

Curtis-Bennett: Threw the bones out of the train?

Mahon: Yes. You know perfectly well all the bones have not been found. There is one leg missing.

Curtis-Bennett: I thought the only thing you had in the Gladstone bag was the boiled flesh. Were there bones too?

Mahon: There were one or two bones.

Curtis-Bennett: Did you take the head away in that bag to Reading?

Mahon: No. It seemed futile. I burnt the head in the kitchen grate, and it took the best part of an afternoon to do it.

Mr Justice Avory: In which?

Mahon: In this grate [indicating], not the kitchen. This is the only grate I did it in.

Curtis-Bennett: But you used other grates to burn other parts of the body?

Mahon: I know I did, but that is the biggest fire. The reason I used the other grates was for speed – fires going in two rooms together.

POSTSCRIPT

Ex-Superintendent Percy Savage, in his book *Savage of Scotland Yard* (1934) explains the origin of the 'Murder Bag':

What is known as the 'Murder Bag' is now part of the equipment of a chief inspector, who takes it with him whenever he is called upon to investigate a case of murder in the provinces. The origin of the 'Murder Bag' is interesting. The first murder case I had after my appointment as chief-inspector was the crime for which Patrick Mahon was hanged for the murder of Miss Emily Kaye at Eastbourne. When Sir Bernard Spilsbury visited the bungalow on the Crumbles, he expressed astonishment that I had been handling portions of putrid flesh with my bare hands, and he pointed out that I had run a grave risk of septic poisoning. He said that no medical man outside a lunatic asylum would dream of doing such a thing, and that I ought to have at least worn rubber gloves. I told him we were not provided with rubber gloves. Sir Bernard, who is nothing if not practical, had a very serious talk with me and my friend Dr Scott-Gillett, who had been of great assistance to me.

We police officers not only had no rubber gloves, but we lacked many other things which were essential to the efficient performance of our duties. If we wanted to preserve human hair on clothing, or soil or dust on boots, we had to pick it up with our fingers and put it in a piece of paper. We had no tapes to measure distances, no compass to determine direction, no apparatus to take fingerprints, no first-aid outfit, no instrument to find the depth of water, no magnifying glass. In fact we had no appliances available for immediate use on the scene of a crime. And so it came about that the 'Murder Bag' was evolved. With the assistance of Sir Bernard and Dr Scott-Gillett, I made out a list of necessary articles for inclusion in the bag, and each chief inspector now takes one with him on every occasion he is called on to investigate a crime in the country.

ALFRED ARTHUR ROUSE
(England, 1930–1)

The Blazing Car Murder

At two o'clock on the morning of 6 November 1930, William Bailey and Alfred Brown were returning home down Hardingstone Lane from a Guy Fawkes night dance, when some fifty yards ahead of them they saw something burning. Given the date, they were less surprised by the sight of a fire than by the sudden appearance of a man who rushed past them, remarking as he did so that 'it looks as if someone is having a bonfire'.

Approaching closer Brown and Bailey saw that the 'bonfire' was in reality a Morris Minor motor car ablaze. They immediately summoned the police, and when the fire was under control a body could be seen collapsed across the front seats, burnt beyond recognition.

The vehicle's owner proved to be one Alfred Arthur Rouse, 36-year-old commercial traveller, and the man recognised by Messrs Brown and Bailey from their encounter on the 6th. Rouse explained to the police officers who interviewed him that he had picked up a hitchhiker on the Great North Road; had stopped in Hardingstone Lane to answer a call of nature and asked his travelling companion to fill the car's petrol tank from a can in the boot. When he looked back the car was ablaze: 'I saw the man was inside and I tried to open the door, but could not as the car was by then a mass of flames . . . I did not know what to do; I saw the two men . . . I lost my head.'

Described by his trial judge as 'a most facile liar', Rouse was found guilty of murdering his passenger, and after an unsuccessful appeal was executed on 10 March 1931.

But why kill a perfectly innocent stranger, and at the same time burn out your own car?

The answer lay in Rouse's personality; a personality which, for some unaccountable reason – he was neither honest nor faithful, or for that matter particularly good-looking – was very attractive to the ladies. But entertaining his amours, and keeping up with the expense of several 'homes', not forgetting various maintenance orders, were beginning to overstretch Rouse's modest income. In short, his 'harem' had become a liability from which he desperately needed to escape.

What if he were to disappear? Start a new life; leave behind him the four-score or more 'affairs', the illegitimate children, the bigamous marriages. What if he were believed to have been tragically killed in a motor accident? We know this is true because when all hope of reprieve was gone Rouse decided to make a clean breast of it – or very nearly – and confessed to the murder, not to a priest, not to a policeman, but to the *Daily Sketch*:

ROUSE'S CONFESSION

It was the Agnes Kesson case at Epsom in June [1930]*

*Agnes Kesson was a Scottish-born waitress who had been found strangled in a ditch at Epsom on Derby Day 1930. After four months of intensive enquiries during which police took more than 400 statements, a coroner's jury returned a verdict that Agnes Kesson had been murdered, though there was insufficient evidence to say by whom. The case has never been solved.

that first set me thinking. It showed that it was possible to beat the police if you were careful enough.

Since I read about that case I kept thinking of various plans. I tried to hit on something new. I did not want to do murder just for the sake of it.

I was in a tangle in various ways. Nellie Tucker was expecting another child* of which I would be the father and I was expecting to hear from 'Paddy' Jenkins similar news. There were other difficulties and I was fed up. I wanted to start afresh.

I let the matter drop from my mind for a while, but in the autumn of last year [1930] something happened which made me think again.

A man spoke to me near the Swan and Pyramid public house in Whetstone High Road. He was a down-and-out, and told the usual hard-luck story. I took him into the public house and he had some beer. I had lemonade. Of course, I paid for the drinks. He told me he usually hung about there.

I met him once again and stood him a couple of drinks. He did not tell me his name, but he did say that he had no relations, and was looking for work. He said he had been to Peterborough, Norwich, Hull, and other places trying to get work, and that he was in the habit of getting lifts on lorries.

He was the sort of man no one would miss, and I thought he would suit the plan I had in mind. I worked out the whole thing in my mind, and as it was then early in November, I suddenly realised that I should do it on 5 November, which was Bonfire Night, when a fire would not be noticed so much.

I think it was on 2 or 3 November that I searched out the man. He was having a drink of beer and we talked.

---

*Her second by Rouse, it was born on 29 October 1930.

When I said that I intended to go to Leicester on the Wednesday night he said he would be glad of a lift up there. This is what I thought he would say.

I made an appointment with him for the Wednesday night for about eight o'clock. I met him outside the Swan and Pyramid, and we went into the bar. He had more beer, and again I had lemonade.

I asked him if he would like something to drink on the journey, and he said he would. I bought a bottle of whisky. Then we both got into the car, which was outside the public house.

We drove first of all to my house in Buxted Road. I got out, leaving the man in the car. My wife was in.* She had seen me draw up near the house and she asked me who it was I had in the car. I said it was a man I knew, but she suspected that it was a woman.

I said: 'All right. I'll drive close up in front of the house, as I am turning round, to let you see that it is a man.'

I did so, as I drove out of Buxted Road, so that my wife could see for herself and would have no grounds for jealousy.

So far as I remember, it was about 8.30 when I started off for the north with the man in the car, though I might be mistaken about the time. I drove slowly because I wanted it to be late when I did what I had in mind. I don't think I travelled more than fifteen miles an hour.

I stopped at St Albans partly for a rest and partly to fill in the time. The man switched out the lights by mistake and a policeman spoke to me, as is already well known.

During the journey the man drank the whisky neat from the bottle and was getting quite fuzzled. We

*Rouse's 'legal' wife, the former Lily May Watkins.

talked a lot, but he did not tell me who he actually was. I did not care.

I turned into the Hardingstone Lane [outside Northampton] because it was quiet and near a main road, where I could get a lift from a lorry afterwards. I pulled the car up.

The man was half-dozing – the effect of the whisky. I looked at him and then gripped him by the throat with my right hand. I pressed his head against the back of the seat. He slid down, his hat falling off. I saw he had a bald patch on the crown of his head.

He just gurgled. I pressed his throat hard. My grip is very strong.

I used my right hand only because it is very powerful. People have always said I have a terrific grip. He did not resist. It was all very sudden. The man did not realise what was happening. I pushed his face back. After making a peculiar noise, the man was silent and I thought he was dead or unconscious.

Then I got out of the car taking my attaché case, the can of petrol and the mallet with me. I walked about ten yards in front of the car and opened the can, using the mallet to do so. I threw the mallet away and made a trail of petrol to the car. I took the mallet away with one purpose in view.

Also, I poured petrol over the man and loosened the petrol union joint and took the top off the carburettor. I put the petrol can in the back of the car.

I ran to the beginning of the petrol trail and put a match to it. The flame rushed to the car, which caught fire at once.

Petrol was leaking from the bottom of the car. That was the petrol I had poured over the man and the petrol that was dripping from the union joint and carburettor.

The fire was very quick, and the whole thing was a mass of flames in a few seconds. I ran away. I was running when I came near the two men, but I started to walk then. It is not true that I came out of the ditch when the men saw me. I was on the grass verge. I did shout to them that there must be 'a bonfire over there'.

I did not expect to see anyone in the lane at that time of night. It surprised me and I decided to change my plans.

I had intended to walk to Northampton and to get a train to Scotland. But when the men saw me I hesitated and went the other way. The men were right when they said they saw me hesitate.

I left my hat in the car. When I was driving, I nearly always did so with my hat off. I forgot, in the excitement, to take it out of the car.

I went to Wales because I had to go somewhere, and I did not know what to do. I did not think there would be much fuss in the papers about the thing, but pictures of the car with long accounts were published, and I left Wales.

I was not going to Scotland, as I said. I just went back to London because I thought it was the best thing to do. London is big.

In my attaché case was my identity disc, which the police still have. I intended to put it on the man in the car so that people would think it was me. I forgot to do so.

I knew that no one would find out that the man had been strangled, because the fire would be so fierce that no traces would be left.

I am not able to give any more help regarding the man who was burned in the car. I never asked his name. There was no reason why I should do so.

POSTSCRIPT

Not surprisingly, the mystery of the identity of Rouse's late travelling companion spread much farther than the confines of the court in which his last fatal hours were chronicled. It is customary in such cases for the police to be deluged with letters, telephone calls and visits from anxious friends and relatives all believing that the mystery man is their missing loved one. Though each and every one of these possibilities must be investigated, most are able to be simply dealt with at no serious cost to time. So it was with the army of reported identifications of the blazing car victim, coming as they did from every point of the compass.

Among those viewed more positively by the police was the case of Thomas Waite. In his *New Light on the Rouse Case,*★ J. C. Cannell, veteran reporter on the long-defunct *Daily Sketch*, recalls being sent to Merthyr, in south Wales, where Mrs Waite had the previous day been to the local police station to express the fear that her son was Rouse's unknown victim. The description given by Mrs Waite matched exactly the information gleaned from Sir Bernard Spilsbury's post-mortem examination – right down to the sooty deposit found in the lungs, prompting Sir Bernard to suggest that the man had, in life, been a coal miner. Thomas Waite had spent many years in the pits of his native Wales. To add emphasis to Mrs Waite's story, Tom's workmates in Brighton, where he had been recently employed, made an independent visit to their local police with his description and a report that he had not been seen at work since a day or two before 5 November. What was more, a man living at Tally Ho

★Published by John Long, London, 1931.

Corner, close to where Rouse claimed to have picked up the stranger, was positive that he had seen Waite there on 5 November. Confirmation that Thomas Waite and the corpse were one and the same was eagerly anticipated, at which stage Thomas Waite himself turned up, protesting that he was sorry to be a nuisance, but was still very much alive.

As if the flood of gratuitous correspondence were not enough, Cannell persuaded his news editor to offer a £100 reward for information as to the dead man's identity, and the *Sketch* was, unsurprisingly, inundated with further letters. But the enigma remained – and is likely to continue to be one of those baffling and insoluble mysteries of true crime.

Whether Rouse himself knew any more than he told in his confession is doubtful, despite his rather tantalising statement in prison to the effect that he didn't see why he should help the police in the matter of his victim's identity as 'they have not helped me'.

For what it was worth, though, Rouse did give a description:

Forty years of age, 5ft 6in. to 5ft 8in. tall, respectably dressed in a light-coloured overcoat, with the appearance of a clerk. Had a slight brogue, and a boxing or sporting tattoo on his right forearm; wearing police boots which he said he had been given by London police. Carried a sports diary.

KURT ERICH TETZNER
(Germany, 1929–31)

The Secret of the Green Opel

By the time he had conceived his 'unique' plan to become the late Mr Rouse in the year 1930, Alfred Arthur had just been pipped to the post. Although Rouse was unaware of it, in Germany Kurt Erich Tetzner had already tried the blazing car scam – without success. Not that it would have made much difference to Rouse's determination had he known – after all, he wasn't going to get caught, was he?

By November 1929 Tetzner had already had ample opportunity to prove his ruthlessness – only a few months earlier he had insured his mother-in-law's life for 10,000 marks knowing her to be suffering from terminal cancer. Up to this point he had been successfully advising the old lady not to undergo surgery, but with the current possibility of rich rewards, Tetzner could hardly get her under the knife quickly enough. When she died a few days after an unsuccessful operation, the gleeful Erich was moved to confide to his wife that this insurance business could prove a very profitable little supplement to his more legitimate commercial concerns.

Tetzner's next victim, he decided, would be himself; or rather, a body charred beyond identification in his burnt-out car.

After a number of false starts when those he had selected from the replies to a 'travelling companion

wanted' ad smelled a rat, Tetzner picked up Alois
Ortner, conveniently for his purpose a motor mechanic; an obliging fellow who, on a lonely stretch of
road outside Ingolstadt, needed no persuading to look
under the car for an imaginary oil-leak. That part had
been easy; crushing Ortner's skull with a hammer proved less so, and after a fierce struggle in which the
mechanic all but bested him, Tetzner decided to cut his
losses and drove off as fast as his tyres could carry him.

With extravagant irony, the luckless Ortner was
picked up by the police lying unconscious on the
roadside. His story they found so unbelievable that
Ortner was taken temporarily into custody suspected
of having attacked a passing motorist!

But at least he had escaped with his life.

On the night of Monday, 25 November 1929, Erich
Tetzner, in his green Opel, picked up a young man on
the road to Etterhausen, in Bavaria. A more co-
operative victim by far than Herr Ortner, the youth
quickly succumbed to the tightening rope around his
neck, and passed into oblivion with hardly a whimper.

It was a grief-stricken Frau Emma Tetzner who
tearfully identified the cinders in her husband's
wrecked and fire-gutted car. Poor Erich!

Insurance investigators are a suspicious group by
nature, and long experience had taught the man in
charge of the Tetzner claim the wisdom of caution in
cases of sudden death in those who had only weeks
previously taken out huge policies on their life – with
three separate insurance companies.

On 30 November the agent of Nordstern Insurance
called on Professor Richard Kockel. Luminary among
the German forensic scientists, and of international
reputation, Kockel had a particular interest in the pathology of fire victims, and it was with this singular

expertise that he was to elevate the case of Erich Tetzner to the position of a German forensic classic.

Kockel received the suspicious insurance investigator in his laboratory at Leipzig University's Institute of Forensic Medicine, and within the hour both men were on their way to the city's South Cemetery where the charred remains of Erich Tetzner awaited imminent burial.

While mourners waited on the very steps of the cemetery chapel, Richard Kockel performed his postmortem. Externally, he noted that the remains comprised the trunk with the upper part of the vertebral column attached, terminating in the base section of the skull; both thighs were present, plus part of the right femur and parts of both arms. Internally, the breathing apparatus still remaining – the mouth, larynx, and part of the windpipe – was noticeably free from the sooty deposits customarily associated with the corpses of those who had been burned while life remained. Furthermore, the small amounts of blood that could be taken from the unburned section of the lungs and heart proved on laboratory examination to be clear of the carbon monoxide contamination characteristic of a victim burned alive. But it was Kockel's observations on the general structure of the frame based on skeletal examination that revealed disturbing discrepancies. The general frailty of the bones indicated a man of slight, almost feminine build, aged about twenty. Kurt Erich Tetzner was twenty-six years old, powerfully built and overweight.

In his report to the Leipzig police authorities, Professor Kockel listed his suspicions that:

1. Whoever the victim in the burned-out car was, it was not Erich Tetzner.

2. The man was dead before the car caught fire.

3. Given the circumstances surrounding the incident, it seemed likely that Tetzner had been responsible for the man's death in pursuance of an insurance fraud.

4. Erich Tetzner was in hiding and likely to contact his wife. Accordingly a watch was put on Frau Tetzner, and a tap put on the neighbours' telephone which she was in the habit of using. On 4 December the detective monitoring the telephone intercepted a call from a man calling himself Sranelli from Strasbourg. While the detective was explaining that Emma Tetzner was out and that the caller should ring again at six o'clock that evening, telephone operators had traced the call to a Strasbourg telephone kiosk. Sranelli – better known as Tetzner – was arrested as he tried to telephone his wife.

When Tetzner appeared before the court at Regensburg on 17 March 1931, it could be fairly thought that he, and he alone, had signed his death warrant. Such was the painfully slow progress of the German legal machine that Erich Tetzner spent long enough in prison to ponder his fate and to retract the confession that he had made to police at the time of his arrest. It had been a detailed statement, and one which chilled to the bone the hushed court to which it was read – Tetzner had originally planned to burn his young victim alive!

Against this stood the prisoner's new defence – that he had accidentally knocked a man down on the road, killing him. Not one to let a good opportunity pass by, he had quickly formulated a way of using the accident to his own financial advantage. Hard-hearted, but if the jury had believed him, not murder.

But it was Tetzner's original confession that the jury carried in their heads into retirement. The self-indictment of a man who killed out of sheer greed. And it was as a greedy, ruthless murderer that they found him guilty.

So ponderous had the whole process been that by the time Erich Tetzner was executed at Regensburg in June 1931, Alfred Arthur Rouse had already kept his appointment with the hangman. Both made an eleventh-hour confession to their identical, wicked crime.

ERNEST ELMES
(England, 1953)

A Man Well Placed

Murder followed by suicide is statistically one of the most frequent homicide syndromes. The pattern usually begins with an unpremeditated killing committed in a fit of anger or temporary loss of reason – frequently associated with alcohol followed by a suicide provoked by panic-induced remorse and fear of retribution.

There is rarely anything to interest the criminologist in such cases; the protagonists are ordinary people, their lives ordinary lives; small dramas for an amateur cast.

And this is how the case of Ernest Elmes might have been described, but for the serendipitous combination of his crime and his occupation.

Elmes was a general handyman in a wire factory at Tottenham, north London, with special responsibility for the boilers. With his wife, 37-year-old Rose Winifred, they comprised the 'perfectly ordinary suburban couple'.

One Saturday in September 1953, Elmes' next-door neighbour, Alan Watson, was in his garden when he heard a shrill scream which he described as a woman's coming from the direction of the Elmes house. Given their apparent devotion to each other, this stuck in Watson's mind.

Some days later, Ernest Elmes presented himself at

Tottenham police station to report the disappearance of his wife, and Detective Inspector Weston, who interviewed Elmes, remembered being decidedly uncomfortable both with his story, and with the man himself. He was certainly in a dishevelled, unwashed state, and his fingernails were bitten down to the quick – though of course these could simply have been the outward signs of the anguish and despair suffered by a man whose wife, so he claimed, had just run out on him – and to top it all, with a policeman! The scratch marks on Elmes' face were less easily explained away, and his story that he and the policeman had fought over Rose had only deepened Weston's feeling of unease.

When Ernest Elmes returned to his job after an absence of several days, he made his apologies to manager John McCave, explaining that his wife had left him. Eloped. With a sailor! To a colleague, Margaret Bowers, he also confided that his wife had run away, run away with a policeman.

In what McCave no doubt saw as a conciliatory gesture for his absence, Elmes suggested that the factory boiler needed cleaning, and that he would be happy to take care of it. The manager agreed, and Elmes set to work.

Now, murder is really a very easy act to commit. Anyone can do it – some do. The difficult part, as they inevitably discover, is disposing of the body. Lucky Ernest Elmes – the general handyman with his own crematorium.

In hindsight, we know that Elmes bludgeoned poor Rose to death with a hammer – the hammer found by police when they searched his home. We know that he laboriously cut up the body – this was proved by the saw marks on the bones recovered from the factory boiler by pathologist Francis Camps. The blood-stained hacksaw blades in the house confirmed his report; that it had been a grisly business was evident from the extensive blood splashes on the walls and floor.

And the motive? She was an ambulance driver whom Elmes had met on a first-aid course, and with whom he had struck up what had at first been an easy-going, platonic, friendship. And then Ernest told her that his wife had left him; a story which she at any rate was prepared to believe, opening the way for a more intimate relationship to develop. Which it did. Perhaps to add credence to the story, Elmes told the girl that he had been questioned by the police about his wife's disappearance. On the Sunday following, she called round to comfort Ernest. She knocked on the door; knocked again; knocked again. Concerned, she went round to the back of the house and broke into the gas-filled kitchen and discovered why Elmes had not answered the front door.

Three

Eating People Is Wrong

ALBERT FISH
(USA, 1928–36)

'If Only Pain Were Not so Painful'

Every day, somewhere, is the last day of somebody's life. For ten-year-old Grace Budd, Sunday, 3 June 1928, didn't seem like her last day on earth – far from it. Despite the fact that Ma and Pa Budd, their eighteen-year-old son, Edward, and young Grace were a long way from being wealthy, carving out a precarious existence in downtown New York, it was a close and a happy family. What was more, Edward had just inserted an advertisement in the newspaper asking for work; things were on the up and up.

Ed's optimism was confirmed when on 3 June an elderly, respectable-looking man calling himself Frank Howard presented himself at the Budds' apartment door clutching a copy of the newspaper in his hand. Howard announced that he was a vegetable farmer down in Farmingdale, Long Island, and that if young Budd didn't mind an open-air life in the country, he was willing to give him a break.

They may have been overwhelmed with gratitude, or simply too trustful of the small grey-haired old man; whatever the reason, Albert and Delia Budd allowed 'Frank Howard' to take ten-year-old Grace to a children's party which, so he claimed, his sister was giving that afternoon. They never again saw Grace alive.

Of course, there was no party. Instead, poor Grace

was taken to Wisteria Cottage, an unoccupied house in Greenburgh. Here, Albert Fish – the man calling himself 'Howard' – choked her to death.

It was six years before anybody heard of Grace Budd again. On 11 November 1934, the Budds found a letter among the morning mail which read, in part:

Dear Mrs Budd,

Some years ago a friend of mine, Captain John Davis, shipped from California to Hong Kong, China, where at that time there was a great famine. It was dangerous for children under the age of twelve to be on the streets, as the custom was for them to be seized, cut up, and their meat sold for food. On his return to New York, my friend seized two boys, one six and the other eleven, killed, cooked, and ate them.

So it was that I came to your house on June 3, 1928, and under the pretence of taking your daughter Grace to a party at my sister's I took her up to Westchester County, Worthington, to an empty house up there, and I choked her to death, I cut her up and ate part of her flesh. I didn't fuck with her. She died a virgin.

Understandably very distressed, Mrs Budd immediately made contact with detective Smith, who had been assigned to the case of Grace's disappearance. From an imperfectly erased address on the back of the letter's envelope, Smith traced 66-year-old Albert Fish to a seedy boarding house on 52nd Street, New York, where he was arrested on 13 December. It was to prove significant that he had in his possession at the time a collection of illustrated newspaper cuttings relating to the crimes of the Hanover mass killer Fritz Haarmann (see page 125).

In detention, Fish signed six separate confessions to

the murder of Grace Budd. And something more. After he had slowly choked the child to death, he had stripped off her clothes, severed her head with a cleaver and sawn her body in half across the navel. Most of the dismembered corpse Fish hid in the house; a part of it he had taken home with him, had cooked in various ways: 'with carrots and onions and strips of bacon' and eaten over the course of the following week.

Between the time of his arrest and the trial at White Plains court house on 12 March 1935, Albert Fish was examined in painstaking detail by Dr Fredric Wertham, one of America's foremost psychiatrists. In brief, Dr Wertham summed his patient up as 'one of the most developed cases of sexual perversion in the literature of abnormal psychology'.

To Dr Wertham, Fish confided that he felt compelled to torture and kill children, often acting on the direct orders of God, whose voice he frequently heard. On the subject of the murder of Grace Budd and the subsequent cannibalisation of her flesh, Fish claimed that the acts raised him to a state of constant sexual ecstasy. Wertham recalled that Fish had described this process in a chillingly matter-of-fact way: 'Like a housewife describing her favourite methods of cooking. You had to remind yourself that this was a little girl he was talking about . . . I said to myself, however you define the medical and legal borders of sanity, this is certainly beyond that border.'

'There is no known perversion that he did not practise,' stated Dr Wertham at Fish's trial, 'and practise frequently.' Fish had admitted grossly molesting at least one hundred children, almost all from poor black ghettos across 23 states from New York to Montana – and murdering fifteen. His perversions extended to inflicting pain upon himself as well as upon others, and he had developed a fondness for sticking needles deep into the flesh around his genital area. An X-ray taken in prison revealed no fewer than 29 needles still implanted in his body; some had been there so long that they had begun to erode. At times he had experimented with forcing needles under his fingernails, but had to give up when the pain became unbearable: 'If only pain were not so painful', he lamented to Wertham. Fish had described his experiences eating his own excrement, and the unsavoury pleasure he took from soaking pieces of cotton in alcohol, pushing them into his rectum, and setting fire to them. Quite clearly Albert Fish was as mad as a hatter – and a very dangerous *chapelier* at that.

It seemed obvious that Fish's defence at trial would be insanity, and so it was. However, despite Dr Wertham's expert testimony and that of Fish's own children who gave evidence of their father beating himself with nail-studded planks on his bare body till he bled, screaming the while: 'I am Christ', the jury found Fish 'Guilty of murder in the first degree'.

At his appeal, there was further lengthy discussion of Fish's eligibility to be considered legally insane, and once again Fredric Wertham's diagnosis of 'paranoid psychosis' was rejected. One of the four psychiatrists called to pronounce Fish sane went as far as to state that in his opinion: 'A man might for nine days eat [human] flesh and still not have a psychosis. There is no accounting for taste . . . it is a matter of appetite and intensive satisfaction, and the individual may do very repulsive things and still be a seer, I mean a very wise man.'

The only hope left was a direct appeal to the state governor. While Albert Fish sat in his cell on Sing

Sing's death row, Dr Wertham made his final impassioned plea: 'This man is not only incurable and unreformable, but unpunishable. In his own distorted mind he is looking forward to the electric chair as the final experience of supreme pain.'

We will never know quite how much Albert Fish enjoyed his own execution; certainly on that chilly morning of Thursday, 16 January 1936, he seemed to be happy enough with the prospect; he even helped to adjust the straps that bound him to the electric chair.

POSTSCRIPT

It was revealed afterwards by a member of the Fish trial jury that a majority of them had, in fact, accepted that the prisoner was legally insane, but were so appalled by the catalogue of his crimes against children that they felt Fish deserved to die anyway. Dr Wertham continued his study into the background of Albert Fish's mental instability, and in 1949 published his findings as *The Show of Violence* (see Bibliography).

ED GEIN
(USA, 1954–7)

Psycho!

Nothing in his training had prepared the deputy sheriff for the sight in front of him now. Experience told him that policing the small town of Plainfield, in the heart of Wisconsin's dairylands, was easy enough if you kept your head down and got on with your neighbours. And that is what he was trying to do on 16 November 1957.

Fifty-eight-year-old Bernice Worden, the widow who ran the local hardware store, had been reported missing from home by her relatives – and that was about as exciting as anything got around Plainfield; a job to be done as effectively as he knew how, while not making too many ripples on the respectable surface of small-town life. Mrs Worden's son had given him one lead. He had seen the pick-up truck belonging to Ed Gein outside the old lady's shop on two occasions on the day she disappeared. This was why the deputy was here at the Gein farm.

Ed had worked the farm with his brother and mother, an overbearing woman who ruled her sons' lives totally. His brother Henry had died in 1944, as had his mother the following year. Gein, lost without his mother's authoritarian 'guidance', turned in upon himself and became reclusive, letting the farm run down. In short, as the neighbours put it, Ed had 'gone weird'. They were soon to find out just how weird.

It was the officer's second visit to the Gein place on that chilly November day; he had called earlier, found that Ed was away from home and left. Gein did not answer the deputy's knock on the farmhouse door this time either, and with the instinctive curiosity that distinguishes his calling, the deputy wandered around to the outbuildings. That was where the horror started.

It hung from the rafters of a lean-to at the side of the house; suspended by the ankles, and headless. Bernice Worden was missing no longer.

But the Ed Gein story only ended with the bizarre killing of Mrs Worden. It had begun with his mother; with her obsessive restraint of his natural sexual instincts; her refusal to permit any contact with the female of the species had bred in the young Ed Gein an unnatural and morbid interest in female anatomy.

After the death of Mrs Gein, Ed took to digging up corpses from isolated graveyards and taking them home to study, to perform acts of necrophilia upon and, according to his own subsequent statement, to eat.

When police officers made a thorough search of the Gein farm, they found an appalling collection of relics fashioned from the corpses of the recently buried – bracelets and lampshades of flayed human skin, preserved heads, a soup bowl cut from the cranium of a human skull; and testament to his cannibalism, a collection of preserved human organs that made the refrigerator look like a slaughterhouse. Gein later caused a sensation when, in his voluntary confession, he spoke ecstatically of the sexual gratification he derived from draping the skin stripped from his victims over his own naked body.

Pathologists estimated that in all, the remains came from fifteen bodies, including a 5l-year-old woman named Mary Hogan whom Gein had shot in 1954 to supplement his collection of corpses.

And among all these grisly souvenirs of murder, necrophilia and anthropophagy stood 'Mother's room' – preserved as a shrine in the midst of carnage; locked since the day she died. It did not escape the notice of psychologists that both the women Gein had killed – Mrs Worden and Mary Hogan – bore a strong resemblance to Mrs Gein.

Not surprisingly, Edward Gein was judged unfit to stand trial and was committed instead to Central State Hospital, Waupon, where he worked as a mason, carpenter and hospital orderly. In 1978 Gein was moved to the Mendota Mental Health Institute, where, always a model prisoner, he died on 26 June 1984, at the age of 77.

As for the Gein family farm, the scene of such unspeakable perversions, it was burnt to the ground by local people shortly after its owner's confinement.

POSTSCRIPT

It is said that Robert Bloch based his chilling novel *Psycho* on the Ed Gein story, though anybody with a knowledge of both may find it difficult to identify the schizophrenic transvestite Norman Bates with the perverted farmer of Plainfield. In 1960, Alfred Hitchcock transformed Bloch's novel into a masterpiece of Gothic cinema. The *New York Times* critic might almost have had in mind the officers who entered the Gein farmhouse when he declared of the film: 'You better have a pretty strong stomach and be prepared for a couple of grisly shocks.'

GEORG KARL GROSSMANN
(Germany, 1913–21)

The Hot-dog Seller

Georg Grossmann was without question as unsavoury a character as one could expect to encounter outside the wildest excesses of his fellow countrymen, the brothers Grimm; a monster from real life, he was possessed of such depraved wickedness as to beggar fiction.

Born in Neuruppen in 1863 (the year, incidentally, that Jakob Grimm died), Grossmann had been a sexual degenerate and sadist from an early age, and by his middle fifties, when he parted company with this world, had already collected three lengthy terms of imprisonment with hard labour for abusing children – in one case the abuse had proved fatal. At his trial it would be revealed that Grossmann also frequently indulged in bestiality and necrophilia.

It was in the month of August 1921 that one of the residents sharing the block in which Grossmann lived, near to Berlin's Silesian railway terminus, felt constrained to call the police on account of the terrible shrieking, shouting and banging that was coming up from Georg Grossmann's kitchen. When the police arrived, the noise had stopped; no shrieking; no banging; just the body of a young woman, dead but still warm, trussed up as if for slaughter on a camp bed.

Grossmann's occupancy of the apartment had dated from 1913, eight years earlier – just before the start of the Great War, in which conflict Georg was not invited to participate because of his thoroughly discreditable police record. During this time the reclusive tenant had commandeered the kitchen, forbidding entry even to his landlord. The number of street girls passing through to service Grossmann's appetite was so large that it was a long time before his neighbours noticed that many failed to re-emerge. Some idea of the magnitude of this Bluebeard's activities is indicated by the discovery of remains in Grossmann's room at the time of his arrest that proved the murder and dismemberment of at least three women in the previous three weeks.

Like his contemporary, Fritz Haarmann, Grossmann's source of victims was the railway station where, not entirely coincidentally, he sold cooked sausages of his own recipe and manufacture. Like Haarmann, the Berlin Butcher was turning his pleasures into profit; and his victims into human hot-dogs. Such was Grossmann's degradation that he almost certainly saved on grocery bills by sampling his own wares, and those portions he found unsaleable were simply thrown into the river Spree.

It would defy common sense to say that his trial, custody in prison, and subsequent death sentence sent Georg Grossmann mad, but it certainly aggravated the existing unbalance of his mind, provoking fits of violent mania which ended in his cheating the executioner by suspending himself by the neck in his cell.

How many women – they were all women – fell prey to the ghastly Grossmann can never be computed, but even conservatively inclined estimates talk of a figure exceeding Haarmann's total of fifty.

FRITZ HAARMANN
(Germany, 1918–24)

The Ogre of Hanover

The trial that was to shock all Europe opened at Hanover's assize court on 4 December 1924. Before public prosecutor Oberstaatsanwalt (attorney-general) Dr Wilde, stood Fritz Haarmann, 45 years old, a homosexual with a previous record of custodial sentences for every kind of theft and fraud, and for offences against children. Beside him in the dock, 25-year-old Hans Grans, also a homosexual, also a thief and a pimp.

But it was no charge of petty misdemeanour that Haarmann and Grans faced now; they stood indicted on 27 counts of murder. The list of victims, all boys between the ages of twelve and eighteen years, was so long that when it was read out to him, Haarmann was obliged to admit: 'That might well be,' and 'I'm not sure about that one.' In fact the prisoner's own estimate of the extent of the deaths was rather higher: 'It might be forty, I really can't remember the exact number.'

In all, during the sixteen days of the proceedings, nearly 200 witnesses were called, comprising for the most part the victims' grieving relatives. One contemporary newspaper reported:

> There were scenes of painful intensity as a father or mother would identify some fragment of the clothing or possessions of their dead son. Here a

    handkerchief, there a pair of braces; a greasy coat,
    soiled almost beyond recognition.

For all this obvious anguish, Fritz Haarmann and his vile companion could express nothing but the deepest contempt. When he was shown a picture of young Hermann Wolf, Haarmann glared indignantly at the boy's father and shouted: 'I would never have looked twice at such an ugly boy as this . . . there's plenty of rubbish around like him, such a person would have been far beneath my notice.'

But if this was sickening to every human soul in that court, there was worse to come. A stunned world was about to hear how Haarmann had killed his victims by biting through their throats; he then filleted the bodies, throwing the skulls and bones into the river Leine, and sold the flesh on the black market for human consumption.

Fritz Haarmann was a son of the city in which he now stood trial, born on 25 October 1879. A lazy and rather weak-minded youth, Fritz was sent to a military school at the age of sixteen as part of his father's desperate attempt to toughen up the boy who was showing an alarming fondness for playing with dolls. Here at New Breisach, Haarmann exhibited symptoms of epilepsy and was released; shortly afterwards he was accused of indecently molesting small children and confined to an asylum from which he escaped. From this point, Fritz Haarmann alternated between theft and prison, with the years 1900 to 1903 spent serving with some distinction in a Jager regiment. His father, after an unsuccessful attempt to have Fritz certified insane, seems to have relinquished all hope for the youth's salvation and abandoned him to the criminal ways to which he so naturally inclined. In

1914, Haarmann earned himself a five-year sentence for robbery which, if nothing else, preserved him from the perils of trench life. Released in 1918, he took up residence at 27 Kellerstrasse, where he continued in his chosen pursuits of stealing, meat smuggling, and – to divert attention from his less honest activities – spying for the police. It was at around this time that the murders started.

The source of Haarmann's victims was Hanover's old central railway station through which still poured a tide of desperate refugees from all parts of Germany, many of them rootless children and youths fleeing from homes broken by war and its aftermath. This human flotsam and jetsam became Fritz Haarmann's natural prey – a kind word at the station, a cigarette, the offer of a hot meal and a mattress for the night. Within 24 hours their flesh was being innocently boiled, grilled or fried by grateful Hausfraus all over the city.

In September 1918 seventeen-year-old Friedel Rothe was reported missing by his parents, last seen in the company of Fritz Haarmann. It may have been because of his underground activities on their behalf that the police made such an unenthusiastic search of No. 27 Kellerstrasse, but they failed to find the unfortunate boy's head where it had been wedged behind the cooker, wrapped in newspaper.

The Butcher of Hanover had another narrow escape when one of his customers took the meat she had bought to the authorities, complaining that it looked like human flesh; she was informed by the police analyst simply that she should consider herself lucky being able to get such a piece of pork in these difficult times!

Haarmann met Hans Grans in September 1919, and

the younger man quickly established a position of superiority within the relationship – often selecting Haarmann's victims for him simply because he coveted a particular shirt or pair of trousers that they were wearing. By now the murderous couple had moved to an alley called Rothe Reihe, to a flat through the front door of which neighbours saw many young men enter who did not come out.

It was not until 17 May 1924 that the Haarmann and Grans reign of terror among Hanover's dispossessed began to draw to a close. On that day the first of a succession of human skulls was fished out of the Leine; by 13 June there were three more. On 22 June, Fritz Haarmann was arrested while attempting indecently to assault a young man named Fromm. While in custody, his lodgings were routinely searched and a pile of clothing and other modest possessions belonging to some youths reported missing were found. More incriminating by far were the splashes of blood on the walls – human blood. Of course, Haarmann confessed; and equally predictably implicated the sinister Grans.

By this time, a dredge of the river, watched by hundreds of spectators, had yielded a varied assortment of 500 human bones, and a group of boys playing in a meadow found a further sackful – in all about 23 bodies' worth.

Haarmann, fearful lest he might be considered insane and sent to an asylum (ghosts from his past no doubt still haunted him) demanded the death sentence for himself, and it was with no trace of regret that the court granted his wish; according to the German practice, Haarmann was beheaded on 20 December 1924. Hans Grans was sentenced to life imprisonment of which he served twelve years.

Shortly before his ignominious departure, Fritz Haarmann made a full, if rather fanciful, confession, littered with abstruse references to his own sexual perversions on which he seemed to lay the blame for his blood lust.

Four

'This was the most unkindest cut of all'

William Shakespeare
Julius Caesar

CATHERINE HAYES
(England, 1726)

A Case of 'Petit Treason'

On Wednesday, 2 March 1726, all London town was alarmed with an account that the head of a man, which by its freshness appeared to have been recently cut off from a living body, had been taken up by a watchman in the dock of McReth's lime-wharf near the Horse Ferry at Westminster, soon after daybreak.

It was brought to St Margaret's churchyard, and laid on a tombstone, but being much besmeared with dirt and blood, the churchwardens ordered the face to be washed clean, and the hair combed, and caused it then to be set upon a high post, in full view of passers-by, hoping to discover an identity.

Mr Henry Longmore, who kept the Green Dragon ale-house in King Street, near Golden Square, being nearly related to one John Hayes, who lodged with his wife on the second floor of Mr Weingard's house in Tyburn Road, noticed that Mr Hayes had not been seen by anybody for some days; and hearing many strange reports and suspicions that he had been murdered, had many times asked Mrs Hayes what had become of him. Sometimes she said he had gone to take a walk in the fields, at other times that he had gone into Herefordshire, or some such story. Finally, when pressed by Hayes' close friend, Mr Joseph Ashby, Mrs Hayes concocted the pretence that her husband had accidentally killed a man in a quarrel, and had been obliged to flee to Portugal.

So preposterous a story far from satisfied Mr Long-more and Mr Ashby, and they determined to view the now celebrated 'Head of a Man' which, having failed to elucidate the matter from its position at St Margaret's, had been removed to Mr Westbrooke, the Parish Surgeon, to be preserved in spirits. It is impossible to describe the consternation of the two gentlemen when they beheld what a cruel and inhuman murder had been committed on their unfortunate friend.

Immediately, Oliver Lambert, one of His Majesty's justices of the peace, issued his warrant for the apprehension of Catherine Hayes, who had in the meantime moved her lodging further along the Tyburn Road to the house of Mr Jones, a distiller.* Here, on the night of 23 March, they found Mrs Hayes, Thomas Billings, a tailor, and Mary Springate. Hayes was committed to the Tothill-Fields Bridewell, Springate to the Gatehouse, and Billings to New Prison.

But remark the wonderful Providence of God in bringing to a still clearer light this hidden work of darkness. For a Mr Huddle, gardener at Marybone [Marylebone], had been walking in the fields when he discovered the arms, legs and trunk of a man's body, wrapped up in two pieces of blanket, lying in a pond near the Farthing-pye House, covered with bricks and rubbish. The head was sent for, where, in the view of

---

*There is an historic public house still standing in South Molton Street (off Oxford Street which was formerly Tyburn Road) called The Hog in the Pound, which claims association with Catherine Hayes. This is an error; Edward Oxford was barman in the Hog at the time of his attempt on the lives of Queen Victoria and Prince Albert as they drove along the route from Buckingham Palace in 1840. The Brawn's Head Inn, in which Hayes and his murderers drank on the night of his death, once stood in New Bond Street, into which South Molton Street runs.

Right: John George Haigh;
and *(below)* Haigh as a boy,
giving little indication of
the monster who was to
emerge

Above: John White Webster kills
Dr Parkman in his laboratory

Left: Miss Emily Kaye, victim of
the Crumbles murder

Below: Victim and killer;
Margaret and Peter Hogg in
happier times

Cutting off the head of John Hayes

Mrs Catherine Hayes executed by burning at the stake

Contemporary sketches from the Second Brighton Trunk Murder

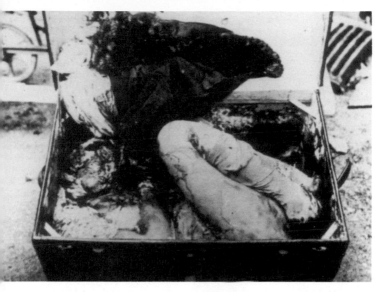

Above: The corpse of Miss Violette Kaye; and *(below)* the corpse of Mr Charles Bessarabo as it was taken from the trunk

Left: Dr Hawley Harvey Crippen; and *(above)* Mrs Cora Crippen as her stage persona, Belle Elmore

Below: The arrest and trial of Dr Crippen

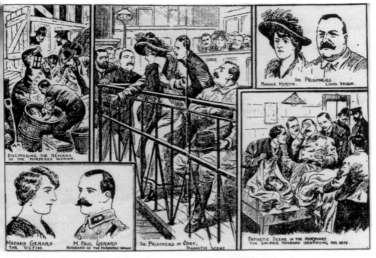

Contemporary sketches of events after the crime of Louis Voisin

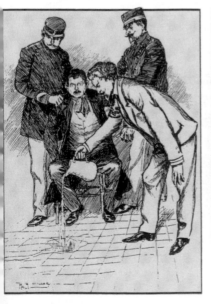

Detective Macé confronts Pierre Voirbo

Marcel Petiot in court

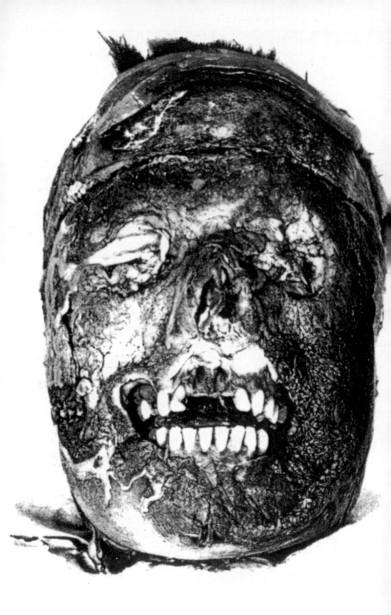

The head of Mary Jane Rogerson

several surgeons and others, it was found to correspond exactly with the body.

When the peace officers, attended by Longmore, went the next day to fetch up Catherine to her examination, she earnestly desired to see the head; and it being thought prudent to grant her request, she was carried to the surgeon's; and no sooner was the head shown to her than she exclaimed: 'Oh, it is my dear husband's head! It is my dear husband's head!' She now took the glass in her arms and shed many tears while she embraced it. Mr Westbrook told her that he would take the head out of the glass that she might have a more perfect view of it and be certain that it was the same; and the surgeon doing as he had said, she seemed greatly affected, and having kissed it several times, she begged to be indulged with a lock of the hair; and on Mr Westbrook expressing his apprehension that she had had too much of his blood already, she fell into a fit. On her recovery she was conducted to Mr Lambert's to take her examination with the other parties.

The Sunday following, one Thomas Wood, a person suspected of being concerned in the murder, was seized in the street and committed to Tothill-Fields Bridewell where he made an ingenious confession:

He had come to town from Worcestershire, and seeking out Hayes, persuaded him to give him a lodging, as he was afraid of falling victim to the press-gangs. After Wood had been in town only a few days, Mrs Hayes informed him of the plot that existed, and endeavoured to persuade him to join her. He was at first shocked at the notion of murdering his friend and benefactor, and rejected the proposals; but at length Mrs Hayes, alleging that her husband was an atheist, and had already been guilty of murdering two of his own children, and besides urging that fifteen hundred pounds which would fall to her at his death, should be placed at the disposal of her accomplices, obtained his consent.

Shortly after this, Wood went out of town for a few days, but on his return found Mrs Hayes, her husband and Billings drinking together in the Brawn's Head Inn, and apparently in good humour. He joined them at the desire of Hayes. When the latter boasted that he was not drunk, although they had had a guinea's worth of liquor among them, Billings proposed that Hayes should see whether he could drink half-a-dozen bottles of mountain wine without getting tipsy, and promised that if he did so he, Billings, would pay for the wine. The proposal was agreed to, and the three murderers went off to procure the liquor. On the way it was agreed among them that this was the proper opportunity to carry their designs into execution, and having procured the wine, for which Mrs Hayes paid half-a-guinea, Mr Hayes began to drink it, while his intended assassins regaled themselves with beer. When he had taken a considerable quantity of the wine he danced about the room like a man distracted, and at length finished the whole quantity; but not being yet in a state of complete stupefaction, his wife sent for another bottle, which he also drank, and then fell senseless on the floor. Having lain some time in this condition, he got, with much difficulty, into another room, and threw himself on a bed.

When her husband was asleep, Mrs Hayes told her associates that this was the time to execute their plan, as there was no fear of resistance on his part, and accordingly Billings went into the room with a hatchet, with which he struck Hayes so violently that he fractured his skull. At this time Hayes' feet hung off the bed, and the torture arising from the blow made him stamp repeatedly on the floor, which was heard by Wood, who also went into the room, and taking the hatchet out of Billings' hand gave the poor man two more blows, which effectually despatched him. A woman named Springate, who lodged in the room over that where the murder was committed, hearing the noise occasioned by Hayes stamping, imagined that the parties might have quarrelled in consequence of their intoxication; and going downstairs she told Mrs Hayes that the noise had awakened her child, her husband, and herself. Catherine, however, had a ready answer to this: she said some company had visited them, and had grown merry, but they were on the point of taking their leave; and Mrs Springate returned to her room well satisfied.

The murderers now consulted on the best manner of disposing of the body so as most effectually to prevent detection. Mrs Hayes proposed to cut off the head, because if the body were found whole it would be more likely to be known, and on the villains agreeing to this proposition she fetched a pail, lighted a candle, and all of them went into the room. The men then drew the body partly off the bed, and Billings supported the head while Wood, with his pocket-knife, cut it off, and the infamous woman held the pail to receive it, being as careful as possible that the floor might not be stained with the blood. This being done, they emptied the blood out of the pail into a sink by the window, and poured several pails of water after it. When the head was cut off, the woman recommended boiling it till the flesh should part from the bones; but the other parties thought this operation would take up too much time, and therefore advised throwing it into the Thames in expectation that it would be carried off by the tide, and would sink. This agreed to, the head was put into the pail, and Billings took it under his greatcoat, being accompanied by Wood; but making a noise going downstairs, Mrs Springate called, and asked what was the matter. To this Mrs Hayes answered that her husband was going on a journey; and with incredible dissimulation affected to take leave of him, pretending great concern that he was under a necessity of going at so late an hour, and Wood and Billings passed out of the house unnoticed. They first went to Whitehall, where they intended to throw in the head; but the gates being shut they went to a wharf near the Horse Ferry, Westminster. Billings putting down the pail, Wood threw the head into the dock, expecting it would be carried away by the stream; but at this time the tide was ebbing, and a lighterman, who was then in his vessel, heard something fall into the dock, but it was too dark for him to distinguish any object.

The head being thus disposed of, the murderers returned home, and were admitted by Mrs Hayes without the knowledge of the other lodgers. The body next became the object of their attention, and Mrs Hayes proposed that it should be packed up in a box and buried. The plan was determined upon immediately, and a box purchased, but being found to be too small, the body was dismembered so it would fit in the box, and was left until night should favour its being carried off. The inconvenience of carrying a box was, however, immediately discovered, and the pieces of the mangled body were therefore taken out and, being wrapped in a blanket, were carried by Billings and Wood to a field in Marybone, and there thrown in a pond.

At the trial, Wood and Billings confessed themselves guilty of the crime alleged against them, but Mrs

Hayes, flattering herself that as she had said nothing she had a chance of escape, put herself upon trial; but the jury found her guilty. The prisoners being afterwards brought to the bar to receive sentence, Mrs Hayes entreated that she might not be burned, according to the then law of 'petty treason', alleging that she was not guilty, as she did not strike the fatal blow; but she was informed by the court that the sentence awarded by the law could not be dispensed with.

After conviction, the behaviour of Wood was uncommonly penitent and devout; but while in the condemned hold he was seized with a violent fever, and being attended by a clergyman to assist him in his devotions, he said he was ready to suffer death, under every mark of ignominy, as some atonement for the atrocious crime he had committed. But he died in prison, and thus defeated the final execution of the law. Billings behaved with apparent sincerity, acknowledging the justice of his sentence, and saying that no punishment could be commensurate with the crime of which he had been guilty. He was executed in the usual manner, and hung in chains not far from the pond in which Mr Hayes' body was found, in Marybone Fields.

The behaviour of Mrs Hayes was somewhat similar to her former conduct. Having an intention to destroy herself, she procured a phial of strong poison, which was casually tasted by a woman who was confined with her, and her design thereby discovered and frustrated. On the day of her death she received the Sacrament, and was drawn on a sledge to the place of execution. When the wretched woman had finished her devotions, in pursuance of her sentence an iron chain was put around her body, with which she was fixed to a stake near the gallows. On these occasions, when women were burned for petty treason, it was customary to strangle them, by means of a rope passed around the neck and pulled by the executioner, so that they were dead before the flames reached the body. But this woman was literally burned alive; for the executioner letting go the rope sooner than usual in consequence of the flames reaching his hands, the fire burned fiercely round her, and the spectators beheld her pushing away the faggots, while she rent the air with her cries and lamentations. Other faggots were instantly thrown on her; but she survived amid the flames for a considerable time, and her body was not perfectly reduced to ashes until three hours later. These malefactors suffered at Tyburn on 9 May 1726.

POSTSCRIPT

Although it is unlikely that Mrs Hayes was the first killer ever to hit on the idea of confusing the issue of identification by distributing her victim piecemeal, it is the first such case to be so extensively recorded, and contain such rich detail.

The absence not only of forensic scientists but also of any regular police force gave rise to the ingenious, if unsavoury, expedient of sticking poor Hayes' head on a pole in St Margaret's in the hope that he might be recognised.

Mrs Hayes' explanation for her husband's disappearance that he had killed a man in a fight, bought off his widow, and absconded to Portugal – can be better understood with an appreciation that the London of the early eighteenth century was a comparatively very violent place. With no resort to a police force, a person relied very much on his own resources to settle disputes, and murder for the most petty grievance was commonplace. This general inevitability of violence, and the absence of life insurance, makes it unsurprising that the widow of Hayes' supposed victim would have accepted the not inconsiderable settlement of twelve pounds per annum as compensation.

But 'murder will out', and the text illustrates how, in the absence of police officers to execute a magistrate's warrant, it is the nearest of kin, or the aggrieved party, that undertakes the task. The fact that Billings, Wood, and Catherine Hayes were each remanded in a different prison shows just how many gaols there were in the capital at the time – in fact about three dozen of them, the most significant of which was Newgate. It was here that the three prisoners would have been confined awaiting execution. Thomas Wood in the meantime succumbed to what became known as Gaol Fever – typhus – which in the year 1754–5 alone was responsible for reducing the population of Newgate by as much as one-fifth.

Billings had a more dramatic fate in store, being strung up before a huge, festive concourse of people at Tyburn, then the official place of execution – about where Marble Arch stands today. Consistent with some attempt to discourage those who might be tempted into committing a similar crime, Billings' body was hung in chains as a semi-permanent deterrent; this was customarily done on the spot where the crime for which the miscreant had suffered took place. Coincidentally, it was another dismemberer, James Cook, who was the last to suffer the ignominy of hanging in chains, in Leicester, in 1834.

As for Catherine Hayes, hers was the most terrible end. The crime of 'petty treason' dated back officially to the year 1351, when according to a Statute of

Edward III, the following classifications of murder were termed 'Petit Treason': a servant killing his master; a wife killing her husband; and an ecclesiastic killing his superior. The punishment was burning in each case, though effectively it was reserved for husband-killers. This barbaric form of execution was repealed only towards the end of George III's reign, in about 1790.

PIERRE VOIRBO
(1868–9)

Blood-Guiltiness

An early example of exceptional forensic investigation by one of France's most distinguished policemen began in January 1869 outside a small restaurant in the rue Princesse in Paris's sixth arrondissement. The proprietor of the eating-house, a man named Lampon, had traced the foul smell and taste of his well water to the severed lower joint of a human leg which, despite the neat job of sewing that had been made on its black glazed calico shroud, was decomposing into the drinking water. On the following morning, 26 January, Gustave Macé, then a commissioner of police, was detailed to the case. Before long the detective was confronting the leg's companion which had also been fished out of the well; it, too, had been sewn up in the same anonymous black calico, but an examination of a stocking which still covered the leg revealed a small identification mark embroided in red cotton – the letter B with a cross on either side of it (+B+). Preliminary examination suggested that the legs were a woman's, and that they had been slowly polluting M. Lampon's well for about a month.

There was good reason to suppose that these remains were connected with some gruesome discoveries that had been made during the previous December. On the 17th a thigh bone had been found in the rue Jacob, and several scraps of flesh had been washed up on the banks of the Seine and seen floating on the Saint Martin Canal. Two days later a thick-set, bearded man had been observed throwing chunks of meat into the Seine – ground bait, he had explained, to attract the fish. Two policemen named Ringue and Champy, on duty on the night of 22 December, recalled stopping a man near the rue Princesse whose description matched that of the hirsute angler. The man in question had been carrying a basket which contained two well-wrapped parcels which he claimed were hams!

If the earlier medical examination had deceived detectives into wasting time looking for missing women, at least the re-examination by that legend of French medical jurisprudence, Dr Tardieu, corrected the mistake, and further drew attention to a recent scar on one of the legs. Meanwhile Gustave Macé was focusing his attention on the wrappings in which the legs had been found. For a start, the needlework suggested the hand of a professional, and following this lead it was not long before Macé had found a Mademoiselle Mathilde Gaupe (alias Dard), by training a waistcoat-maker, lately turned night-club singer – and resident in the rue Princesse. Mademoiselle confided that she numbered among her friends a tailor by the name of Voirbo, a young man-about-town for whom she did odd jobs and who, in return, had carried her water up from the nearby well – the well that also served M. Lampon's restaurant.

Further enquiries revealed that for some time Voirbo's close companion had been an ageing dandy named Désire Bodasse, and the coincidence of his disappearance two months previously did not go unremarked in the offices of the Sûreté. It was Bodasse's aunt who added the vital last link to the identification of the disembodied legs – the embroidered initial B[odasse] flanked by crosses was the work of her own hand, and the scar found on the leg – souvenir of a recent fall upon a broken bottle – convinced the poor woman further that the tragic remains were those of her nephew.

The puzzling part was that his neighbours in the rue Dauphine swore that old Désire was still alive, since lights were often seen at his window and he was known to have lived alone. Still, the fact remained that nobody had actually seen Bodasse, and when police finally tired of their vigil and entered the apartment they could see why. Judging by the dust carpeting the furniture, the rooms had not been occupied in many long weeks. On the other hand, the large number of cheap candles burnt to stumps gave ample proof of where the light originated; in short, somebody had been at great pains to preserve the impression that Désire Bodasse was still alive and well.

Pierre Voirbo had never been long out of Gustave Macé's thoughts, and when his previous record indicated a thoroughly dishonest heart and a very greedy hand, the man who had so recently been refused a 10,000 franc loan by his old friend Désire, who had only recently been identified as cashing in a similar Italian share certificate to those missing from Bodasse's deserted apartment, was put under constant surveillance. When Voirbo failed to incriminate himself, he was taken into police custody and questioned directly about the matter of Désire Bodasse's death. Then he was questioned about the ticket for a steamship bound for America the next day that was found in his pocket. He was questioned about his wife's claim that he had just come into possession of a number of high-value Italian securities. And through-

out this interrogation, Voirbo stubbornly refused to
incriminate himself with a single word. Of course, he
lamented, he was as anxious about his dear friend's
mysterious disappearance as everybody else; if only
there were more he could do.

During the days that Pierre Voirbo had been held as
a suspect, commissioner Macé had been engaged in a
minute examination of the cellar in his prisoner's
house in the rue Mazarin. Here he found two wine
casks, and suspended from the bung of one of them
was a sealed metal container. When it was opened, the
riddle of Monsieur Bodasse's Italian securities was
solved – 10,000 francs' worth of them, minus the 500-
franc certificate already cashed by Voirbo. All Macé
needed now – and he needed it desperately if he was
ever to bring a charge of murder against Voirbo – was
proof that his suspect did, indeed, kill and dismember
his one-time friend Désire Bodasse. The more he
paced the tiled floor, the more the detective became
convinced that this was the grim scene of that last
destructive act, convinced that Voirbo had used the
heavy bench behind him as a crude operating table.
But if he could not find the evidence, then the case was
all but lost.

Now, enshrined in French investigative procedure
is what is known to Maigret readers the world over as
the 'reconstruction of the crime', in which the accused
will frequently play his own leading role. So it was
that Pierre Voirbo found himself back at the rue
Mazarin. Macé, with all the drama of a player on the
stage of the Opéra, stood in the centre of the tiled
floor, a jug of water in his hand. 'I am going to pretend
that this jug contains blood not water.'

Simulating the dripping of blood as it must have
departed the mutilated corpse of the late Désire

Bodasse, Macé and the circle of officers watched expectantly, mesmerised as the liquid flowed over the tiles, settling in the depressions caused by uneven wear, causing observable pools to form. Voirbo, inscrutable until now, became plainly anxious.

Round the places where the pools had formed, a chalk mark was made before the floor was dried. As the tiles were carefully lifted from the areas within, the coagulated blood on which Gustave Macé had staked his reputation was exposed – indelible proof of murder, and worse.

Pierre Voirbo confessed his crime; admitted luring Bodasse to his home and bludgeoning him to death with a flat-iron when he refused to lend Voirbo money. The catalogue of grisly details was carefully noted, down to filling the dismembered head with molten lead through the mouth and ears, and throwing it off the Pont de la Concorde to disappear beneath the Seine.

Voirbo never got the reward his captors felt he so richly deserved. He cheated Monsieur de Paris and his mechanical blade, preferring instead to cut his own throat with a razor smuggled into his prison cell in a loaf of bread while he awaited trial. As for Gustave Macé, he went on to become chief of detectives for the whole of Paris.

BELLE GUNNESS
(USA, 1908)

Man Slaughter

Born Bella Poulsdatter near Trondheim, Norway, in 1859, the girl who was to earn a reputation as one of America's worst mass murderers first set foot in the New World in 1883, making her home in Chicago and there marrying fellow-countryman Max Sorensen in 1888.

In the course of time the Sorensens moved to a homestead in Austin, Illinois, where Belle settled down to a predictable routine of farming and child rearing.

1900 saw the turning of the first page of a catalogue of 'bad luck' that was to characterise the rest of Belle's life; ill fortune, some would say, that had a suspicious way of proving very profitable for Belle. In short, Max Sorensen died.

It is impossible to know exactly how far the $100 insurance and the money raised by the sale of the farm comforted the widow Sorensen, but putting a brave face on things, Belle returned to Chicago and invested in a lodging-house. Poor Belle; hardly had she got the sheets on the beds than disaster once again visited in the form of a fire which gutted the rooming-house, leaving its owner with no more than the huge insurance claim for comfort.

Undeterred, Belle put her capital into a bakery business, and who knows what treats might have been in store for the sweet of tooth had not her old adversary, the fire bug, chosen to consume Belle's business one night.

No doubt wisely, Belle took a hint from the insurance company's churlish suspicions and their abject refusal to do further business with such a high-risk client. It was time for a change in direction; and that direction was east, to a remote smallholding at La Porte, in the neighbouring state of Indiana, where she became Mrs Belle Gunness – a name which was soon to send shivers of incredulity and horror throughout America.

Unhappily, Peter Gunness did not long survive his wedding, and when a hatchet accidentally slipped from a high shelf dealing him a mortal blow on the head, it was as much as insurance money could do to console the grieving widow.

At about this time, Belle must have tired of bilking the insurance companies – or more likely lived in fear of the inevitable investigation. Whatever the reason, she was now to develop an alarmingly successful means by which a woman alone, with her children to support, could soften the hardship of widowhood:

> Rich, goodlooking widow, young, owner of a
> large farm, wishes to get in touch with a
> gentleman of wealth with cultured tastes.
> Object, matrimony.

One specification that Belle thought it best not to publicise was that intended suitors should also be without-family or close friends, which was a perfect description of the commercial traveller through whom the 'rich good-looking widow' planned to get even richer. Having selected her candidate from the first batch of letters, Belle replied as follows:

> I have been overjoyed by your answer to my

advertisement, because I feel sure you are the one man for me. I feel you will make me and my dear babies happy, and that I can safely entrust you with all that I possess in the world. But I will be candid with you and tell you exactly how I stand. There must be no concealment on either side. Now as to the farm, there are seventy-five acres of land, and also all kinds of crops – apples, plums, and currants. All this is pretty near paid. I am alone with three small children – two girls and a boy. I lost my husband by an accident five years ago . . . and find that it is too much for me to look after things and manage the children as well. Anyway, my idea is to take a partner to whom I can trust everything . . . I have decided that every applicant I have considered favourably must make a satisfactory deposit of cash or security. I think that is the best way to keep away grafters who are on the lookout for an opportunity. I am worth at least $20,000, and if you could bring $5000 just to show you are in earnest, we could talk things over.

The uncompromisingly mercenary tone of the letter clearly did not discourage the salesman, nor did it seem to have deterred the subsequent parade of hopefuls who beat a path to the La Porte farmhouse. Nobody is quite sure how many gentlemen of 'wealth and cultured taste' came knocking on Belle's door, but whatever the number, none ever left. Nobody *can* be sure how long the Belle Gunness enterprise might have gone on had she not encountered a piece of unforeseen bad luck.

Her troubles started through a piece of Belle's own carelessness. When she lured Andrew Holdgren to Indiana, she did not know that he had a brother, or that he had confided his matrimonial aspirations to that brother. After five months without hearing the sound of wedding bells, Holdgren wrote to Mrs Gunness craving some word of Andrew. Belle replied, apparently desperate with anxiety:

I would do anything to find him. He left my house seemingly happy and since that time in January I have not seen him . . . I would go to the end of the world to find him.

Which Holdgren obviously thought was an excellent suggestion, and proposed visiting La Porte to spearhead the search. But fate had decided otherwise.

On 28 April 1908 Belle's old enemy struck once more – and this time she did not survive to collect the insurance. On that Tuesday morning the farmhouse was burnt to the ground. When police investigated the conflagration they found four charred corpses – the one without a head was later identified as Mrs Gunness, the three smaller bodies, those of her children Myrtle, aged eleven, Lucy, nine, and Philip, five.

On 23 May Roy Lamphere, a man periodically employed by Belle to help out on the farm and other more personal duties, was indicted by a Grand Jury on four counts of murder and one of arson. In the event, Lamphere was convicted only of arson, and imprisoned for 21 years.

Meanwhile the police, suspicious as they are paid to be, investigated the farm with picks and shovels. They solved the enigma of Andrew Holdgren – his dismembered body, wrapped in oil-cloth, was one of the first to be dug up. There were thirteen others, all cut up and neatly parcelled, and there might have been more had the team dug further.

It was many years later that Roy Lamphere began to

talk about life on the farm, and about that fatal night in April 1908. He confided that he not only knew about the mass murders at La Porte, but had assisted Belle in disposing of the victims. A more startling revelation was that the burned body identified as Belle Gunness was not, in reality, his former employer and lover, but a female vagrant who had been lured to the farm.

So where, if Lamphere was telling the truth, was Belle Gunness? In retrospect it is almost certain that she did perish in the fire, that it was her body. But then again, having been acquitted of murder, why should Roy Lamphere feel obliged to tell lies? Whatever the answers to these and all the other questions that remain unanswered, one thing is certain: the wealthy widow was never heard from again.

POSTSCRIPT

Although we can view in hindsight such historic crimes as the classic La Porte killings and see them as complete, almost inevitable, narratives, to investigators and reporters trying to make sense of events at the time, it is an uncertain, often frustrating voyage of discovery, with clues unfolding only slowly with which to craft a logical case. Small details emerge, later to be discarded; others to be misinterpreted, finding their true position in the puzzle only at some distance in time.

The following 'diary' of the Belle Gunness case derives from the index of the *New York Times*, and sees the drama unfold as information became available for daily publication to an eager readership.

1908

6 May   Bodies of five murdered persons unearthed in the yard of Mrs Belle Gunness's farm at La Porte. Roy Lamphere, an employee of Mrs Gunness, is believed to be responsible for her murder, that of her children and of the five persons found.

7 May   Four more skeletons found in farmyard; the testimony of a drayman indicates that the bodies may have been transported to Mrs Gunness for burial. Police are trying to determine whether Mrs Gunness was operating a private cemetery in Chicago before moving to La Porte. Her sister states that Belle was 'money-mad'.

8 May   Mrs Gunness described as a religious fanatic who got into crime as a result of the sudden wealth she inherited on the death of her first husband, Max Sorensen. Editorial suggests Mrs Gunness's complicity in the murders.

9 May   Women believed to be Mrs Belle Gunness and her mother were taken from a train at Utica and detained at Syracuse. Meanwhile another body was found at the farm, bringing the total to ten.

10 May   Additional missing persons are believed to have been victims of the La Porte murderer, though no new bodies have been discovered. An editorial criticises the Syracuse police for rashly arresting two women in the belief that they were Mrs Gunness and her mother.

11 May   About 15,000 sightseers visit the Gunness farm.

12 May   A solution to the La Porte murders is believed to be imminent.

13 May   La Porte police are confident that new evidence will draw a confession from Roy Lamphere, accused of burning the Gunness farmhouse.

14 May   The Indiana authorities are reported to have evidence to support the belief that Mrs Gunness had an accomplice in the farmhouse murders.

15 May   Parts of a human jawbone and pieces of skin are found in the cellar of the Gunness farmhouse.

16 May   District Attorney R. Smith is reported as being satisfied that the jawbone found in the cellar belonged to Mrs Gunness.

17 May   New evidence suggests that Mrs Belle Gunness may have fled to Europe.

18 May   Sunday sightseers flock to the Gunness farm.

20 May   False teeth belonging to Mrs Gunness found in the ashes of her burnt farmhouse, proof, it is said, that she died in the fire.

22 May   Police believe that a Miss M. O'Reilly, of Rochester, New York, may also have been a victim of the La Porte murders as jewellery marked with her name has been found in the ruins of the Gunness house.

23 May   Mr Roy Lamphere is indicted by the Grand Jury on four counts of murder and one count of arson. Police still searching the La Porte farm found a human skull in the cesspool.

26 May   Mrs Gunness is now believed to have escaped from the farm dressed in men's clothing. The body once claimed to have been hers is now thought to be that of Miss O'Reilly who disappeared last autumn.

29 May   Belle Gunness reported to be living in Brooklyn.

30 May   Property belonging to Mrs Gunness brings high prices at auction.

3 June   Sheriff Smitzer reveals details of J. G. [Truelson's] confession to the Gunness farmhouse murders.

5 June   Miss O'Reilly, whom [Truelson] claims was murdered at the farm, is found alive and well in Saratoga; she has never been to La Porte in her life.

21 June Police scientists discover that Mrs Gunness poisoned the first of her ten victims with arsenic and strychnine.

24 Nov. Lamphere's defence attorney attempts to prove that Mrs Gunness committed suicide two months after the fire in which she is alleged to have perished.

27 Nov. Roy Lamphere found guilty of arson, but not of murder; he is sentenced to the penitentiary for 2–21 years.

LOUIS VOISIN
(England, 1917–18)

Written out of Reputation★

The first of the pieces was found in the early morning of 2 November 1917. A street-sweeper was about his business in the Bloomsbury district of west London when he became inquisitive about a bundle left beside the railings of Regent Square's central green; wrapped up in the meat sack and blood-soiled sheet were the torso and arms of a woman. Enclosed with the remains was a piece of paper bearing the cryptic message 'Blodie Belgium' scrawled in pencil. Although it was to be some time before the head was found, the trail of a laundry mark (II H) on the sheet eventually led to Madame Emilienne Gerard, a French national who had been living at 50 Munster Square. Significantly, Mme Gerard had not been seen since the night of 31 October.

A routine examination of Emilienne Gerard's apartment enabled the police to patch together a little of the missing woman's background, while from above the fireplace the rounded features of one Louis Voisin gazed out from its frame, the eyes seeming to hover over his own signed IOU for £50 lying on the mantel shelf. Voisin, an expatriate Frenchman, a

★'I hold it as certain, that no man was ever written out of reputation but by himself.'

(William Warburton, *The Works of Alexander Pope*)

butcher by trade, and Mrs Gerard's lover by inclination, was traced to the basement of 101 Charlotte
Street, which accommodation he shared with another
woman-friend, compatriot Berthe Roche (also called
Martin).

Voisin attempted no denial of his acquaintance with
Madame Gerard; indeed, he had been with her on 31
October, the last day she had been seen, when he
offered to keep an eye on her cat while she was visiting
her husband in war-torn France. By this time, Scotland Yard's legendary Detective Chief Inspector
Frederick Porter Wensley had taken charge of the case
and, influenced as much by his instinctive mistrust of
the Frenchman as by the pathologist's report that the
dismemberment had exhibited the kind of rudimen-
tary anatomical knowledge that a butcher might possess, Voisin was taken to the police station at Bow
Street for questioning.

With the assistance of Detective-Sergeant Read,
who spoke French, to supplement Voisin's broken
English, Wensley learned that the butcher had known
Emilienne Gerard for eighteen months or a little
longer, she having once served him in the capacity of
housekeeper. On her disappearance, Voisin could
shed no light, but for the fact that he believed she had
departed for the Continent.

On the following day, Chief Inspector Wensley
decided to apply the one test which might conclusively
link his suspect with the Regent Square shambles.
Speaking through his interpreter to avoid any misunderstanding, Frederick Wensley asked Voisin if he
had any objection to writing out the words 'Bloody
Belgium'; Voisin hadn't, and with the painstaking
deliberateness of the barely literate, proceeded to ins-
cribe 'Blodie Belgium'. It was the same mis-spelling

and broadly the same writing as the note found with
the torso. In his memoirs★ Frederick Porter Wensley
recalled a great sense of anticipation as he asked: ' "Perhaps you're not feeling quite yourself, would you like
to try again?" Five times he wrote, each time using the
same spelling, but the handwriting varied in size. The
final copy bore a very close resemblance in every particular to that of the original. I knew then that it was
only a question of time before other points in the case
would be cleared up.'

One of those 'other points' was the very seminal
requirement to identify positively the remains found
in Regent Square. True, they had been wrapped up in a
sheet belonging to Emilienne Gerard, and that lady
was missing from home, but this was not evidence to
go to court on. Not long after the first discovery, a
parcel containing the matching legs had been found
near Regent Square, but the key to the puzzle, the
head, was still missing. For all the police could prove,
the remains could have been those of somebody
entirely unconnected with Mme Gerard and her disappearance.

It was Detective-Sergeant Alfred Collins who was
able to make that final connection. An officer of great
enthusiasm and long experience, Collins had been
assigned to search the basement at 101 Charlotte
Street. It was in a low cellar that he prised the top off a
barrel of sawdust to see the dead face of Emilienne
Gerard looking up at him. The bludgeoned head had
been found, along with the two hands with their tell-
tale fingerprints. The head matched the other remains;
a positive identification had at last been made.

Charged with murder, Louis Voisin simply

★*Detective Days*. Cassell, London, 1931.

shrugged and muttered: 'It is unfortunate.' He was rather more forthcoming after a couple of days in the cells had impressed on him just how 'unfortunate' his position was. It was desperate, and after the uncharacteristically chivalrous gesture of exonerating Berthe Roche from any part in the death of Madame Gerard, Voisin cobbled together a statement: 'I went to Madame Gerard's place last Thursday, at 11 a.m., and when I arrived the door was closed but not locked. The floor and carpet were full of blood. The head and hands were wrapped up in a flannel jacket . . . They were on the kitchen table . . . The rest of the body was not there . . . I remained five minutes stupefied. I did not know what to do, I thought a trap had been laid for me. I commenced to clean up the blood and my clothes became stained. Then I went back to my house, had lunch, and later returned to Mme Gerard's apartment and brought the parcel back to my place. I kept thinking this must be a trap. I had no intention to harm Madame Gerard, why should I kill her? I didn't want any money, and I owe her nothing.' In fact, according to his own IOU, he owed her £50. Voisin concluded with a somewhat incoherent account of Madame Gerard's 'taking somebody to the flat that night'. It was, in all, a profoundly silly statement, but the best he could come up with in the difficult circumstances.

In January 1918 Louis Voisin and Berthe Roche stood before Mr Justice Darling at the Old Bailey, jointly charged with the murder of Emilienne Gerard. Sir Bernard Spilsbury's examination had indicated that a number of the blows to Madame Gerard's head had been delivered by a much weaker hand than Louis Voisin's, and the wounds were consistent with having been delivered by both prisoners. Nevertheless, at the judge's direction, Berthe Roche was acquitted of murder on the second day of the trial, leaving Voisin alone to face the dread sentence of death, read by Lord Darling in French. The Butcher of Charlotte Street was executed on 2 March 1918.

Berthe Roche, for her contribution to the affair, had been sentenced to seven years' penal servitude, and went insane in prison. After completing a little over a year of her punishment she died in a mental institution.

POSTSCRIPT

Chief Inspector Wensley always had reservations about the legal issues involved in giving Voisin the 'Blodie Belgium' test, and his apprehensions were to some degree justified at the trial, when the prisoner's counsel argued that the circumstances in which his client wrote the incriminating words made it inadmissible as evidence. The judge, however, ruled that in the present case it had been quite proper for the police to attempt to establish the identity of the author of the 'Blodie Belgium' note, and that it would, on the contrary, have greatly *helped* Voisin's case had his handwriting *not* resembled the scribbled note. The fact that there was not the slightest suggestion that the test was complied with involuntarily by the prisoner, in Lord Darling's opinion, enabled the evidence to be presented in open court.

Nevertheless, at his subsequent appearance before the Court of Appeal, the 'Blodie Belgium' statement again formed the backbone of Voisin's grounds for appealing against verdict and sentence.

Finally, Mr Justice A. T. Lawrence settled the matter in summing up their Lordships' observations:

The question whether the prisoner had been duly cautioned before the making of the statement was one of the circumstances which must be taken into consideration, and one on which the Judge must exercise his discretion. It can not be said as a matter of law that the absence of a caution made the statement inadmissible. It might tend to show that the person was not on his guard as to the importance of what he was saying or as to its bearing on some charge of which he had not been informed. Voisin had written the words quite voluntarily. The mere fact that there were police officers present, or that the words were written at their request, or that Voisin was being charged at Bow Street Police Station did not make the writing inadmissible. There was nothing in the nature of a 'trap' or the 'manufacture' of evidence. The identity of the dead woman had not been established, and the police, although they were detaining the appellant in custody for enquiries, had not decided to charge him with the crime.

It is desirable in the interests of the community that investigations into crimes should not be cramped, and the Court is of the opinion that they would be most unduly cramped if it were held that a writing voluntarily made in the circumstances proved in this case was inadmissible in evidence. The mere fact that a statement was made in answer to a question put by a police officer is not in itself sufficient to make it inadmissible in law. It might be, and often is, a ground for a Judge to exclude the evidence, but he should do so only if he thought the statement was not voluntary in the sense which I [Mr Justice

Lawrence] have mentioned, or was an unguarded answer made in circumstances which rendered it untrustworthy, or made its admission against the prisoner unfair.

It was a piece of supreme irony that the 'Blodie Belgium' message, conceived by Voisin to throw the police off his scent, ended up hanging him.

JAMES M'KAY
(Scotland, 1927–8)

Murder in the Family

Despite the fact that 'murder in the family' has always topped the homicide statistics, matricide is unexpectedly rare. Of course, the black book of crime has been punctuated by such hard-hearted rogues as Donald Merrett, Sidney Fox and, more recently, Jeremy Bamber, but these have all been crimes of avarice – murders committed to claim insurance or to secure an inheritance.

And so it seemed in the case of James M'Kay, although his case was complicated by the fact that, despite pleading insanity at his trial, and having that plea rejected, M'Kay was clearly as mad as a hatter.

Mrs Agnes Arbuckle, whose only sin was to have given birth to her worthless son James, had lived her blameless life in a house in Main Street in the Gorbals of Glasgow – until October 1927. It was on the 12th of that month that James M'Kay had enlisted the help of John Russell in getting a large – and, Russell observed, extremely heavy – tin trunk out of Mrs Arbuckle's kitchen and into M'Kay's lodgings. On the following day the trunk was returned by a considerably worse-for-wear James, clothing grimy and dishevelled, face dirty, shoes caked with mud, and as neighbour Mrs Meiklejohn described him so graphically in court: 'His hair standing up on end and his eyes staring in his head.'

It was shortly after this that various portions of Agnes Arbuckle's dismembered body began to be found.

On Saturday morning, 15 October, George Geddes (ironically of the Royal Humane Society) in company with George Bisset were towing a barge up the river Clyde when they saw a strange-shaped bundle on the opposite bank – about where the M'Neill Street Housing Scheme stood. When they recovered the parcel and discovered its contents – dismembered human remains – Geddes and Bisset lost no time in passing responsibility for the future care of their find into the hands of the Central police, who in turn despatched it to the mortuary. In fact the only person who really wanted to look very closely at it was Professor John Glaister who catalogued the parcel's contents as: one head, two legs sawn off below the knees, one thigh, and the left arm and hand from which the ring finger had been chopped (a further rummage in the packaging revealed the finger, but no ring). The head had been severely battered and burned on one side. Also in the bundle were a piece of striped shirting, a woman's apron, a short curtain, and a Glasgow newspaper dated 9 October 1926. Each of the pieces of flesh had been wrapped in tissue paper, the lot bundled up in a bed sheet and tied.

On the following day, Sunday the 16th, police announced that the dismembered corpse recovered from the Clyde had belonged to Mrs Arbuckle, the remainder of her mortal remains having been found buried under coal in the bunker at her home. At the same time, detectives were bringing in Mrs Arbuckle's 37-year-old son under arrest.

In December 1927 James M'Kay was arraigned before Lord Ormidale at the Glasgow circuit court, where the jury set aside the plea of insanity in favour of a simple verdict of 'guilty of murder as charged'. As he was being led out of court, M'Kay turned to his relatives in the public gallery and called out breezily to his wife: 'Cheer up.'

The motive for murder, as outlined by the Advocate-Depute, Mr J. M. Hunter, was robbery. M'Kay was badly in need of money, and by his mother's untimely death he stood to gain about £100 from a variety of sources. On the subject of the prisoner's personality, what sort of man, Mr Hunter asked the jury, after killing and dismembering his own mother, would then remove the dentures from her mouth and try to sell them around town?

In M'Kay's defence, Mr James M'Donald KC emphatically denied his client's involvement in his mother's death – indeed, how she came to be murdered was still a complete mystery to him. 'Assume,' he continued, 'that this man had come home drunk and found his mother dead. In his drunken frenzy he did not know what to do. He felt how he might be suspected of causing her death for he was alone with her in the house.' It was credible that when he found his mother lying dead on the floor he got into such a state of frenzy and became so alarmed that he did his best to conceal the body, and that was the explanation. That also accounted for the lies he told afterwards.

It was the first murder case appeal to be heard by Edinburgh's High Court of Justiciary since the passing of the Criminal Appeal (Scotland) Act. M'Kay's defence counsel was objecting to the admission of certain evidence presented in the court, and the failure of the trial judge fully to consider the medical evidence. There was no reason to suppose that it was other than M'Kay had claimed at his trial – that he had gone to visit his mother and found her lying dead on the floor. For reasons that could only be the product of a guilty conscience, M'Kay had feared being accused of her murder and decided to hide the body.

Not a very impressive defence, and the court was not impressed; the appeal was dismissed, and James M'Kay was hanged on 24 January 1928 at Duke Street Prison, Glasgow.

DR BUCK RUXTON
(England, 1935–6)

'What Motive, and Why?'

On the morning of 29 September 1935 Susan Haines Johnson, an early autumn visitor to the southern uplands of Scotland, was crossing the stone bridge over the Gardenholme Linn along the Edinburgh–Carlisle road outside the town of Moffat. As she looked down, Miss Johnson saw what looked like a human arm protruding from a package at the bottom of the steep gully. The startled Miss Johnson relayed this apprehension to her brother Alfred, who himself made a closer inspection and turned up several other more or less identifiable pieces of human body. By late that Sunday afternoon Sergeant Sloan of the Dumfriesshire Constabulary was in attendance, accompanied by Inspector Strath. The two officers further combed the tangled bankside of the Linn, and by day's end had accumulated a formidable shambles at Moffat mortuary. Next day the search was resumed and the finds examined by Drs Pringle and Huskie from Moffat.

On the following morning, 1 October, Professor John Glaister of the Forensic Medicine Department of Glasgow University was summoned, along with Dr Gilbert Millar of the University of Edinburgh and two senior CID officers, to view the tree-lined ravine which was becoming one of the most famous spots in the British Isles. From the scene of the recent

discoveries, Millar and Glaister repaired to Moffat
cemetery with its tiny mortuary to begin what was to
become one of the outstanding achievements of forensic medicine. Their inventory of the remains so far collected makes grim reading:

Of the four bundles recovered during the initial
search, the first was wrapped in a blouse and contained two upper arms and four pieces of flesh;
the second bundle comprised two thigh bones,
two legs from which most of the flesh had been
stripped, and nine pieces of flesh, all wrapped in a
pillow-case; the third was a piece of cotton sheeting containing seventeen portions of flesh; the
fourth parcel, also wrapped in cotton sheeting,
consisted of a human trunk, two legs with the
feet tied with the hem of a cotton sheet and some
wisps of straw and cotton wool. In addition,
other packages opened to reveal two heads, one
of which was wrapped in a child's rompers; a
quantity of cotton wool and sections from the
Daily Herald of 6 August 1935; two forearms
with hands attached but minus the top joints of
the fingers and thumbs; and several pieces of skin
and flesh. One part was wrapped in the *Sunday
Graphic* dated 15 September [which was subsequently to provide an important clue].

The remains were all badly decomposed and infested
with maggots, so their immediate transfer to the
Anatomy Department of Edinburgh University was
ordered in the interests of preservation. Under Dr
Millar's supervision these remains, and those
discovered around the Gardenholme Linn over subsequent days, were washed in a bath, treated with ether
to destroy the maggots, and left in a preservative solution of formalin until their removal to Edinburgh's

Forensic Medicine Laboratory where the reconstruction and detailed examination was to be carried out. In all, seventy pieces of what appeared to be two bodies had been collected, and it was immediately clear that the extensive mutilation of the features was the result of a deliberate attempt to frustrate identification. For example, the ears, eyes, nose, lips and skin of the faces had been removed, and some teeth extracted; the terminal joints of the fingers had been removed presumably to prevent identification from fingerprints. Nevertheless, one of the heads could be confidently ascribed to a young woman, while the other was initially thought to be male. A statement to this effect was issued and published in the press.

Two hundred miles south of Edinburgh, at No. 2 Dalton Square, Lancaster – home and surgery of Dr Buck Ruxton the news reported in the *Daily Express* under the headline 'Ravine Murder' was being very gratefully received: 'Do you see, Mrs Oxley,' the doctor explained to his charlady, 'it is a man and a woman, it is not our two.'

Dr Ruxton had been born in 1899 to a Parsee family living in Bombay. Christened Bukhtyar Rustamji Ratanji Hakim, he abbreviated his name first to Buck Hakim and later, in England, by deed poll to Buck Ruxton. Ruxton gained his Bachelor of Medicine and Bachelor of Surgery degrees at Bombay University, and subsequently served in the Indian medical service in Baghdad and Basra. Ironically, as it was to prove, Dr Ruxton attended Edinburgh University where, although he failed to secure his fellowship of the Royal College of Surgeons, he did secure a partner in the person of Miss Isabella Kerr, who had been managing a café in the city, and had at the time been married to a Dutchman named Van Ess. Ruxton and Isabella never

married, though when he secured the practice at
Dalton Square they lived together as Dr and Mrs Ruxton, and she bore him three children. The household
was completed by Mary Jane Rogerson, a cheerful girl
of twenty whose duty it was to help with the children.

The Ruxtons' was not an entirely harmonious
relationship, dominated as it was by his insane – and
quite groundless – jealousy. Although there was no
doubt that a considerable affection existed between the
couple, the quarrels became more violent as they
became more frequent with Ruxton's growing obses-
sion with his wife's imagined infidelity, occasioning at
least two recorded visits from the local constable.

In 1934, two years after a desperate suicide attempt,
Mrs Ruxton left her husband and fled to the comfort of
her sister's home in Edinburgh. She was finally persuaded by a hysterically sobbing Ruxton to go back to
Lancaster, but it was clear that the relationship was
nearing crisis. A year after her return Isabella Ruxton
was being wrongly accused of entertaining an affair
with a young local man named Edmondson, the son of
family friends. On 7 September 1935 Mrs Ruxton
again escaped to Edinburgh, this time with her friends
the Edmondsons. Although there was absolutely no
foundation to his suspicions, Ruxton began a tirade of
abuse on her return that was to last most of the following week – until Mrs Ruxton took the family car up to
Blackpool where it was a harmless annual custom for
her to meet her two sisters for the day and enjoy the
illuminations. To Buck Ruxton it was obvious that
she had gone to meet a new lover.

Isabella Ruxton returned on that Saturday night, 14
September, as she had said she would. She was never
seen alive outside 2 Dalton Square again; nor was
Mary Rogerson.

It was not until 4 October that Ruxton went to the police and officially reported the two members of his household missing – and then only under considerable duress. To Mary Rogerson's concerned stepmother and stepfather he had spun some preposterous yarn about Mary being pregnant and Mrs Ruxton taking her away to 'get it seen to', and neither of them being seen since. Wisely, the Rogersons paid a visit to the police and gave a description of Mary Jane. Then, quite coincidentally, one of Ruxton's charladies had been questioned by the police on a quite separate matter – the murder in Morecambe of a woman named Smalley. The doctor was now also concerned that local gossip was beginning to connect the disappearance of his wife and maid with the gruesome discoveries at Moffat which had become headline news throughout Britain.

On the evening of 11 October a distressed Dr Ruxton once again blustered into the Lancaster police station waving a copy of the *Daily Express* and demanding to see the Chief Constable, Captain Henry J. Vann: 'My dear Vann, can't you do something about these newspaper reports. Look at this. This newspaper says that this woman [Body No. 1] has a full set of teeth in the lower jaw, and I know, of my own knowledge, that Mary Rogerson had at least four teeth missing in this jaw.' The more he talked, the more excited Ruxton became: 'Can't you publish it in the papers that there is no connection between the two and stop all this trouble?'

On 12 October Dr Ruxton was invited to call in at the police station to answer some further questions. At seven o'clock the following morning Captain Vann announced: 'Listen carefully to me. I intend to prefer a very serious charge against you. You are charged that between 14 and 29 September 1935 you did feloniously and with malice aforethought kill and murder one Mary Jane Rogerson.'

'Most emphatically not. Of course not. The farthest thing from my mind. What motive and why? What are you talking about?'

On 5 November Ruxton was also charged with the murder of his wife.

Meanwhile, the forensic team at Edinburgh University were performing minor miracles. Professor Glaister had enlisted the help of Professor James Couper Brash of Edinburgh University's Department of Anatomy, assisted by Dr E. Llewellyn Godfrey. The dental examination was entrusted to Dr A. C. W. Hutchinson, Dean of the Dental Hospital and School at Edinburgh, and Mr A. Johnstone Brown. Later in the investigation (he was out of the country at the time of the discoveries) Professor Sydney Smith would lend the great weight of his experience.

Professor Brash had begun the painstakingly slow reconstruction of the remains. The collections of parts which until then had been roughly divided into boxes marked Body No. 1 and Body No. 2 were taking on separate identities. The size and shape of the heads were so dissimilar as to be differentiated at a glance and formed the basis of the identification. The degree of determination on the killer's part to destroy the identity of his victims, and the consequent problems this raised for the pathologists can be gauged by the mutilation of one of the heads alone:

Head No. 1: The head had been severed from the trunk immediately below the level of the chin, and had been much mutilated by removal of the skin and underlying tissues. The nose and both ears had been cut off, and both eyes removed. A large piece of the scalp was missing from the right side of the head, and most of the skin of the forehead and face had been removed. The lips had been almost entirely cut away, the two upper central incisor teeth had been drawn, and the tongue protruded slightly in the gap. Some skin remained on each cheek, down to the chin and below it.

Furthermore, the neat job that had been made of the dismemberment, using only a surgical knife, clearly indicated a degree of anatomical knowledge. The removal of other parts of the bodies which would have more accurately revealed the cause of death suggested that the murderer was also in possession of extensive medical knowledge. Nevertheless, when news of the disappearance of Isabella Ruxton and Mary Jane Rogerson was communicated to Edinburgh along with their descriptions, it was possible to build constructive comparisons with Body No. 1 and Body No. 2; how convincing the match was can be seen on the comparison charts on pages 174–5.

Early in the examination it had been observed that Head No. 1 and Head No. 2 were markedly different in size and shape. Known photographic portraits of the two missing Lancaster women indicated that Head No. 1 could not be Mrs Ruxton, and Head No. 2 could not be Mary Rogerson. The 'positive' identification was achieved by means of a photographic comparison of the skulls with the portraits – a technique never before used in criminal investigation.

Two photographs were used of each of the women – a studio portrait of Mrs Ruxton (called Portrait A) and a snapshot showing the left-side view of the same woman (Portrait B). Of Mary Rogerson only two photographs could be found (Portraits C and D), both

	Mary Jane Rogerson	Body No. 1—Female
Age . . .	Twenty years (8 October 1935).	Certainly between 18 and 25. Probably between 20 and 21.
Stature . . .	About 5 ft.	4 ft. 10 in. to 4 ft. 11½ in. (without shoes).
Hair . .	Light brown.	Hair from scalp and body light brown.
Eyes . .	Blue. 'Glide' in one.	Removed.
Complexion .	Light. Freckles on nose and cheeks.	Ears, nose, lips and most of skin on face removed; complexion of remainder of skin consistent.
Teeth . . .	Old extraction of six teeth, four of them named.	Old extraction or loss of eight teeth, including the four named.
Neck . .	Short neck.	Very small larynx very highly situated.
Tonsils . .	Subject to tonsillitis.	Microscopic evidence consistent with recurrent tonsillitis.
Vaccination Marks .	Four on left upper arm.	Four on left upper arm.
Finger-nails . .	Maidservant.	Trimmed but not regularly manicured; scratches indicating some form of manual work.
Scars . . .	1. Abdominal scar— appendix operation.	1. Trunk missing.
	2. Operation for septic thumb which had left a mark.	2. First segment of right thumb denuded of tissue; no scar on left thumb.
Identifying Peculiarity	Birth marks (red patches) on right forearm near elbow.	Skin and soft tissues removed from upper third of forearm, and lower two-thirds of front only.
Size and Shape of Feet	Left shoe as evidence.	Cast of left foot fitted shoe.
Form of Head and Face	Two photographs in different positions.	Outlines of photographs of skull in same positions fitted.
Finger-prints . .	Numerous imprints from house at 2 Dalton Square.	Positively identified as the finger-prints of both hands and palmar impressions of left hand.
Breasts . . .	Age 20, unmarried.	Single breast, appearance and structure consistent.

	Isabella Ruxton	Body No. 2—Female
Age . . .	34 years 7 months (3 October 1935).	Certainly between 30 and 55. Probably between 35 and 45.
Stature . . .	5 ft. 5 in. to 5 ft. 6 in.	5 ft. 3½ in. (without shoes).
Hair . . .	Soft texture, mid-brown with patch of grey slightly to right of top of head.	Scalp completely removed; a few adherent hairs light to medium brown. Eyelashes dark brown. Available body hair mid-brown.
Eyes . . .	Deep-set; grey-blue.	Removed.
Complexion . .	Fair.	Ears, nose, lips and skin of face removed.
Teeth . . .	Denture replacing three named teeth in gap which would show during life; old extraction of one other named tooth.	Old extraction or loss of fifteen teeth, including the four named.
Fingers and Nails .	Long fingers. Recognisable nails—bevelled, brittle, growing tight at corners, rounded at ends, regularly manicured.	Terminal segments of all fingers removed.
Legs and Ankles .	Thick ankles. Legs of same thickness from knees to ankles.	Soft tissues removed from legs.
Left Foot . .	Inflamed bunion of left big toe.	Hallux valgus of left foot; tissues removed over metatarso-phalangeal joint down to bone and joint opened. X-rays showed exostosis of head of metatarsal.
Size and Shape of Feet	Left shoe as evidence.	Cast of left foot fitted shoe.
Nose . . .	Bridge uneven.	Removed, but bone and cartilage arched.
Form of Head and Face	High forehead, high cheekbones, rather long jaw. Two photographs in different positions.	Corresponding features. Outlines of photographs of skull in same positions fitted.
Breasts . . .	Pendulous breasts: three children.	Appearance and structure of pair of breasts consistent.
Uterus . . .	Three children.	Separate uterus. Could not be assigned but structure consistent.

taken by an amateur and consequently losing some clarity of detail when enlarged to life-size. The two skulls, by now cleaned of their remaining tissue, were each photographed from four angles, matching as closely as possible the positions of the heads in the portraits. From the life-size prints of the skulls and the portraits, distinctive shapes and features were traced in ink on transparent paper; subsequent superimposition revealed that Portraits A and B (Mrs Ruxton) fitted well over the outline of Skull No. 2; similarly, Portraits C and D (Mary Rogerson) were found to fit Skull No. 1. Further elaborate photographic techniques were employed to provide the positive and negative images from the skulls and portraits which, when superimposed, also showed remarkable consistency. It should, however, be emphasised that impressive though this evidence was, it was not *conclusive* in the sense required by the court – indeed, defence counsel objected to the admission of the photographs at all, on the grounds that they were 'constructed evidence, so liable to error'.

Ascertaining cause of death presented predictable problems. In Body No. 1 (thought to be Mary Rogerson), the neck and trunk with its internal organs were never recovered, making cause of death impossible to establish, though swelling of the tongue was consistent with asphyxia. Body No. 2 (thought to be Mrs Ruxton) exhibited a congested state of the lungs and brain which, associated with the damaged condition of the hyoid bone in the throat, indicated manual strangulation.

The police investigation had also been progressing, and while missing-person enquiries launched over a large area around Moffat had failed to yield the names of likely victims, another team of forensic officers had been working on the materials in which the dismembered remains had been wrapped. A major breakthrough came with the identification of the pages of the *Sunday Graphic* for 15 September 1935 as being from what in the newspaper trade are called 'slip editions' – that is, issues covering events of a purely local interest and circulated only in that area. The 'slip' in question contained news of the Morccambe Festival and was sold only in that town, Lancaster, and the immediate surrounding district.

Mrs Jessie Rogerson was brought up from Morecambe to see if she could identify any of the materials associated with the human remains. There was Mary Jane's blouse – no doubt about it, it had a distinctive repair patch under the arm sewn on by Mrs Rogerson herself. Through another lead from Mrs Rogerson, the child's rompers were later identified by a Mrs Holme as part of a bundle of children's clothing she had passed on to the Ruxtons during their stay with her as boarders the previous summer. Dr Ruxton had had good reason to feel uneasy, every justification for thinking that fingers were pointing in his direction.

But if things looked bad for the doctor now, the narrative of his peculiar conduct that was paraded before the court would have been burlesque had two women not lost their lives in so dreadful an act of butchery.

Ruxton's trial opened at the High Court of Justice, Manchester, on Monday, 2 March 1936, before Mr Justice Singleton. Mr J. C. Jackson KC, Mr Maxwell Fyfe KC and Mr Hartley Shawcross were instructed by the Director of Public Prosecutions on behalf of the Crown. For Dr Ruxton stood one of the greatest criminal advocates of his day, Mr Norman (later Lord) Birkett KC, assisted by Mr Philip Kershaw KC.

The proposition that was to be put so convincingly to the jury over the next eleven days was outlined by Mr Jackson in his opening speech:

Now, it does not need much imagination to suggest what probably happened in that house. It is very probable that Mary Rogerson was a witness to the murder of Mrs Ruxton, and that is why she met her death. In that house the bedrooms are on the top floor; the back bedroom was occupied by Mary Rogerson, in one of the front slept Mrs Ruxton with her three children, and on the same floor was also the doctor's room. You will hear that Mrs Ruxton had received before her death violent blows in the face and that she was strangled. The suggestion of the prosecution is that her death and that of the girl Mary took place outside these rooms on the landing at the top of the staircase, outside the maid's bedroom, because from that point down the staircase right into the bathroom there are trails of enormous quantities of blood. I suggest that when she went up to bed a violent quarrel took place; that he strangled his wife, and that Mary Rogerson caught him in the act and so had to die also. Mary's skull was fractured: she had some blows on the top of the head which would render her unconscious, and then was killed by some other means, probably a knife, because of all the blood that was found down these stairs.

As had been expected, the medical evidence was presented with the same skill as that with which it had been gathered, and a faultless rendition of his findings by Professor John Glaister earned him this accolade from the judge: 'No one could sit in this court and listen to the evidence of Professor Glaister, either in examination-in-chief or in cross-examination, without feeling that there is a man that is not only master of his profession, but who is scrupulously fair, and most anxious that his opinion, however strongly he may hold it, shall not be put unduly against the person on his trial.'

It was nevertheless this unassailable scientific testimony that weighed so heavily against Ruxton, and there was very little that his counsel could do to shake the foundations of the prosecution case. In fairness, though, it must be emphasised that Norman Birkett's courageous championing of his client was nothing short of what might have been expected from so eminent a defender, and his attention to detail, to any hint in favour of his client was untiring.

In the absence of any credible witnesses on the prisoner's behalf, Dr Ruxton himself stood sole testimony to his innocence. On the whole he displayed himself rather badly, being prone to outbursts of hysterical sobbing, and rambling, illogical accounts of his own behaviour, and his refusal to acknowledge the truth of even the clearest evidence that might incriminate him did much to emphasise the impression of a guilty man bluffing.

In accordance with British legal tradition, Norman Birkett, by calling Ruxton to the stand, had entitled himself to make his closing speech for the defence after the prosecution address instead of before it – in this way his words would be the last the jury would hear before his Lordship's summing-up:

It seems scarcely necessary to have to say to you that if you are satisfied of the fact that in the ravine on that day were those two bodies, identified beyond the shadow of a doubt, it does not prove this case. If, for example, the word of the

prisoner was true, 'They left my house,' there is
an end of the case. Even though their bodies were
found in a ravine, dismembered, and even
though those were the bodies, this does not prove
the case against the prisoner. The Crown must
prove the fact of murder, and you may have
observed how much of this case has been mere
conjecture. It is not for the defence to prove
innocence; it is for the Crown to prove guilt, and
it is the duty of the defence to propound a theory
which would be satisfactory to your collective
mind . . .

It is never incumbent upon the prosecution in a
charge of murder to prove motive, but they say,
'We will show you the motive; here it is – jealousy because of infidelity'. I ask you to accept
with the greatest reserve evidence spoken to after
the event, such as that which has been given in
this court from the servants and others . . . The
doctor is arrested for murder, and how it colours
the mind. This is clear, and I do not seek to deny
it, that there were intervals and periods of the
greatest possible unhappiness. You will remember that phrase employed by Dr Ruxton, a phrase
so revealing and so powerful – 'We were the kind
of people who could neither live with each other,
nor live without each other.' Unhappiness was
no new thing . . . The Crown said this was a
record of marital unhappiness, grievous quarrels;
she had left him and under the persuasion of her
sister had returned, and there in that family was
this canker, this jealousy, and so he would kill
her. I suggest to you it is fantastical, and to suggest that was the motive and that was the occasion is, in my submission, not to strengthen this

case in any particular but on the contrary to weaken it. For years that unhappiness has subsisted, and there was nothing revealed to you upon the evidence which on that occasion should prompt him to do that which the Crown lay at his charge.

After an impeccably painstaking and impartial summing-up, the jury required just a little more than one hour to return a verdict of guilty against Buck Ruxton. An appeal was, of course, lodged on Ruxton's behalf, and heard before the Lord Chief Justice Lord Hewart, Mr Justice du Parq and Mr Justice Goddard. Their Lordships, rightly, dismissed the appeal and Ruxton was left to face the hangman on 12 May 1936 at Strangeways Prison, Manchester.

On the following Sunday, a popular newspaper published what purported to be a sealed confession written by Dr Ruxton and left with the instructions that it should be opened in the event of his execution. However, serious doubt is cast on the provenance of this confession by a letter received from his client by Mr Norman Birkett on the morning of the execution; in it Ruxton thanks his counsel for the efforts made to save his life, and concludes: 'I know that in a few hours I shall be going to meet my Maker. But I say to you, sir, I am entirely innocent of this crime.'

BRIAN DONALD HUME
(England, 1949–50)

'I Got Away with Murder'

In the early evening half-light of 5 October 1949, an
Auster light aircraft emerges from the clouds and flies
out beyond the coast of Essex towards the open North
Sea, where its pilot drops two parcels into the icy
water. 'Mission accomplished', as the plane's former-
RAF occupant might have expressed it as he landed the
craft safely at Southend's municipal aerodrome. Or at
least, part of the mission had been accomplished. On
the following day the pilot arrived at Southend in a
hire car and took the same plane by the same route,
where a third bundle, larger than the others, wrapped
in felt and bound with ropes, was thrown into the sea.

Not exactly everyday behaviour, but who was there
to notice?

It was a fortnight later, on 21 October, that things
began to go wrong for the airman with the strange
pastime. A farm labourer named Sidney Tiffen was
wildfowling from his punt on the Essex marshes at
Tillingham when he saw a felt-covered parcel lying on
the flats. Naturally inquisitive – who wouldn't be? –
Tiffen cut the rope and folded back the covering from
the bundle. It probably put the unfortunate man off
opening parcels for life – if not off punting the Essex
flats. What he saw there in the mud in front of him was
a human torso, minus head and legs, and with the arms
pinioned behind the back with a leather strap. The

remains were modestly clad in a cream silk shirt and blue silk underpants. A practical man, as well as a startled one, Sidney Tiffen had the presence of mind to secure the 'bundle' by one arm to a stake in the mud before making off at speed to the nearest police station.

By the following morning the mutilated corpse had been recovered from the water, and via Chelmsford mortuary had arrived for post-mortem at the London Hospital Medical School, Whitechapel; the pathologist was Dr Francis Camps.

Examination indicated that the probable cause of death could be guessed from the five stab wounds in the chest. Subsequent to death, the head and lower limbs had been removed with a sharp blade and saw. Dr Camps also found a number of bones in the chest broken, consistent with crash injuries; Camps went so far as to suggest that the torso had been thrown out of an aircraft into the water.*

It was the fingerprints that identified the Essex Torso. Fingerprints that matched the police record of Stanley Setty, born Sulman Seti in Baghdad 46 years previously. Setty was a small-time crook who made his dishonest income through dubious car deals and by acting as 'banker' for others on the edge of gangsterdom. Setty had been reported missing from his home in London's Lancaster Gate since 4 October. On that day he was known to have received a cheque for £1000 in settlement of a car sale.

Acting on Dr Camps' theory that the body had been thrown from a plane, Scotland Yard investigations led to the United Services Flying Club at Elstree where,

---

*Camps was able to make this informed suggestion because during the war it had been his job to examine the bodies of pilots whose parachutes had failed to open.

on 5 October, an Auster sports plane had been hired by
Brian Donald Hume. When he took the aircraft out en
route for Southend he had been carrying two parcels.
It was the same man who had picked up the plane from
Southend Municipal Aerodrome on the following
morning accompanied by a further, larger parcel.

Hume, it transpired, was also well known to the
police. Like Setty a petty crook, he lived with his wife
Cynthia and three-month-old daughter in Finchley
Road, Golders Green. But that was not all Scotland
Yard had up their sleeve when they interviewed
Donald Hume on 26 October. They had found
bloodstains in the plane that he had piloted, and they
found a taxi driver who had taken a £5 note from
Hume – part of the cash received from the Yorkshire
Penny Bank by Stanley Setty when he cashed his
£1000 cheque.

After a momentary lapse into histrionics during
which he put his head in his hands and wailed: 'I'm
several kinds of bastard, aren't I?' Hume coped with
the situation instinctively – in other words, he told a
pack of lies.

The fact was – according to Hume's statement – he
did fly some bundles out over the estuary and drop
them from the plane. He had met two men, Mac and
Greenie, who had persuaded him to hire a plane to
engage in a little harmless smuggling. On 5 October
Mac, Greenie and a third man called The Boy arrived
at Hume's Golders Green maisonette with two parcels
containing, so Mac had claimed, plates for printing
forged petrol coupons which had to be disposed of – in
the sea, from a light aircraft.

When Hume returned, mission accomplished, he
found Mac, Greenie, The Boy and another parcel
waiting for him. But as he had already been paid £50

and was offered a further £100 he made no fuss about the second drop. It was only when the news broke that part of Stanley Setty had been found embedded in the Essex marshes, and The Boy had telephoned with the advice to keep quiet about his recent airborne activities, that Hume was in any way suspicious; by that time it was too late.

As well as an extensive search for the enigmatic Mac, Greenie and The Boy, police officers also searched extensively in Hume's flat, discovering that the recently cleaned living-room carpet showed evidence of extensive blood staining.

On 18 January 1950 Brian Donald Hume appeared before Mr Justice Lewis at the Old Bailey, charged with the murder of Stanley Setty. In mid-trial his Lordship was taken fatally ill, and it was necessary to reopen the proceedings before a new trial judge – Mr Justice Sellers – and a fresh jury.

Understandably, the prosecution case relied heavily on the evidence of the blood-stained carpet, inferring that the soiling had resulted from the murder and dismemberment of Stanley Setty. No, protested Hume, he had nothing to do with Setty's death; however, he had not been completely frank in what he had told the police about the bundles. He had dropped the large one on the living-room floor while carrying it to the car; and one end had split open spilling blood out on to the carpet. By this time, he whined, he was so scared of his involvement, and so frightened by the terrible trio who *had* killed Setty, that he said nothing.

Yes, the whole story was becoming quite preposterous. The jury were so bewildered that they were unable to agree on a verdict of any kind, and had to be discharged.

And so Donald Hume's trial began for the third

time. On this occasion the prosecution decided to offer
no evidence on the charge of murder, and Hume was
formally found 'Not Guilty'. Wisely, the prisoner had
agreed to plead guilty to the lesser charge of being an
accessory, for which misdeed he earned himself
twelve years' imprisonment.

POSTSCRIPT

Donald Hume was released from Dartmoor in the
spring of 1958 after earning maximum remission for
good behaviour. On 1 June the *Sunday Pictorial*
published a story headed: 'I KILLED SETTY . . .
AND GOT AWAY WITH MURDER.' For his confession, printed over the succeeding four issues, Hume
was paid £2000 (some put the figure as high as £10,000)
and, though he could not be tried again for the same
crime, found it expedient to spend part of the money
on a one-way ticket to Switzerland and the rest of it on
a few months of high living.

By January 1959, the man who was now calling
himself Donald Brown found his bank account was in
serious need of repair, and in escaping from an abor-
tive attempt to rob a Zurich bank on 30 January, he
shot and killed 50-year-old taxi driver Arthur Maag.
Thus Hume escaped the executioner for a second time
– for there was no capital punishment in Switzerland.
He was sentenced instead to life imprisonment in
Regensdorf, and when, in August 1976, he was judged
to have become insane Hume was returned to Britain –
in ankle chains and manacles – and confined in
Broadmoor. On 19 April 1988, at the age of 67,
Donald Hume was moved to a hospital for low risk
patients at Southall, west London, where he remains.

REGINALD DUDLEY and
ROBERT MAYNARD
(England, 1974–7)

Another First for Forensics

It was a brisk early autumn morning on 5 October 1974 on the north bank of the river Thames at a spot called Cold Harbour Point, near Rainham, Essex. For Richard Leighton, the traditionally placid pastime of bird-watching was about to be invested with a new and terrible association – the upper part of a man's torso, half in, half out of the water.

Over the following ten days, sundry other dismembered parts of the same body were discovered washed up into nooks and crannies over a nine-mile stretch of river; collected together at Guy's Hospital they became the preoccupation of Dr Alan Grant, who found himself confronting the problem of attempting an identification – not the least of his troubles being the absence of a head and hands. Nevertheless, Dr Grant was able to announce with some confidence that the remains had been in the water for about five days prior to the first discovery, and that the body had been severed with a knife and saw. Despite the unavailability of the skull, congestion formed in the lungs was consistent with a severe head injury being the cause of death.

Although detectives investigating the case were privately convinced that the corpse was that of William Henry Moseley, a 37-year-old small-time crook operating in north London (and blood samples taken from Moseley's wife and children compared with that taken from the torso suggested a family connection – see table below), it was to be nearly a year before any further progress could be made in the case.

On 7 September 1975 the bludgeoned and shot body of Michael Cornwall was unearthed in Chalkdell Wood in Hatfield, Hertfordshire, by a small boy engaged in digging for 'buried treasure'. It was known that Cornwall and Moseley had been close friends, and the circumstances of their demise made it unlikely that the deaths were not in some way connected.

Parent 1	Parent 2	Children's Groups Possible	Children's Groups Impossible
O	O	O	A, B, AB
O	A	O, A	B, AB
O	B	O, B	A, AB
A	A	O, A	B, AB
A	B	AB, B, O, A	All possible
B	B	O, B	A, AB
O	AB	A, B	O, AB
A	AB	AB, A, B	O
B	AB	AB, A, B	O
AB	AB	AB, A, B	O

Research into hereditary factors in blood-grouping (mainly for the purpose of establishing paternity) cannot state with certainty that a child comes from specific parents; it can, however, ascertain whether a child is *not* the offspring of a given couple

It required the matchless skills of Professor James Cameron at a second post-mortem on 24 October to supplement Dr Grant's report and positively identify the remains of William Moseley. Cameron was able to recover from the gallbladder a comparatively uncommon 'metabolic' or pure cholesterol gallstone, a condition for which Moseley had been undergoing treatment. Medical records also proved invaluable when an x-ray of the dismembered torso was compared with one taken of William Moseley during a mass chest x-ray campaign; the eight points of similarity provided further convincing evidence of identification. Professor Cameron's supplementary observations added that the victim had been severely tortured before death, having the toenails on one foot pulled out and the sole of the foot burned.

This information, plus what was known of Moseley's 'business connections', led police to infiltrate the criminal underworld in their search for a lead on the killings and dismemberment. These enquiries yielded the information that just before Moseley had been 'eliminated', two men had been discussing his death – Reginald Dudley, 55, a crooked jeweller, and 40-year-old Robert Maynard, a petty crook. Detectives also learned that this same Reginald Dudley had been involved in a fracas with the same William Henry Moseley who had thrashed him soundly, much to the amusement of everybody in gangland except Dudley, who had sworn revenge. It now appeared that it had been no empty threat!

As for Michael Cornwall, he had been returned to the streets of London in October 1974 after a spell 'inside'. Hearing of the untimely death and piecemeal disposal of Moseley, and with rather more bravado than good sense, Cornwall went in search of the men rumoured to have distributed his friend along the Thames.

With staggering naivety, which for all we know may have been provoked by genuine affection, Michael Cornwall soon found himself not only

hunting Reginald Dudley, but enjoying domestic bliss
with his daughter Kathleen. On 22 August 1975 Cornwall disappeared.

From the outset there had never been any doubt in
the mind of Commander Albert Wickstead that they
were dealing with gangland killings. Since taking
charge of the case soon after the discovery of
Moseley's remains, Wickstead had continually
exploited his unique familiarity with the London mob,
their habits and habitats. The result was that in April
1976 seven people – including Dudley and Maynard –
were committed for trial by the Epping magistrates.

The Old Bailey proceedings, which lasted a sensa-
tional seven months, were the longest in British
criminal history. In the end, on 16 June 1977, three of
the seven accused were acquitted; Reginald Dudley
and Robert Maynard were convicted of the double
murder and sentenced to life imprisonment. Kathleen
Dudley, who had proved that blood is thicker than
water, was handed down a two-year suspended sentence for conspiring to cause Michael Cornwall grievous bodily harm. Another crony, Charles Clarke, was
jailed for four years for his part in the conspiracy.

POSTSCRIPT

The most remarkable feature of this otherwise quite
unremarkable tale of gangland rivalries was the positive identification of William Moseley's remains – the
first time this had been achieved without a head. But
for the brilliant pathologist who had solved the riddle,
there was one more surprise to come.

On 28 July 1977, six weeks after the trial had ended
and three years after the first pieces of William

Moseley had been fished out of the river, Professor Cameron took delivery of a dismembered head. It had been found wrapped in a woollen balaclava and sheets of newspaper in a public lavatory in Islington, north London. The first thing that impressed Cameron's team at the London Hospital was how cold and damp the head was – quite consistent with thawing out after deep-freezing. The last piece of William Moseley had been found, and with it confirmation of James Cameron's initial conviction that death had been occasioned by a severe head injury.

DENNIS ANDREW NILSEN
(England, 1978–83)

Dismembering a Body

It was on Thursday, 3 February 1983, that residents of the flats at 23 Cranley Gardens, in the quiet north London suburb of Muswell Hill, found that their lavatories would not flush properly.

The job had already defeated the local plumber before, on the following Tuesday evening, help arrived in the person of Dyno-Rod's Mike Cattran.

Cattran's first job was to inspect the manhole at the side of the house. It was never the pleasantest of jobs, but even so, the stench that rose from the pit when the cover had been removed was appalling even by his professional standards. Aiming the beam of a torch down twelve feet to the bottom of the hole, the plumber was disturbed to see a layer of whitish sludge, flecked with what looked horribly like blood; it was against all his better instincts that the Dyno-Rod man climbed down into the manhole finding, when he reached the bottom, chunks of rotting meat, some with hair still attached to the skin.

When a full search of the drain was carried out next day by the police, further fragments of flesh and bone were fished out and quickly identified by pathologists as human. Detective Chief Inspector Peter Jay clearly had a murder on his hands.

Among the residents of No. 23, occupying the attic flat, was 37-year-old Dennis Nilsen – 'Des' as he preferred to be called. When Nilsen arrived home from his job at the Denmark Street Job Centre on the evening of Wednesday, 8 February, it was to be met by a trio of detectives. Nilsen expressed some surprise that the police should be interested in anything as mundane as blocked drains, and when told of the remains that had been found, replied: 'Good grief, how awful.'

Acting on an inspired guess, Inspector Jay rounded on Nilsen with: 'Don't mess about, where's the rest of the body?'

To the detective's great surprise Nilsen turned and replied quite calmly: 'In two plastic bags in the wardrobe. I'll show you.'

On the way to the police station, Detective Inspector McCusker turned to Nilsen in the back seat of the car and asked casually: 'Are we talking about one body or two?' Dennis Nilsen looked up: 'Fifteen or sixteen since 1978: three at Cranley Gardens and about thirteen at my previous address at Melrose Avenue, Cricklewood.'

And so began the extraordinary story of Britain's most prolific serial killer.

There was never any question that Dennis Nilsen was guilty – he had dictated 30 hours of uncannily detailed confession over the period of eleven days – the question was how guilty he was, or rather, how accountable he could be held for his guilt.

At first, after consultation with solicitor Ronald Moss, Nilsen had decided to plead guilty. Apart from saving the court a great deal of time and the taxpayer a great deal of expense, it would have extended to the families of his victims the mercy of not having exposed in court, and to the world at large, the worst of Nilsen's excesses.

By the time his case had come to the Old Bailey's Number One Court on 24 October 1983, Dennis Nilsen had changed his solicitor for that colourful champion of underdogs, Mr Ralph Haeems, on whose advice he changed his plea to 'diminished responsibility' due to mental disorder.

Mr Ivan Lawrence, acting for Nilsen, opened his defence by declaring that it was not his intention to prove that his client was insane, but that at the time of each of the killings he was suffering from such abnormality of mind that he was incapable of forming *the specific intent to murder*.

Dr James MacKeith of the Bethlem Royal Hospital testified that Nilsen had difficulty in expressing emotions and exhibited symptoms of maladaptive behaviour – their combination, he declared, was 'lethal'. It was a conclusion sharply opposed by the Crown prosecutor, Mr Alan Green; Green reminded the court of Nilsen's calculation in killing and disposing of his victims, and the cunning way in which he had sought to establish insanity by telling obvious lies – in other words 'he was a jolly good actor'. In the end Dr MacKeith was unwilling to describe the defendant's responsibility as diminished, as that was a legal and not a medical definition.

The second psychiatric witness for the defence, Dr Patrick Gallwey, fared little better in trying to get the court to accept what he called 'Borderline False Self As If Pseudo-Normal Narcissistic Personality Disorder' – as unwieldy a concept as it was a title, and no clearer when abbreviated to 'False Self Syndrome'.

When the defence had completed its case, the Crown, as is customary in pleas of 'diminished responsibility', was permitted to bring to the witness box its own 'rebuttal' psychiatrist to contradict the expert testimony of Gallwey and MacKeith. Dr Paul Bowden, after declaring himself unable to find any abnormality of mind as described by the Homicide Act,* went on to state that in his opinion Dennis Nilsen simply wanted to kill people – a condition which was lamentable, but in no way excusable on psychiatric grounds: 'In my experience, the vast majority of people who kill have to regard their victims as objects, otherwise they cannot kill them.'

As for the trial judge, Mr Justice Croom-Johnson, it was clear from his summing up of the medical evidence that he considered Nilsen not insane, but thoroughly evil: 'There are evil people who do evil things. Committing murder is one of them,' and: 'There must be no excuses for Nilsen if he has moral defects. A nasty nature is not arrested or retarded development of mind.'

And, so, although the best part of the proceedings for a whole week were occupied with evidence given by the opposing psychiatrists, the debate ended as confused and unresolved as it had begun. It remained for the members of the jury to make up their own minds as to whether or not the prisoner was sane. After 24 hours of deliberation that jury decided, by a majority vote of 10–2, that Dennis Nilsen was sane and guilty of the six counts of murder as charged, and of the two attempted murders.

---

*The Homicide Act of 1957 reads, in part: 'Where a person kills or is a party to a killing of another, he shall not be convicted of murder if he was suffering from such abnormality of mind (whether arising from a condition of arrested or retarded development or any inherent causes or induced by disease or injury) as substantially impaired his mental responsibility for his acts and omissions in doing or being a party to the killing.'

Nilsen was sentenced to life imprisonment with a recommendation from Mr Justice Croom-Johnson that he serve no fewer than 25 years. Nilsen himself accepts this sentence and in truth does not expect to be released. In 1984, he was transferred from Wormwood Scrubs to Wakefield Prison in Yorkshire, where he remains to this day.

POSTSCRIPT

Since news of the Nilsen case broke on to the front pages of the world's press in February 1983, millions of words have been written about Dennis Nilsen, though none with more depth and understanding than Brian Masters' outstanding, award-winning *Killing for Company* (Cape, London, 1985).

Masters originally contacted Nilsen while the latter was on remand in Brixton Prison, seeking his co-operation in a written study of the case. Nilsen agreed, and between the two there arose what Masters described as 'a trust which enabled us to discuss his past and his offences in complete frankness'.

Nilsen revealed himself not only as an intelligent, articulate and sensitive man, but one capable of intense self-examination. During his time in prison he has produced a staggering 50 volumes of journal, in which he looks deeply into himself and his crimes, recalling and describing details with chilling clarity. It is not difficult to take the point of Dr Bowden and Alan Green – that the meticulous manner of the murders and disposal makes a plea of diminished responsibility difficult to sustain:

> I got ready a small bowl of water, a kitchen knife, some paper tissues and plastic bags. I had to have

a couple of drinks before I could start. I removed the vest and underpants from the body. With the knife I cut the head from the body. There was very little blood. I put the head in the kitchen sink, washed it and put it in a carrier bag. I then cut off the hands and then the feet. I washed them in the sink and dried them. . .

NICHOLAS BOYCE
(England, 1985)

The Lucan Jinx

Not all men who kill – or women – are monsters of the breed typified by Ruxton and Nilsen – or Belle Gunness; murderers in cold blood, assassins who can hack through a body with none of that sweating terror by which a normal person might at once become paralysed. Some are ordinary people who are haunted by a nightmare of their own creation, from which they can never awaken. Nicholas Boyce was one of those for whom the memory of his bloody initiation into the ranks of The Butchers proved too powerful a spectre to lay.

Unable to bear his wife's humiliating taunts of 'lazy good-for-nothing', and despite his Bachelor of Science degree too unimaginative to find a better solution, Boyce bludgeoned and strangled her after a blazing row in early January 1985. He elected to dispose of the body by dismembering it, and according to his own recollection took five hours with a carving knife and a saw in the bath of their small council flat in London's East End: 'I cooked the bones and boiled the flesh and later put the parts in plastic bags and left them in different parts of London.' In fact, he left them in various builders' skips in Kilburn and Islington, on Hackney Marshes and in Westminster outside a take-away food bar. On these motoring trips he was accompanied by his young children.

Mrs Boyce's head, as is so frequently the case with dismemberment, was singled out for special treatment and was encased in concrete before being thrown into the Thames.

Five days later, on 18 January, Nicholas Boyce walked into Bethnal Green police station and confessed.

The background is the familiar one of domestic strife compounded by violence, and leaving aside the brutal manner of the murder (pathologists assembling the recovered pieces of Christabel Boyce testified to 'a ferocious attack') and the gruesome dismemberment, it would have failed to make a leading story in the national press. But there was an irresistible feature of the crime that Fleet Street could not ignore: the headlines told the story – 'Lucan Nanny No. 2 Murdered', 'Second Lucan Nanny Killed'.

Richard John Bingham, seventh Earl of Lucan – known as 'Lucky' to his friends – disappeared on 7 November 1974, leaving behind, in the London home of his estranged wife Veronica, the brutally bludgeoned body of the Lucan children's nanny, Sandra Rivett. At the inquest in June 1975, a coroner's jury returned a verdict of 'Murder by Lord Lucan'.*

Christabel Boyce, then Christabel Martin, was the girl who had taken over the care of the Lucan children.

Ironically she had also preceded Sandra Rivett in the job, and filled in when Sandra was off duty – had she been off duty on 7 November 1974, Christabel might have met her tragic end a decade earlier, and by a different hand.

---

*For students of legal procedure, this was the last time that a coroner was permitted to name a murder suspect at an inquest.

Although there have been reported sightings from every corner of the globe, and although some believe him to be dead, Lord Lucan remains in law a fugitive. As for Nicholas Boyce, we know exactly where he is; serving six years in prison.

Five

Dismemberment While Alive

SUCHNAM SINGH SANDHU
(England, 1968)

The Scattered Seed

On Thursday, 4 April 1968, Suchnam Singh Sandhu, a
39-year-old Punjabi Sikh, took a day's leave from his
job as a machine minder to a manufacturing chemists.
He had spent the morning lounging about in his
pyjamas at home in Fanshawe Avenue, Barking.
Suchnam Singh was an educated man, with a good
command of the English language; indeed, he had
been a schoolmaster back in his native village of Jullundor in the Punjab. His two younger daughters were
out at school and his wife was also away for the day.
The only other occupant of the house that morning
was his eldest daughter, nineteen-year-old Sarabjit
Kaur.

In common with many eldest children – of whatever
culture – Sarabjit was her father's favourite, and he
entertained great ambitions for her to become a
doctor. She had attended the Delhi School of Nursing
in India, and Suchnam Singh's main motive for bringing his family to England in September 1967 had been
to further her career. Unfortunately, before leaving
India, she had secretly fallen in love with her cousin,
who, besides being of a lower caste, was also a married
man. When she arrived in Britain, Sarabjit had
dutifully enrolled as a medical student at the East Ham
College of Technology, but had continued to correspond illicitly with her Indian lover. At some stage,

Suchnam Singh must have discovered his daughter's secret, and his disappointment and frustration at what he could only see as her shameful behaviour knew no bounds. He had begun to show her actual physical abuse, beating her and, on one occasion, had even tried to choke her.

Sarabjit found it necessary to leave home in November 1967, moving into a flat in Uphall Road, Ilford. Soon afterwards, she visited a local GP, Dr Gabriel Merriman, who broke the news – almost certainly considered by his patient 'bad' news – that she was pregnant, and referred her to the ante-natal unit of Barking Hospital. Sarabjit attended just once, on 20 November, when she was diagnosed as being twenty weeks pregnant. She must have decided, with formidable courage in the circumstances, to admit her plight to her parents, because they arrived one day at her flat and took Sarabjit and all her possessions back to the family home. Suchnam Singh now almost certainly arranged for an Indian doctor to perform an illegal abortion on his daughter, as there is no official record of a birth or of any further medical treatment. Subsequently, Sarabjit remained at Fanshawe Avenue as a member of the family.

On the morning of 4 April, Suchnam Singh and his daughter had a heated argument, at least according to his account. Sarabjit had come downstairs from her bedroom and told her father that she had just taken a large overdose of Phenobarbitone tablets, and had written a suicide letter in which she claimed that she was killing herself because her father refused to allow her to live with the man she loved. Suchnam Singh, probably as much from panic as from anger, lost control and, grabbing a hammer which was used to break up coal, hit his daughter twice on the head, causing her to drop unconscious to the ground, to all appearances dead. She had also taken the fatal overdose, but it had not yet had time to take effect.

Suchnam Singh dressed and made the fifteen-minute journey to a hardware shop in Ilford High Road. He bought a high-tensile hacksaw, returned to the house, and changed back into his pyjamas.

He then placed Sarabjit's limp body in a large plastic bag and, using this to protect the room from the gore, Suchnam Singh began the grisly job of dismembering his eldest daughter. As he sawed at her neck, she revived momentarily and made a grab for the blade, tearing her thumb. Unperturbed, Singh finished the decapitation, then sawed through the torso at the belly and the legs at the knees. The upper torso, still dressed in a pink cardigan, a blue pullover, a blue Indian dress with white embroidery, a cotton vest and a bra, with four white metal bangles still on the left arm, was then wrapped in a square of green material and put into an olive-green suitcase. The lower torso, with the pants still on it, and the feet, were wrapped in green and black material and placed in a reddish-brown case. The head was wrapped in some old torn towelling and put into a cotton bag along with the financial page of the *Daily Telegraph* dated 27 March to pad it out. The cotton bag was placed in a blue duffel bag. Suchnam Singh then emptied the considerable amount of blood from the plastic bag into the bath and threw his bloodstained pyjamas and the hacksaw blade into the dustbin. The hammer was later disposed of somewhere in Barking.

That same evening, Suchnam Singh travelled up to central London by public transport, carrying with him the olive-green suitcase. Arriving at Euston Station, he saw from the destination board that a train was scheduled to leave for Wolverhampton at 10.45 p.m. from platform seven. After buying a ticket at the booking office, Singh waited for the train to arrive at the platform before passing through the barrier. The train was still unlit as he entered a carriage and tucked the suitcase under a table. He then got off the train, went back through the barrier and returned home, carefully tearing up and throwing away his ticket. Singh then collected the other suitcase and took it to Ilford High Road. He claimed later that he had intended to give himself up at Ilford police station, but, in the event, walked past the building until he reached the bridge over the River Roding, from where the second suitcase was thrown, and he returned home again.

Next morning, Singh strapped the duffel bag containing his daughter's head to his moped's carrier, and set out for work as usual. Crossing Wanstead Flats, he stopped and dumped the duffel bag near some bushes, barely nine feet from the main road, before continuing on his way.

The first evidence of Suchnam Singh's dreadful crime had already been discovered. After the Euston train's arrival at Wolverhampton at 12.52 a.m. on 5 April, two drivers who were going off duty noticed an abandoned green suitcase in an empty carriage. Dutifully taking it to the left luggage office, they left the clerk, Leslie Stevens, to open it . . . and then to call the police.

Detective-Sergeant Leslie Whitehouse of the Wolverhampton Police took charge of the immediate situation, but Scotland Yard's expertise was also requested. Detective Chief Superintendent Roy Yorke and his sergeant, DS George Atterwill, travelled up to the Midlands through the night. The torso was taken to Wolverhampton Royal Hospital, where pathologist Dr Richard Marshall set to work unravelling its secrets, while the police searched and fingerprinted the empty railway carriage, and began to interview British Rail staff to discover how the suitcase had arrived on the train. The officers were fortunate in the fact that a census of the train had been carried out by British Rail at each stop that night, and it had not been very crowded. They were soon able to ascertain that the suitcase had been on the train all the way from Euston. The ticket collector at Euston also recalled that a 'coloured man' had passed through the barrier carrying a suitcase and had returned later without it.

The next big break had come by lunchtime the next day, when a woman spotted the second suitcase under the bridge at Ilford. When Detective Sergeant Stephenson arrived, he opened the case to reveal a foot sticking out of the material. The case, it transpired, had first been seen at 11.15 a.m. Detective Superintendent Emlyn Howells at Ilford immediately contacted the Yard men at Wolverhampton. An examination of the various pieces side by side soon revealed to Professor Robert Warwick of the Anatomy Department at Guy's Hospital Medical School that they belonged to the same body; all that was missing was the head.

The question was, whose body was it?

Professor Warwick's deductions were these. That she was an Asian woman between the ages of 18 and 30: she was not a virgin and had recently had some sort of inexpert gynaecological operation. She had taken a lethal overdose of barbiturates, but this was not the immediate cause of death. The body had been cut up with a hacksaw blade which was blue on one side and yellow on the other. After consultation with Indian experts, they were also able to deduce from the style of

clothing and its place of origin, and from the fact that
the woman didn't shave herself, that she was most
probably a Sikh. An appeal to the Indian community
also elicited the useful information that the pattern on
the pullover found on the torso was unique to the area
around Jullundor in the Punjab. Sandal marks and
callouses on the feet further indicated that the woman
had only recently begun to wear European shoes, and
was therefore almost certainly a recent immigrant to
Britain.

Police enquiries now followed two separate directions. A thorough search for the head was imple-
mented, using helicopters to follow the Euston to
Wolverhampton railway track and making use of
divers to drag the River Roding. These operations
yielded no result. Secondly, officers began the tedious
process of going through the records of hospitals and
clinics, searching for Indian women who had had
recent gynaecological problems.

On Wednesday, 8 May, a Mr Howard Perry was
cycling across Wanstead Flats when he was halted in a
traffic jam. Just off the road, he noticed a duffel bag in
the bushes that looked in better condition than his
own, so he picked it up. The head had been found.

The police were alerted and it was again DS
Stephenson whose doubtful privilege it was to transport it to Ilford mortuary; they now had a face and a
cause of death – two heavy blows to the head with a
blunt instrument.

Meanwhile, the enquiries at hospitals had begun to
bear fruit. A young Indian girl named Sarabjit Kaur
had attended Barking Hospital. Her general prac-
titioner, Dr Gabriel Merriman, was traced, and with
the aid of a photograph of the head, he was able pro-
visionally to identify her. From there the victim was

traced back to her flat in Ilford and her former landlady was able to name Suchnam Singh as her father and to provide an outdated address, at Sibley Grove, Bow.

The police arrived at Fanshawe Avenue to interview Suchnam Singh on Saturday, 11 May. He began by denying that he even had a daughter called Sarabjit Kaur, but when a search of the house unearthed two photographs of the girl, Singh decided to change his story. His daughter had left home in February, he now claimed, and he had not heard from her since, nor did he have any idea where she might be. He also protested ignorance of Sarabjit's pregnancy. Suchnam Singh was then removed to Ilford police station for questioning. On the first day he stuck rigidly to his story, though he ventured the unprompted remark that he thought she might be dead. On the second day Singh asked to see Chief Superintendent Yorke and made a full statement in which he stated that his daughter had taken an overdose of Phenobarbitone and had accidentally struck her head on a sewing machine as she fell to the ground. He had discovered her dead body and had left the house with the intention of informing the police. He had been in such a state of shock that he had nearly been run down by a car, and had then come upon a cousin, who had persuaded Singh that things would look bad if he went to the police. The cousin, Hardyal Singh Sandhu, had then helped with the disposal of the body. When Hardyal Singh was interviewed by the police, he denied any knowledge of or involvement in the affair and the police were inclined to believe him.

The dismemberment, at least, was verified by traces of blood found in the trap under the bath. Sarabjit Kaur's body was later conclusively identified from fingerprints found on her clocking-in card at the factory where she had worked, and on a physics text-book found in the house in Fanshawe Avenue.

Suchnam Singh Sandhu was tried at the Old Bailey in November 1968. His story of his daughter's suicide was not believed, and it took the jury barely 90 minutes to find him guilty. Singh was sentenced to life imprisonment.

Much was made at the trial of the ancient Sikh custom that the bodies of those who had died in disgrace should be dismembered and the parcelled pieces despatched in all directions to expunge the shame. Whether this throwback to a past Indian culture actually provided the motivation for Suchnam Singh's actions, or whether this can be treated as a red herring thrown in by a desperate defence, must remain open to question.

Although Suchnam Singh's confession was generally accepted, there are some grounds for believing that his actions were considerably more premeditated than he was prepared to acknowledge. His place of work, from which, significantly, he had taken leave, gave him access to the large plastic bag in which he cut up the body, and also to Phenobarbitone tablets, which Sarabjit had never been prescribed by any doctor. So who administered the fatal overdose? A distraught daughter? Or an angry, disillusioned and humiliated father?

JOHN BOWDEN et al.
(England, 1980–1)

'A Good Boy, Gentle and Kind'

At four o'clock on the morning of 9 November 1980, police officers were despatched to a council maisonette in Harris Street, Camberwell, in response to a telephone call from a neighbour. Accustomed as they were to facing the less romantic aspects of life in the south-east of the metropolis, they were quite unprepared for the sight that confronted them when they entered the flat – floors, walls, and furniture in most of the rooms were soaked in blood; but what turned their stomachs most was that in the middle of this gory shambles, four people were sleeping as peacefully as if they had been enjoying the luxury of a three-star hotel suite, the remains of a take-away Chinese meal sharing table space with pools of congealing blood. The three men and one woman were taken immediately into custody, leaving detectives to solve the riddle of the source of the spilt blood.

It did not take long. Shortly after daybreak the first of the dismembered parts of a man's body was discovered in a black plastic rubbish bag on waste ground in Camberwell; this was followed by a further bag of grisly relics comprising two legs and a right hand.

In their examination of the headless torso, forensic investigators identified a number of distinctive tattoos: on the left forearm 'Satan' was written, with the letters 'OZ' or 'OS' and a cross in a circle. On the other forearm was the name 'Don' possibly the victim's own. The knuckles of the hand that had been recovered had the word 'LOVE' spelled out, and it was a fair assumption that 'HATE' would be found on the missing hand. These tattoos would have provided valuable clues if help from the public were needed in identifying the man. However, on the following day, 11 November, a matching head was found in another plastic bag in Harris Street and identified as 47-year-old former boxer, Donald Ryan.

Meanwhile the four suspects being detained by police for questioning had been charged with Ryan's murder, and at a brief magistrate's hearing on the 13th were remanded in custody pending their trial at the Central Criminal Court.

It was exactly a year later, on 19 November 1981, that the trial opened at the Old Bailey of 34-year-old mother Shirley Brindle, her lover, grave-digger Michael Ward, John Bowden and David Begley.

Prosecuting counsel, Mr Evan Stone, recounted to a court shocked into silence how unemployed Ryan had been lured back to Brindle and Ward's home in Harris Street on the Saturday with the intention of robbing him. All five sat around consuming large volumes of cider, and at some point Bowden and Begley battered Ryan over the head with an empty bottle. Having rifled his pockets of a meagre £20, they next submerged the semi-conscious man in a bath of near-boiling water. In what was one of the most 'appalling and horrifying' stories ever told in a court of law, Mr Stone proceeded to describe how Donald Ryan's still-living body was slowly cut to pieces with a saw, machete and electric carving-knife.

In the midst of this dreadful activity two boys,

sixteen-year-old Paul Boyce and Michael Ward's cousin, Martin McDonough, called at the flat. The door had been opened by Ward, stripped to the waist, blood smeared on his face and dripping from his hands. The lads were left in the blood-spattered sitting-room, listening to the hammering and banging and scuffling going on upstairs: 'You may think it not surprising that they were frightened, and left,' observed Mr Stone. 'You may think they were lucky to do so.'

While the men finished off bagging up the pieces of Donald Ryan's body, Shirley Brindle had popped out to get them all a meal from the nearby Chinese restaurant, which they ate back at the flat before setting off for a night's drinking at the Red Bull.

John Bowden had clearly not seen enough blood for one day, because during the course of the evening he got into a brawl with Patrick O'Connor, the result of which was that O'Connor was rushed to hospital to have his face sewn up with 30 stitches.

Before making their nocturnal sortie to dispose of the packaged remains of Don Ryan, Brindle, Ward, Bowden and Begley paid a visit to Mrs Mary Ward and, for reasons known best to themselves, told her what had happened. It was Mrs Ward who subsequently alerted the police.

So harrowing was the evidence, so awful the photographs of the scene of the carnage and of the remains of Donald Ryan, that before the end of the trial three members of the jury were ill. Nevertheless, on 26 November Bowden, Ward and Begley were convicted of murder, and Shirley Brindle of unlawful disposal of the body.

In sentencing 26-year-old labourer John Bowden to life imprisonment with a recommendation that he serve no fewer than 25 years, the judge remarked: 'Bowden is a man who obviously enjoyed inflicting pain, and even killing. There never was a more horrific case of murder than this!'

To which Bowden replied, on being sentenced: 'You old bastard! I hope you die screaming of cancer!'

Despite his parents' claim that John was 'a good boy, gentle and kind', Bowden had already collected an impressive criminal record and received several custodial sentences for blackmail, robbery, assault, wounding, and carrying offensive weapons.

But when the cell door at Parkhurst finally closed behind John Bowden, the world had not yet heard the last of him. In 1982 he and another prisoner seized the assistant governor and held him at knife-point until the Home Office promised to investigate their grievances.

Six

'Pigs will eat anything . . . absolutely anything'

Mr Nicholas Purnell, QC
at the trial of John David

ARTHUR and
NIZAMODEEN HOSEIN
(England, 1969–70)

The Disappearance at Rooks Farm

It was on the evening of Monday, 29 December 1969, that Mrs Muriel Freda McKay disappeared. When *News of the World* deputy chairman Alick McKay arrived at 7.45 p.m. to find the front door unlocked and his wife missing from their home in Arthur Road, Wimbledon, his worst fears seemed to be confirmed by the telephone wires which had been wrenched from the wall, and the contents of his wife's handbag strewn carelessly across the floor.

Given the reputation of the newspaper on which Mr McKay served, and the unhealthy interest already being shown on the front page of its sister paper the *Sun*, police investigating the report were far from convinced that this was not just an elaborate publicity stunt. Nevertheless common sense cautioned that they should treat it as at least a *possible* case of kidnapping, so the enquiry was put in the hands of a team of officers led by Detective Chief Superintendent Bill Smith and Detective Inspector John Minors.

For his part, Alick McKay began what for him was the worst nightmare he would ever endure; waiting by his reconnected phone for some kind of a message, something that would reassure him that his wife was safe, was still alive.

At one o'clock on the following morning McKay

received the first of many calls from a man described
by the operator connecting them as having 'an American or coloured voice'; the call came from a public telephone box at Bell Common, Epping:

'We are from America – Mafia M.3. We have your
wife. You will need a million pounds by Wednesday.'

'This is ridiculous! I haven't got a million.'

'You had better get it. You have friends, get it from
them. We tried to get Rupert Murdoch's wife. We
couldn't get her, so we took yours instead.* You have
a million by Wednesday night or we will kill her.'

'What do I have to do?'

'All you have to do is wait for the contact. Have the
money or you won't have a wife.'

A second call confirming the demand was received
two days later, followed by a letter postmarked in
Tottenham, north London, written by Mrs McKay,
pleading: 'Please do something to get me home. I am
blindfolded and cold. Only blankets. Please co-
operate for I cannot keep going . . . I think of you con-
stantly . . . What have I done to deserve this
treatment. Love Muriel.'

In total, eighteen telephone calls were made by the
kidnappers to Mr McKay before he received any clear
indication of how the money was to be delivered.
Then, on 22 January, a ransom note giving detailed
instructions accompanied two more letters from an

*The kidnap had been bungled from the very start. The real target
was indeed Anna, the wife of *News of the World* chairman Rupert
Murdoch. Murdoch had just returned with his wife to his native
Australia for a holiday, and the company's dark blue Rolls-Royce,
usually driven by the Murdochs, was entrusted to Alick McKay.
The Hoseins, trailing the car, had seen it parked outside the house
in Arthur Road and arrived at the wrong conclusion.

understandably distressed Muriel McKay. In one she confessed she was 'deteriorating in health and spirit'.

The ransom note ordered McKay to hand over the money in two halves – the first to be delivered on 1 February. Despite this apparently clear instruction, Alick McKay was to receive three more telephone calls, one more ransom note, and two more letters from his wife. This latest demand ended: 'Looking forward in settling our business on the 1st February at 10pm as stated in last letter in a very discreet and honest way, and you and your children will be very happy to join Muriel McKay, and our organisation will also be happy to continue our job elsewhere in Australia . . . You see we don't like to make our customer happy, we like to keep them in suspense, in that way it's a gamble . . . We give the order and you must obey. M3.'

Although he had been warned not to involve the police, it was a law officer who took McKay's son Ian's place behind the wheel of the car on the night of the drop. First he was instructed to go to a telephone kiosk on the A10 at the corner of Church Street in Edmonton. Here he received a message sending him on to another callbox at the corner of Southbury Road where instructions were waiting, written on a cigarette packet, to leave the suitcase containing £500,000 – the bulk of which were forgeries, with real notes at the ends of the bundles – on a bank at High Cross where two paper flowers would mark the spot. 'Ian McKay' was then to return to the first telephone box where he would be told the whereabouts of his mother.

In spite of the almost farcical complexity of the drop, the kidnappers did not collect the money, and Alick McKay was the recipient of an irate call from the spokesman for 'Mafia M.3' complaining about the heavy police presence around the spot where the money was left. In fact there was an overkill of more than 150 policemen – some disguised as Hell's Angels on motorcycles – and over fifty unmarked police cars, so that the whole operation inevitably bore some similarity to a Keystone Cops one-reeler.

The second attempt to hand over the money – on 6 February – proved to be even more cumbersome than the first, and police officers impersonating Mr McKay and his daughter Diane were directed from the Edmonton telephone box to one in the East End of London, at Bethnal Green Road, and from there by underground train on the Central line to Epping. From this point their instructions were to take the money, in two suitcases, to Bishop's Stortford and leave them beside a beige mini-van parked in the Gates Garage forecourt.

Once again the kidnappers were deprived of their booty when, at 11 p.m., a couple named Abbott came across the suitcases and, thinking they had been lost by their owner, contacted the local police who thoughtfully removed them. However, if the villains had had a stroke of bad luck, the waiting policemen had some welcome good fortune. Lying in wait, they had seen a dark blue Volvo car cruise several times past the garage, its driver taking an uncommon interest in the van parked there. The car was found to be registered to 34-year-old Arthur Hosein, an Indian Muslim from Trinidad who, with his brother, 22-year-old Nizamodeen, had bought and worked the run-down Rooks Farm at Stocking Pelham, Hertfordshire, since 1967.

The Hosein brothers were immediately taken into custody and held while a minute search of the farmhouse revealed a number of connections with the kidnap of Mrs McKay, including the exercise book in which she had written the letters to her husband. Meanwhile, forensic experts had identified Arthur Hosein's fingerprints on the ransom notes and the cigarette packet left in the telephone box. Both men were charged on Tuesday, 10 February, and remanded in custody by the Wimbledon magistrates.

The trial of Arthur and Nizamodeen Hosein opened at the Old Bailey on 14 September 1970, despite the continuing absence of Mrs McKay's body. Both prisoners were charged with murder, kidnapping and blackmail, and scientific experts were called by the Crown to connect the Hoseins with the kidnapping. Apart from indisputable fingerprint identification from the ransom notes, a handwriting expert showed the court an enlarged photograph of the note written in capital letters on a page torn from a lined exercise book, which he overlaid with a transparency showing the perfectly matching indentations on a sheet of paper found in Nizamodeen Hosein's bedroom.

After the jury had justly found the Hoseins guilty on all counts, both men were sentenced to life imprisonment for murder, and Arthur received a further 25 years, and his brother fifteen, on the other charges. Asked if he had anything to say, Arthur Hosein shouted: 'Injustice has not only been done, it has been seen and heard by the gallery to have been done. They have seen the provocation of your lordship and they have seen your immense partiality.'

Despite the most meticulous search of Rooks Farm and its surrounding acres, Muriel McKay's body was never found, and it is widely supposed that she was drugged and then shot, cut up and fed to the Hoseins' herd of Wessex Saddleback pigs.

JOHN LAWRENCE DAVID
(England, 1987–8)

No Angel

It was the kind of news story that headlines are made of 'Murder Woman Eaten By Pigs', 'Murdered Miriam Dished Up As Pork Pie'. The kind of story that is so bizarre, so grotesque, that it becomes irresistible.

It began, as do so many tragic crimes of murder, with a missing person. Mrs Miriam Jones, a 24–year-old despatch courier and part-time barmaid, went missing from her home in Reading on 8 April 1987, after a night out with her ex-lover.

On 12 April a squad of twenty officers of the Berkshire police force began an inch-by-inch search of Richard McCarthy's pig farm between Fifield and Holyport. During a week of investigation, sometimes wading in manure and slurry eighteen inches deep, police found a number of pieces of chewed bone. Forensic pathologists confirmed that the remains were human and not, as had been suggested, those of a dead pig. At the same time a blue suspender belt was found, which clearly did not belong to a pig, and some fragments of clothing later identified by the victim's mother.

The day following the grisly discoveries, John Lawrence David, 23 years old, of Bracknell, was charged with Mrs Jones' murder and remanded in custody by magistrates.

In December 1988 the jury at Reading Crown Court

was told that David, a hanger-on with the Windsor Chapter of Hell's Angels, had been Mrs Jones' regular lover since they met at the Cider House, an Angels' pub where she worked. At the beginning of April she told him the affair was over and she was returning to her husband (whom David, in a bizarre twist of logic, looked upon as his best friend).

Mr Nicholas Purnell QC, prosecuting, said that David, unable to bear rejection since his mother deserted him at six months old, had gone to Miriam's bedsit in Wantage Road on the evening of 8 April and demanded sex. When she refused, David strangled her and drove the body, wrapped in a blanket, to the pig farm where he doused it with petrol, set fire to it, and left the pigs to do the rest: 'Among the trees were over 100 pigs and piglets. Pigs will eat anything – flesh, clothing, bones, absolutely anything.'

On 6 December, John David, who had confessed to the murder, was sentenced to life imprisonment.

POSTSCRIPT

At the conclusion of the trial senior police officers revealed that for the man who was considered too much of a weakling to join the Hell's Angels, it was his second murder. Twenty-two-year-old Jacqueline Cheer was found dead at her home in Maidenhead just before Christmas 1984, after breaking off her relationship with David.

The investigation into Jacqui Cheer's death was so badly mismanaged that on the scant evidence available a coroner found that she had died from natural causes – asphyxia during convulsions due to a viral infection. In reality she had been brutally raped and strangled, though no test for strangulation was made, and the photograph of the body which showed marks round the neck and bruises was never shown to the pathologist.

Seven

'But we knew the work they had been at,
By the quicklime on their boots.'

Oscar Wilde
The Ballad of Reading Gaol

DR HAWLEY HARVEY CRIPPEN
(England, 1910)

The Worm that Turned?

It is disturbing to observe the way in which some of the country's most notorious killers have, with the passing of years, exchanged the dark mantle of the blackguard for the purple robe of popular folk-hero. The murderous and thoroughly unscrupulous Richard Turpin was an early beneficiary of the whitewash brush, and the theme of elevation has recurred regularly until our own time: for example, to the brothers Kray, whose empire of terror crumbled only on their arrest, conviction and imprisonment for double murder in 1969. Ronnie and Reggie Kray now have the nearest thing to a fan-club in the Free Reggie Kray Campaign.

Between Turpin and the Krays, chronologically, stands the diminutive figure of Dr Hawley Harvey Crippen, a man who, far from being vilified as a cruel killer, has been sentimentalised as 'the worm that turned', the little man who fought back.

Nobody can deny that the true story of Dr Crippen would defy the romance writer to invent – and the myth that has emerged epitomises the theatricality of murder as no other has: he murders a spiteful, domineering wife, a lacklustre music-hall entertainer working under the stage name Belle Elmore, in favour of a young mistress, Ethel Le Neve, with whom he is desperately in love; he cuts up the body and disposes of

it – heaven knows where. Crippen and Ethel put on
disguises (Ethel dressed as a young boy) and take a
steamship to America, to the New World. Unfortunately, the captain is something of an amateur
detective, and via the newly invented wireless telegraph system alerts Scotland Yard to his suspicions
about two of his passengers. Meanwhile the police
have found a few fragments of Mrs Cora Crippen
buried in the cellar. There is a subsequent chase across
the Atlantic by Chief Inspector Walter Dew (also in
disguise) who overtakes and arrests the fugitives
aboard ship. Then follows the ritual of the trial at the
Old Bailey – the most famous criminal court in the
world – where Crippen is literally fighting for his life
in the shadow of the gallows. He loses the battle and,
maintaining the atmosphere of high drama to the very
last act, Crippen is hanged, and according to his last
wishes is buried holding a photograph of his beloved
Ethel and surrounded by her love letters. Ethel herself
is acquitted and builds a new life for herself. These are
the ingredients of a very successful story, and one too
well known to be repeated in detail here.

But consider this: Crippen did not, as his mythology might suggest, kill in a moment of blind
passion, his back broken by the final straw; his was a
cold, calculated murder, planned over months, certainly never out of his mind from the time he bought
five grains of hyoscine from Messrs Lewis and
Burrows on 7 January 1910, until he administered that
fatal dose to the unlucky Cora three weeks later.

Then, having rendered her dead, the little doctor set
about the gruesome job of cutting his wife's body into
pieces. When Inspector Dew prised up the bricks from
the cellar floor at Hilldrop Crescent he found what
remained of Crippen's handiwork.

It was the young Dr Bernard Spilsbury on his first major murder case who was left to describe the putrid mass, caked in quicklime, which it had been his misfortune to examine:

> Medical organs of the chest and abdomen removed in one mass. Four large pieces of skin and muscle, one from the lower abdomen with old operation scar, 4 inches long – broader at lower end. Impossible to identify sex. Hyoscine found 2.7 grains. Hair in Hinde's curler [a type of patent hair grip] – roots present. Hair 6 inches long.

That was all. No head, no limbs, no bones. No bones. Crippen had literally filleted his wife! What he did with the missing parts is anyone's guess. They were never found.

Was it Crippen's undoubted and undying love for Ethel Le Neve, interwoven with the public's undoubted and undying love of romance, that transformed this butcher into a hero?

Almost certainly.

HARRY DOBKIN
(England, 1941–3)

Right Time, Right Place

Nineteen forty-two: a time for killing. England was engaged in one of the bloodiest wars in the world's history, and London was receiving such nightly pounding from the Luftwaffe that death was becoming a commonplace. It was against this backdrop that Harry Dobkin sought to camouflage one more corpse.

During the year from April 1941 to May 1942, 49-year-old Dobkin had been employed as a firewatcher by a firm of solicitors to guard their document store situated behind the already blitzed shell of the Baptist chapel in St Oswald's Place, Kennington. Perhaps bombs, like lightning, never strike in the same place twice; at any rate, Harry Dobkin's watch was never troubled.

There was one fire, though; in the cellar beneath the ruined chapel in the early hours of 15 April 1941. At the height of the Blitz one more fire didn't attract too much attention, and became just another routine call-out recorded on the fire brigade log. It was to be more than a year before anybody really thought about that blaze.

To be precise, it was fifteen months later, on 17 July 1942. A workman engaged in clearing up and making safe the partially destroyed chapel prised up a large paving stone at the end of the cellar and found a charred skeleton.

Even in times of war when mortality figures, including civilian casualties, are high, the well-oiled machinery for dealing with deaths in unusual circumstances is still strictly followed. The police must be informed, and the coroner, who will appoint a pathologist to determine the cause of death. It was an unlucky day for Harry Dobkin when the pathologist chosen was Dr Keith Simpson.

When the remains had been removed to Southwark mortuary, Simpson began a post-mortem that was to become a legend, a piece of medical detective work so thorough and imaginative that those pathetic remains took on again the dignity of an identity.

Simpson's first observation was that this was no bomb casualty. For a start, war victims do not bury themselves under massive stone slabs; and they never dismember themselves.

The blackened mass that lay on the mortuary slab had been clumsily dissected by a person with no knowledge of anatomy; the head and arms had been severed from the trunk, and in an obvious attempt to conceal the victim's identity the flesh had been deliberately stripped from the face. Around the body, particularly in the region of the neck and shoulders, was a deposit of quicklime. Whether this was simply an attempt to mask the smell of putrefaction or whether Dobkin, in his ignorance, had hoped that it would speed decomposition, we do not know. In fact, the lime had the opposite effect – that of preserving what was left of the body tissues from the ravages of maggots and beetles. Remarkably, Dr Simpson was able to present his immediate opinion that the remains were those of a woman, just over five feet in height, between 40 and 50 years old, and suffering from a fibroid tumour. She had died within the previous twelve to eighteen months. Cause of death could with some confidence be ascribed to manual strangulation on account of the characteristic fracture of the tiny hyoid bone in the throat (see figure below).

Certain now that they were dealing with murder, the police left Dr Simpson to the finer points of his examination, and themselves made a check on all missing-person reports filed around the estimated time of the victim's death.

This search revealed that on Saturday, 12 April 1941, a woman had reported her sister missing from home. The sister's name was Mrs Rachel Dobkin, recently estranged wife of Mr Harry Dobkin. It was now that people began to remember the fire in the chapel cellar – it had been just a few days after Mrs Dobkin's disappearance; in a place patrolled by Mr Dobkin.

By the time Harry Dobkin came to trial at the Old Bailey, Keith Simpson and his team had worked a

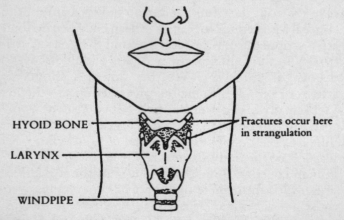

HYOID BONE

LARYNX

WINDPIPE

Fractures occur here in strangulation

Injuries to the internal structure of the neck which may indicate death by strangling

forensic miracle. They had established, beyond any doubt, the identity of the corpse in the cellar. It was no longer simply a middle-aged woman, 5ft ½in. tall, who had been strangled. It was Mrs Rachel Dobkin.

An interview with Mrs Dobkin's sister, Polly, had provided two vital clues to the investigation. The first was that Rachel had been suffering from a fibroid tumour; the second was that her dentist was Barnett Kopkin of Stoke Newington. Although the lower jaw of the corpse in the cellar had become detached and was missing, the upper jaw showed extensive dental repair, treatment which Dr Kopkin, keeping as he did meticulous records, was able to describe exactly.

In a final demonstration of forensic brilliance, Miss Mary Newman, head of the Photography Department at Guy's Hospital, had a negative of the skull superimposed on to a known portrait of Rachel Dobkin – a technique first developed in the Ruxton case six years earlier (see page 167). Miss Newman, in her evidence to the court, gave this description: 'I first of all photographed this portrait that was given to me and obtained a negative of that, and then enlarged it to the same size as the photograph of the skull. To do this I measured carefully the distance between the centre of the two orbits to correspond with that of the skull. I then made an exposure of an x-ray film and produced a positive of the portrait, then from the negative of the skull and the positive film of the portrait I re-exposed them on an x-ray film, and this gave me a transparent positive of the skull and a transparent negative of the portrait. Those two films I then placed together superimposed and re-photographed them.'

The fit was perfect; the identity complete.

On 26 August 1942 Detective Inspector Fred Hatton of the Met's 'M' Division arrested Harry Dobkin on the charge of murdering his wife. Three months later, Dobkin was tried, convicted and sentenced to death; seven days into the New Year, he was hanged at Wandsworth Prison.

Russian-born Dobkin had married Rachel Dubinski in September 1920, via the traditional Jewish custom of a marriage broker. Few marriages have been so short-lived, and within three days they separated. Things would have turned out very differently indeed had Mrs Dobkin not become pregnant in those few days. As it was, she gave birth to a son nine months later and obtained a child maintenance order against her husband. Dobkin proved a reluctant payer, and over the years was imprisoned several times for defaulting.

It began, no doubt, out of desperation, but Rachel Dobkin developed the embarrassing habit of lying in wait for Harry and haranguing him in the street over money. It was a habit that persisted until 1941 – when the 'child' was twenty years old!

Before his execution, Dobkin confessed to his wife's murder, and to trying to burn the dismembered pieces of her body in the chapel cellar that 15 April. He had, he said, simply run out of patience, run out of money.

DR MARCEL PETIOT
(France, 1944–6)

Alias Doctor Death

It just had to stop. The residents of rue Lesueur, in Paris's fashionable Etoile district, had put up with it long enough.

Nobody could really remember the first time the black, greasy, foul-smelling smoke had risen from Dr Petiot's chimney, but they were determined that this should be the last. On 11 March 1944 the police were called in to investigate; they had to agree – the smell was awful.

Pinned on the door of the house, police found a card directing visitors to Petiot's consulting rooms at 66 rue Caumartin and, as the instructions also offered a telephone number, the doctor was summoned immediately.

By now events were beginning to get out of control at rue Lesueur; the chimney which had previously only been a nuisance was threatening to become a serious fire hazard, showers of vermilion sparks being belched out with the nauseous smoke. With the realisation that the whole chimney had caught fire from the inside, the police summoned the fire brigade, who broke into the house via the cellar. The police rearguard which followed now found not only the cause of the smoke, but the reason for its unpleasant odour – it was the pile of dismembered corpses which were being used to fuel the boiler.

At this point Dr Marcel Petiot made his timely
entrance and explained with a hint of pride that, yes,
they were 'his' corpses. Or rather, they were the
remains of pro-Nazi collaborators who had been
assassinated by the French Resistance and entrusted to
him to dispose of. Perhaps it could be ascribed to
wartime patriotism, but Petiot's far-fetched story was
taken in, swallowed, and the man released from
custody with all but a pat on the back.

Wisely, Marcel and Mrs Petiot, along with their
seventeen-year-old son, left 66 rue Caumartin and
disappeared.

It is an interesting phenomenon that few 'successful'
criminals are entirely free from an arrogance that
seems to oblige them to draw attention to themselves.
This was certainly true of Marcel Petiot; and it put his
head on the guillotine.

It was after the fall of Paris, when the newspapers
were looking for something to replace the war reports,
that the case of the corpses in the cellar received its full
share of publicity.

Seemingly unwilling to leave well alone, Petiot
embarked on a correspondence with the magazine
Résistance informing them that he had been a member of
the Resistance (in reality he had joined the Free French
Forces just six weeks previously) and – a complete
change from his former story – the bodies found in rue
Lesueur had been dumped there by the Gestapo. This
offered the police an opportunity to reopen the case
which they grabbed with both hands, and it took them
little enough time to identify the handwriting on the
letter signed 'Captain Henri Valery' as belonging to the
man better known to them as Dr Marcel Petiot. He was
arrested on 2 November 1944.

During his first days in custody, Petiot confessed to killing no fewer than 63 people, though like the 27 found in the cellar they were supposed to have been mostly German soldiers.

When his trial opened at the Seine Assizes on 15 March 1945, a rounder picture of Petiot began to emerge. Not exactly the courageous underground freedom-fighter (though this, to be fair, was in some part true), but a thoroughly degenerate and callous criminal.

Unable to keep his hands off other people's property, the young Petiot's stealing had always been of the meanest kind – at school he had pilfered from his class-fellows before graduating to robbing letter-boxes. While serving during the First World War he had engaged in the despicable practice of stealing desperately needed drugs from a casualty station to sell on the black market. Even when he was entrusted with the honourable civic authority of Mayor of Villeneuve, Marcel Petiot had found it impossible to resist plundering municipal supplies. But he was not on trial here for simple theft. Dr Petiot was facing an incredible 27 separate charges of murder; 27 lives which had ended in the death-house at rue Lesueur.

It was a stunned court that listened, horrified, to the evidence of police discoveries at 21 rue Lesueur. Apart from the ghastly spectacle of carnage produced by corpses in every stage of butchery, the cellar yielded countless fragments of human bone and 33 lbs of char-red body tissue. In the house itself, a sound-proof chamber had been constructed with a spy-hole cut in the door, the purpose of which, the prosecution advanced, was to provide the sadistic doctor with entertainment as his helpless victims writhed in the death agonies produced by lethal injections.

The routine search of an outhouse revealed yet more horrors when a heap of bodies and parts of bodies was found marinating in a pile of quicklime, and a further lime-pit was found in the stable. Professor Henri Griffon, director of the police toxicology laboratory, had examined the heavily limed remains, and in a remarkable understatement commented, '. . . they emitted a piquant and very disagreeable odour'.

It was the prosecution's contention that Petiot had been luring wealthy Jews to the rue Lesueur under the pretence of arranging their escape from certain persecution at the hands of the occupying German forces – but it was beginning to look as though, with Dr Petiot around, the Germans had insurmountable competition!

The refugees would arrive with their cash and portable valuables of which Petiot would relieve them before releasing them from their now burdensome lives. The cellar of the death-house told the rest of the story.

But there was one more poignant piece of evidence with which to trouble the minds of an already appalled jury. In June 1943, Dr Petiot had been observed removing a large number of suitcases from 21 rue Lesueur and loading them into a truck driven by his brother. When the 47 pieces of luggage were later traced to a house in Villeneuve they were found to contain an incredible 1,691 articles of clothing, including 29 suits, 79 dresses, and 5 fur coats. From these garments all identifying marks had been painstakingly removed.

As for the prisoner's behaviour in the dock, he provided the entertainment that the always crowded public gallery expected. By turns abusive, violent, witty and sarcastic, Petiot maintained throughout his examination that he was a good, patriotic Resistance worker ridding the motherland by stealth of the despised Gestapo. When asked for corroboration of this fanciful suggestion, Petiot refused, saying that it would be unprincipled of him to reveal names and details. Even if this were so, it would not have prevented fellow freedom-fighters volunteering information on his behalf; none ever did.

At the end of a frequently harrowing three weeks, the trial jury declared Marcel Petiot guilty of 24 of the 27 murder charges on the indictment. On 26 May 1946 Doctor Death was led from his cell in the Santé Prison to stand beneath the fearful edifice of the guillotine. It is characteristic of the man that when refused permission to relieve himself, Petiot replied nonchalantly: 'Well, when one sets out on a voyage, one takes all one's luggage with one.' They were his last words.

Eight

'I will become a dem'd, damp, moist unpleasant body!'

Mr Mantalini
in Charles Dickens' *Nicholas Nickleby*

THE SHARK-ARM CASE
(Australia, 1935)

The Shark It Was That Died

Australian Anzac Day is a curious affair. Celebrating, as it does, one of the most humiliating blood-baths of modern military history, there is an ambiguous air abroad in the streets of Sydney when the annual Anzac Day holiday comes around. Nowadays, when veterans of both World Wars are thin on the ground, the Anzac parade of rag-tag remnants of the slouch-hatted, sun-bronzed heroes of the Big Brown Land is a spectacle of almost unbelievable pathos; a whole battalion of men represented by one, leather-skinned septuagenarian, banner in hand, medals clinking to the motion of his wheelchair, pushed perhaps by a great-grandson, himself in the uniform of a scout or cadet.

Sydney-siders seem to react with a mixture of shame-faced patriotism – pride at having a tradition to remember – disdain, and the more reliable Australian reflex of not letting any good excuse pass them by for downing huge amounts of alcoholic cheer. But still there's a strange unease in the air.

Anzac Day, 25 April 1935, found a different generation of Australians. Caught in the slough of an economic depression, a day off work – if you were lucky enough to be working – was cause enough for celebration, and crowds flocked to any cheap entertainment that was on offer. The attraction at Coogee certainly pulled them in. For a few bob they could enjoy the spectacle of a fourteen-foot-long, live tiger shark, caught recently by local fishermen. And if, on that sultry afternoon, they had known of the dramatic 'extra show' that was to be played at Coogee, every sensation-seeker in Sydney would have flocked there.

Until that particular afternoon, the tiger shark had been something of a disappointment. In a state of deep shock and resentment at its capture, the creature had refused to eat, bare its teeth, or even move about very much; in fact the spectators had viewed its sinister dimensions with little more than the respect due from a people who share their recreational amenities with such killers. By and large, they moved on from boredom rather than horror.

Then, at precisely five o'clock, in front of the sleepy Anzac crowd, the shark suddenly went berserk, thrashing wildly with its tail, snapping its huge jaws, torpedoing in circles around its tank; the audience gasped in horror and revulsion as a dark mass emitted from the foaming jaws obscured the creature's dark form. As the disgusting mess dissipated in the tank the crowd caught its breath again, unable to believe its eyes. Surfacing from the slime spewed from the shark's belly was either a showman's trick or something so macabre as to suspend belief – the out-stretched fingers of a human hand, attached, as it gradually emerged, to a burly, tattooed human arm, a length of rope floating out from the wrist.

Eventually the crowd dispersed, and the police took over – Anzac Day 1935 was something none of them would forget in a hurry.

The exploding shark presented an enigma to the authorities. It had been captured eight days earlier – how could it have stomached a perfectly preserved human relic for this length of time?

There was, and is, no shortage of experts on 'shar-kology' in Sydney, where man and killer fish still have an uneasy truce in their mutual enjoyment of the warm coastal waters. The arm, said local expert Dr Copple-son, had been preserved because the shark had been in a state of shock since its capture and had subsequently eaten nothing. He added that, from his many years' experience seeing victims of sharks, the police could not assume the creature in question had amputated the man's arm. The marks were not consistent with the work of a shark's teeth – the limb had been hacked off with a sharp knife, the fish had merely taken advantage of a floating snack. Gradually the light dawned on local officials that they had a most remarkable case on their hands – doubly remarkable in that of the thousands of sharks that patrolled the coasts of Australia, it should be this one that was caught; and instead of digesting its gruesome meal within the customary thirty-six hours, had preserved the evidence for more than eight days.

But what were they to do with it now they had it?

Clearly, the single arm begged the question: What happened to the rest of the body? In an attempt to find the corpse, searches were made by beach patrols, divers and by air force aerial units; all without success. Dissection of the shark's body also failed to reveal any further portions of the unfortunate victim.

In an operation taking several weeks, the fragile flakes of skin from the tips of the fingers were removed and stabilised sufficiently to allow fingerprints to be taken from them. This process has subsequently been widely used in identifying corpses suffering extensive putrefaction (for a full description of the technique see my *Murder Club Guide to North-West England*, Harrap, 1988, page 101). A search of criminal records proved the prints to belong to James Smith, described as 'construction worker, billiard-marker, engineer, road labourer, and boxer; age 40'; known to the police as a forger and petty thief. Furthermore, Smith's wife had reported him missing after leaving on a fishing trip on 8 April. Mrs Smith later identified the tattoo depicting two sparring boxers on the severed arm.

The question now was not *who* had died, but how and where, and in what circumstances?

Either through fear of some unpleasant consequences, or from genuine ignorance of the facts, Mrs Smith could provide no clue to the identity of her husband's companion on the late, fatal fishing trip. Nevertheless, police investigators did eventually locate the seaside cottage in which the anglers had stayed; it was deserted. Subsequent questioning of the house's owner revealed that a mattress and a tin trunk were missing. If Smith had been killed at the cottage, a tin trunk might be a singularly handy receptacle. A boat belonging to the cottage had also been plundered of three mats and a coil of rope; a coil of rope matching the description of that tied to the wrist of the severed arm. One reconstruction was that the killer had tried to cram the body into the tin trunk and, finding it an impossible fit, had lopped off one of the arms and lashed it to the outside of the trunk with rope from the boat; the trunk was then dumped offshore, the surplus arm providing a shark's breakfast. Improbable as the hypothesis might have sounded, it certainly accorded with the known facts; it was also the theory favoured by the celebrated English forensic pathologist, Sir Sydney Smith, who, by lucky coincidence, was in Sydney at the time on his way to a meeting of the British Medical Association in Melbourne. It was Smith's task to determine whether, as police now suspected, James Smith's arm had been severed after he had been killed, or, as contrary theories suggested, the limb had been chewed off by the shark while the man was still alive, which would have favoured either accident or suicide.

In his autobiography, *Mostly Murder* (Harrap, 1959), Sir Sydney describes the results of his examination: 'I found that the limb had been severed at the shoulder joint by a clean cut incision, and that after the head of the bone had been got out of its socket the rest of the tissues had been hacked away. In my opinion it was certain that it had been cut, and not·bitten off by a shark. The condition of the blood and tissues further suggested that the amputation had taken place some hours after death.'

Enquiries into James Smith's recent activities identified him as the 'minder' of the *Pathfinder*, a fast little motor launch whose smart appearance belied the fact that she was involved in a very dirty business indeed. A whole can of worms was prized open with this discovery which offered little doubt that Smith had been caught up in the evil machinations of a thriving underground drugs trade.

At the time of the 'murder' Sydney was virtually the world centre of heroin and opium smuggling; the business was getting uncomfortably overcrowded, the profits smaller, and the gangland overlords greedier. The result was an ugly dog-eat-dog war of hijackings, sinkings, torture and murder, involving half the seedy underworld of Sydney. Intelligence sources had discovered that the *Pathfinder*, going about its unlawful business, had recently been scuppered; James Smith had escaped with his life, but was left without a job – a dangerous man who knew too much to be wandering around without employment.

What the police needed now was to trace the owner

of the *Pathfinder*, and in spite of the dense blanket of silence imposed by the gangsters' 'code', the man was run to ground – Reginald Holmes, described as a boat-builder, of McMahon's Point.

Reg Holmes seemed unexpectedly co-operative: yes, he had employed James Smith to look after the *Pathfinder*, and had been sorry to have to let him go when the boat was so 'mysteriously' sunk. Naturally he knew nothing about smuggling, but he did suspect that Smith was being blackmailed – by a man named Patrick Brady, owner of a seaside cottage to which he believed Smith had recently gone for a holiday!

In no time, Brady was in custody, picked up on a minor forgery charge; investigating officers began to feel that at last they were in the lead; at last, with the help of Reginald Holmes, the Shark Arm Case would be laid to rest. But that optimism reckoned without interference from the twilight world of Australia's drug-runners.

It was a couple of days after the arrest of Patrick Brady that a speedboat, wildly out of control, careered across Sydney Harbour, hotly pursued by every available police launch in the area. After a frantic chase, the boat was captured. Its driver, beneath a mask of blood, turned out to be an hysterical and terrified Reginald Holmes. Holmes's story was that a stranger had shot at him near his home and wounded him in the forehead. Holmes had taken off, chased by his unknown assailant, and had finally managed to lose him in his boat.

Clearly, somebody was determined that Holmes would be out of circulation by the time of the inquest. In a gesture of almost unbelievable stupidity, the police rejected the commonsense expedient of placing Reg Holmes in protective custody and, after treatment for a superficial head-wound, Sydney's star witness was turned loose on the streets again – a stool-pigeon back on the shooting range.

The would-be hit-man must have thought he was dreaming; surely, he could never have expected a second chance at Holmes. But that was exactly what the police had given him, and in the small hours of 13 June – the day set for the inquest on James Smith's arm – Holmes was put beyond the call of all but the celestial coroner. Under one of the railway arches of Sydney Bridge, at Dawes Point, Holmes's body was found collapsed over the steering wheel of his car; dead, with bullets in the chest and groin. The police had lost their witness, and with him any chance of a case against Brady.

On its twelfth day, the inquest on Smith was halted by order of Mr Justice Hulse Rogers of the Australian Supreme Court, who ruled that: 'A limb does not constitute a body', and a body had 'always been essential for the holding of an inquest'. This was based on an English statute enacted in 1276, subsequently ignored in all modern legal decisions, and ultimately forgotten – except by Mr Justice Hulse Rogers.

Three months later, Patrick Brady was brought to trial before Justice Sir Frederick R. Jordan. Understandably the case fell flat on its face without Holmes on the witness stand. Brady, in evidence on his own behalf, pointed a finger of suspicion at one Albert Stannard. Stannard, he claimed, had been at the cottage with Smith at the time of his disappearance. As for the attempts on Holmes's life, Brady had the perfect alibi – he had been in police custody at the time! Unsurprisingly, Patrick Brady was acquitted.

In their desperation to salvage some dignity, the police authorised a £1000 reward for information link-ing the murders of Holmes and Smith. But it was too late; the blanket of silence had fallen over the Sydney underworld once again.

Two further trials, against Albert Stannard and his bodyguard John Patrick Strong, also fell apart. At the first, the jury could not agree, and at the subsequent retrial Stannard and Strong were acquitted due to lack of evidence and their own unshakeable alibis.

On 12 December 1935, just nine months after it had been opened, the file on the Shark-Arm Case was closed. But the rumours persisted. Perhaps Reginald Holmes had not been the innocent victim that he had played so convincingly; was it possible that he was, in fact, being blackmailed by James Smith? And why was he seen drinking in friendly – some said almost celebratory – fashion with Brady on the day after Smith's disappearance?

In the murky drama of gangland intrigue, all the players are potential victims, many are potential murderers; the only truly innocent party in the whole of this grisly scenario was the shark!

JAMES CAMB
(At sea and England, 1947–8)

Murder in Cabin 126

At the time of her unplanned rendezvous with the Grim Reaper, 26-year-old Eileen Isabella Ronnie Gibson (stage name 'Gay') had achieved some success as a stage and radio actress in South Africa and was now on her way home to England as a first-class passenger aboard the Union Castle liner *Durban Castle*; the ship had departed Cape Town on 10 October 1947.

At 40 minutes past midnight on 18 October, Miss Gibson retired to her cabin after dining and dancing in the ship's restaurant with shipboard acquaintances Mr Frank Hopwood and Wing-Commander Bray. At three o'clock the bell rang in the pantry on A deck summoning Frederick Steer, the night watchman, to Gay Gibson's cabin on B deck; cabin number 126. In fact, when he arrived Steer noticed that *two* lights were showing outside the cabin door, indicating that its occupant had summoned both the steward and the stewardess.

The night watchman knocked, opened the cabin door, and had it closed in his face; but not before he had seen the figure of a man on the other side of Miss Gibson's door – a man he recognised as the 31-year-old promenade-deck steward James Camb; the one the crew called 'Valentino'.

Although Steer reported the incident to his superior, James Alfred Murray, chief night watchman, and Murray in turn reported it to the Second Officer of the Watch, nothing further was done. It was, after all, up to the passengers what they got up to in the privacy of their cabins.

On the following morning, Gay Gibson failed to turn up for breakfast, and a search of the ship failed to find her. More out of formality than in any hope of success, the captain of the *Durban Castle* ordered the ship reversed and a fruitless search was made for a 'body overboard'.

The incident in cabin 126 in the early hours of the morning now took on a distinctly more sinister importance, and Frederick Steer informed Captain Patey of Camb's nocturnal visit to the missing passenger's cabin. Camb denied that he had done any such thing, though further suspicion was aroused when marks like fingernail scratches were found on the steward's wrists and neck. A careful examination of the Gibson cabin revealed blood-flecked saliva stains on the bedsheets.

The *Durban Castle* docked on the night of 24 October, and James Camb was handed over to the police at Southampton. Told that he would be charged with murder, Camb replied: 'I did not think it would be as serious as this.'

Clearly realising that Steer's unshakeable identification placed him beyond doubt at the scene of Gay Gibson's disappearance, James Camb concocted a not unique defence of natural death and panic.

Yes, he told the jury at Winchester Assizes in March 1948, he was in the cabin all right – by invitation. When they had passed each other on deck on that fateful night Camb – jokingly, he claimed – had said to Miss Gibson: 'I have a good mind to bring a drink down and join you' (in her cabin). We have only his word for it that she replied: 'Please yourself; it's up to you.'

Apparently it did please him, and by around 2 a.m. James Camb was sitting on the bed of cabin 126, Gay Gibson beside him. After chatting generally for ten or fifteen minutes, the couple exchanged their sitting position for a horizontal one, and according to the prisoner: 'There was a certain amount of preliminary love play, and then sexual intercourse took place.'

'When sexual intercourse took place, what were your relative positions?'

'I was lying on top of Miss Gibson. I was face down.'

'What happened in the end?'

'She suddenly heaved under me as though she were gasping for breath.'

'What happened to her body?'

'It stiffened for a fraction of a second and then relaxed completely limp.'

'What did you do when her body showed these symptoms?'

'I immediately got off the bed. She was completely relaxed as though she was in a dead faint. One eye was just slightly open. Her mouth was a little open too. There was a faint line of bubbles, which I assumed to be froth, just on the edges of the lips. It was a muddy colour and appeared to be blood-flecked. I was stunned for a moment. First of all I listened and felt for heart-beats. I could not find any, and I attempted, by massaging the stomach towards the heart, to bring back circulation.'

After 25 minutes of unproductive massaging, the full horror of his situation struck steward Camb. Realising the girl was very dead, he 'hoped to give the impression that she had fallen overboard, and deny all knowledge of having been to that cabin, in the hope that the Captain's further enquiries would not be too severe. I lifted her up and pushed her through the porthole.'

Well, it was not an *entirely* implausible story; stranger things *have* happened. And which of us could say with certainty how we ourselves would have behaved if confronted with the situation described so graphically by the prisoner in the dock?

But there are always two sides to be considered in any trial. And the hypothesis presented by the Crown prosecution in this case was that Camb was far from being a welcome visitor to first-class cabin 126. That having insinuated himself into Miss Gibson's room he had pressed his unsolicited attentions on her, and when she fought him off, strangled her, during the course of which her desperate clawing at the hand tightening around her throat had badly scratched the intruder's wrists. At some stage in her unequal fight for life, Gay Gibson must have managed to press the bells for the steward and stewardess. Had she not, had Frederick Steer not answered that summons, had James Camb not been seen, he might just have got away with it.

The body of Gay Gibson was never recovered from the Atlantic, and the trial of James Camb was one of the very few to take place without the hard evidence of a corpse. That being so, the medical evidence was of vital importance. On the prosecution side, leading pathologist Dr Donald Teare stated emphatically that the blood-stained saliva on Gay Gibson's sheets, and the fact that her bladder had opened just before death and stained the bed with urine, were consistent with manual strangulation.

No less eminent expert witnesses were called on

behalf of the defence. It was the contention of Dr Frederick Hocking that the evidence described by Dr Teare was equally consistent with death from natural causes.

The jury, in the end, chose to believe the former, and on 23 March 1948, after a retirement of just three-quarters of an hour, James Camb was found guilty of the murder of Gay Gibson and sentenced to death.

However, James Camb did have one stroke of luck. At the time his execution was scheduled to take place, Parliament was still debating the 'abolition' clause which the Commons had added to the Criminal Justice Bill, and the Lords had subsequently taken out. As a consequence, the Home Secretary thought it only fair to suspend executions until the matter was resolved. Camb was especially fortunate as the clause was finally deleted and hanging recommenced.

POSTSCRIPT

It must be added that although the matter was never raised in court, Camb had already acquired a reputation for importuning passengers; hence his nickname among the crew: 'Valentino'. Twice he had entered women's cabins, tried to molest them, and was repelled only by the fiercest struggle. On a third occasion he tried unsuccessfully to strangle a female passenger in a deck shelter. Unfortunately for Gay Gibson, none of the victims reported the incidents.

James Camb was released from prison on licence in September 1959 and, having changed his name to 'Clarke', found employment as a head waiter. In 1967 he was sentenced to two years' probation for indecently assaulting a thirteen-year-old girl. While still on probation, 'Clarke' was again found guilty of interfering with minors, and this time his licence was revoked and the man who killed Gay Gibson was returned to prison to complete the life sentence handed down to him for that crime.

PETER HOGG
(England, 1976–85)

The Ladies of the Lake

December. An unfriendly month on any remote surface of Britain's landscape, not least the boulder-strewn peaks and valleys of the Cumbrian Lake District.

Wast Water, on the western edge of the county, could never be called Lakeland's most beautiful stretch of water, though what it lacks in tourist attractions it does not lack in majesty. The wildest of the lakes, it is also the deepest, and even beneath the summer sun there is a kind of eerie menace in its black waters. Now, at year-end, the wind blows a lament across its surface causing a rippling, a shivering. Below the surface, the water is still; and silent as the grave. But for those whose pleasures lie in this sub-aqua world, it is another kingdom with its hills and valleys, its swaying vegetation, its creatures. That was how it seemed to Nigel Prith as he followed a rocky ledge that jutted out a hundred feet or more beneath the surface. Ahead, through his goggles, Prith could see what looked like a rolled-up carpet; then the ledge dropped down steeply into the seemingly bottomless centre of the lake. The drama of the underwater landscape quickly dispersed any curiosity the diver might have felt about the 'carpet', and it was not until two months into the following year, 1984, that official activity around the lake brought the incident back to the forefront of his mind.

The local police were searching Wast Water for traces of a French student, 21-year-old Veronique Marré, who had disappeared from the Wasdale youth hostel the previous summer. Following Prith's directions, police frogmen dived again into the blackest depths of the lake, emerging with confirmation of a weed-logged bundle anchored to the rocky ledge with a block of concrete.

When this sunken booty was dragged up to the lake's edge, dripping water and slimy fronds, there were few among the officers who surrounded it who would not have given anything to have been somewhere else. Few in whose minds the pretty French girl's last written words did not echo with a cruel irony: 'I wish I could stay here for ever.' Gingerly, the plastic sheeting was unwound; a sharp intake of breath; brains forcing eyes to look at the water-logged body at their feet.

The plump, middle-aged woman who lay there, incongruous and pathetic in her underwear, was not by any stretch of the imagination Veronique Marré; in fact, Mademoiselle Marré is still missing. This was another mystery altogether.

As luck would have it, the killer of the woman known popularly as 'The Lady in the Lake' had not made a very thorough job of removing clues to his victim's identity. It was the gold wedding ring on the woman's hand that bore the important information: 'Margaret 11.11.63 Peter' engraved on the inside. In a perfect example of police/press/public cooperation, a woman in Guildford recognised the names from a newspaper report – Margaret and Peter Hogg. She was sure because she had once kept house for the couple who had married on 11 November 1963.

Information from the Surrey police records revealed

that 37-year-old Mrs Margaret Hogg had been reported missing from her home in Cranleigh in October 1976, and had not been seen since. Peter Hogg, an airline pilot, had expressed his opinion that Margaret had run off with a banker named Graham Ryan, with whom she had been having a quite open affair. Despite Ryan's absolute denial that he had eloped with Margaret Hogg, her husband successfully cited Ryan as a co-respondent in his divorce case, and the luckless banker ended up paying Hogg's legal costs. Despite this bewildering finale, the matter seemed at an end. Until 29 February 1984, that is, when Margaret Hogg turned up a very long way from Cranleigh.

Peter Hogg was immediately taken into police custody where according to Detective Chief Inspector Blake, the officer in charge of the case, he was 'most co-operative'. In short, he made a statement admitting killing his wife and dumping her body into Wast Water. At his trial for murder in March 1985, Hogg's unsettled married life was again scrutinised, his wife's constant infidelity again invoked in order to establish a defence of provocation. It was revealed to the court how, after spending the week with her lover at a cottage in Dorset, Mrs Hogg returned to the marital home on Saturday, 11 October 1976. On the following day she had planned to meet Ryan again, but never kept the appointment; that afternoon the Hoggs had one of their now familiar brawls during which blows were struck by both partners. It was the au pair's day off, their eldest son was at boarding school, the youngest staying with friends, so the violence was a little less restrained than usual. According to Peter Hogg's statement: 'I lost control completely, grabbed her throat and squeezed until she stopped squirming around. Then I looked into one of her eyes . . . and knew immediately she was dead.'

Next morning, Monday, 13 October, Hogg telephoned his son's school at Taunton arranging to collect the boy by car at the start of the half-term holiday, thus, by giving the strong hint that he would be staying overnight in Taunton, providing himself with an alibi for the time taken to drive through the night to the dark shores of Wast Water. From the lake's edge, he paddled the wrapped and weighted body of Margaret Hogg in an inflatable dinghy to the middle of the lake. It is an irony that had he rowed out a little further, Peter Hogg's dreadful cargo might never have returned to haunt him; just a couple of yards and it would have missed the rocky ledge on which it settled, and sunk into the unfathomable oblivion for ever.

As his trial drew to a close, sympathy for Peter Hogg was running high, and he was finally convicted only of the lesser charge of manslaughter; even then his sentence was a modest four years' imprisonment.

Both justice and the requirements of the law had been satisfied. Only one question remained. What became of Veronique Marré?

POSTSCRIPT

Cumbria's second 'lady of the lake' was pulled to the surface in September 1988. Like Margaret Hogg, she had been found unexpectedly by an underwater diving enthusiast; and like Mrs Hogg she had died of manual strangulation.

The victim of this apparently copycat murder was identified as 41-year-old Sheena Owlett, missing from her home in Wetherby, East Yorkshire, since the late spring of the same year. Although he had excused her absence to the neighbours, warehouseman Kevin Owlett had not reported his wife's disappearance to the police – for reasons which became obvious at his trial.

Life for the Owletts – like the Hoggs – had been one of constant uneasy tension punctuated by outbursts of aggression that all too frequently erupted into actual physical abuse; in both cases the catalyst had been sexual infidelity.

One early morning, after a bout of particularly heavy drinking, Sheena and Kevin Owlett began their last quarrel. After the preliminary exchange of taunts and accusations came the punches, the blows with a wine bottle, the grabbing by the throat.

What happened next, the almost military precision with which Mrs Owlett's body was despatched, went a long way to dashing any hope Owlett may have entertained of a manslaughter verdict. After driving the corpse in the boot of his car the 100-odd miles to Crummock Water, Owlett weighted the body by winding it in a heavy metal tow-chain and roping it to the cylinder block from a car. He had then lashed the bundle to a plastic beer barrel so that it was buoyant enough to tow behind as he swam to the centre of the lake. As soon as the screw top was removed from the barrel it filled with water, enabling the whole grisly package to sink.

It had been ingenious and, like Peter Hogg's before it, Kevin Owlett's guilty secret might have been shrouded by the lake for years; for ever. But for a million-to-one chance, they might both have got away with murder.

Nine

'Is that your bag?'
'I believe it is'

Patrick Mahon,
questioned and arrested at Waterloo Station

BELA KISS
(Hungary, 1916)

A Case of Stolen Identity

The story begins at Czinkota, a remote village in Hungary, some way beyond Budapest. It was early summer of the year 1916 – in the middle of a World War. Had it not been in the middle of a World War, the chilling crimes of Bela Kiss might have remained undiscovered. As it was, Hungary was short of petrol for its war effort, and the authorities were commandeering every drop of it they could lay their hands on.

At the lower end of the village of Czinkota lay the dilapidated, rambling house and workshop of the local tinsmith and amateur fortune-teller, Bela Kiss. A combination of the house's sinister appearance and the reputation of its owner for having superhuman powers of malevolence served to keep most of the villagers at bay. When Kiss was conscripted into the army he need not have bothered with the padlocks and bars.

An old crone named Kalman, who claimed to have worked as an occasional cleaner for Kiss at one time, was the only person in living memory to have been inside the house. And when she was caught peeping through a keyhole it cost her her job – and all she had seen was a row of petrol casks! Which is how Bela's casks of petrol became woven into local folklore as such trivialities can be in small rural communities.

It was not until the sergeant and his two constables

arrived in their search for petrol that anybody had the temerity to enter the tinsmith's house. But with the promise of a rich prize inside and the praise of their superiors it was not long before the officers found themselves on the other side of the padlocks, a knot of curious but cautious villagers whispering at a safe distance.

There in the attic, exactly as the old woman had described them, were seven large metal casks, each welded tightly shut. But war is war, and petrol is petrol and as the lid of the first barrel succumbed to the sergeant's crowbar all three peered in at their booty.

There was no petrol in the cask. Just a dead body. The naked and trussed body of a young woman, the ugly red marks around her throat giving witness to the way she had died.

One cask open. Six still sealed. Five, four . . . The sight now before the policemen's eyes was beyond their worst nightmares; for with a sense of horror that two years of war had not blunted, they looked down on seven human corpses, all women, all naked, all bound, all strangled.

But this was not the end of the story, by no means the last page of this catalogue of carnage. Meticulously kept records revealed that Bela Kiss had formed liaisons with more than a score of women through the expedient of the newspaper matrimonial advertisements; they had all been lured to the death-house. Of the fates of seven we have just learned; the garden around the ramshackle building yielded up a further ten, and the wood beyond a further dozen before they stopped digging.

In no time at all the police and military, having for the moment forgotten the issue of the war in Europe in the face of mass murder closer at hand, had combined their resources to trace Bela Kiss through his military records. First to the army hospital where he had been treated for wounds received in combat, and thence to the grave which was his last resting place. It seemed a neat, if otherwise unsatisfactory conclusion to the monstrous crimes of the butcher of Czinkota.

And the matter would certainly have been left there, were it not for official red tape, the requirement for every matter to be cross-checked and referenced backwards, forwards and sideways before it can be laid to rest. One of these necessary formalities was that an officer be sent down to the hospital where Bela Kiss breathed his last to confirm the official notification of his death. This duty completed, the policeman remarked to one of the staff nurses that she was very lucky to be alive being so close to a monster like Kiss. Intrigued, she asked the sergeant more. At the end of his story, the poor girl could hardly believe her ears: 'What, that young boy? Murder thirty women?' 'Oh, no, you must be thinking of a different patient,' the policeman explained, 'Bela Kiss was over forty.'

Which was quite correct. The boy who died of his wounds had been named Mackaree – had been, that is, until Bela Kiss had stolen his identity, leaving the boy to go to his grave with the reviled name of Bela Kiss. The new 'Mackaree' was never found, though he was supposedly sighted in Budapest after the war. In 1924 he was reported to have joined the French Foreign Legion under the name 'Hofmann', and he was said to have been seen for the last time in New York in 1932.

HERA BESSARABO
(France, 1914–20)

'The Truth, the Truth . . .'

Mexico at the turn of the century; a mysterious country soaked in the exotic glamour of its Aztec history; a land of opportunity for those with the courage and determination to carve themselves a place beneath the sun. It was here that Madame Bessarabo spent the first years of her married life. She was Madame Jacques then.

As Hera Myrtel, she had been born in Lyons France, on 25 October 1868. A sensitive, creative girl, she both read and wrote poetry eagerly, and until the bankruptcy of the family business Hera had worked as an assistant to her father. It was in her 26th year that Mlle Myrtel had travelled to South America and there met Paul Jacques, a traveller in silk who was twenty years her senior. It was shortly after their return to Paris in 1904 that, as Madame Jacques, she became mother to baby daughter Paule, and as Hera Myrtel became mother to a series of literary works of dubious quality which she had printed at her own expense. She clearly felt that this entitled her to collect a 'salon' – mostly of young men, most of whom became lovers. The Jacques's marriage, to give it credit, had lasted for almost twenty years before succumbing dramatically on 8 March 1914. Despite a previous attempt by his wife to poison his soup with corrosive sublimate Monsieur Jacques had stayed put at 107 rue des Sèvres, and on the eve of his leaving for a business trip to Mexico, became the victim of a fatal shot, fired, so the coroner's court ruled, by his own hand. The following year Hera Jacques returned to Mexico.

One day, the police in Mexico City were confronted by an apparently distraught Madame Jacques sobbing out a somewhat preposterous story of four hooded horsemen who had ridden up to the ranch, dragged her head ranch hand from the house, and with the verbal receipt: 'This settles the account', shot him dead and ridden off.

It was undeniable that Mexico was – and is – a violent place; and ranchers and travellers were troubled with more than their share of banditti. Despite a serious police attempt, the four killers were never traced.

However, sympathetic as the authorities had been, local gossip was far less charitable.

As time went lazily by, Madame made the acquaintance of a Roumanian wood merchant named Bessarabo. Actually, Bessarabo was not his real name, but to him at least it seemed preferable to the less romantic Charles Weissman with which he was christened.

With almost indecent haste, Madame sold the Jacques hacienda and moved into Mexico City, where her beauty and Bessarabo's wealth made her the toast of the French colonists.

After their marriage, the Bessarabos and young Paule returned to France and a life of civilised gaiety among Paris society. But the good times were not to last, and by the time the rumbling thunder of 'the war to end wars' rolled over Paris, Madame was preoccupied with a young French soldier, while Monsieur sought refuge in the comforts of a young typist whom he had installed in a discreet country retreat.

Despite the end of the war, there was no ceasefire for the battling Bessarabos, and on the occasions when the couple were obliged to be in each other's company there were spiteful quarrels. On one occasion – it was the evening of 8 July 1920 – Madame Bessarabo, in a particularly violent fit of pique, pulled a gun on her husband and with words roughly translating as: 'Get out or I'll lay you out', fired at him – a shot which would surely have found its mark if the quick-thinking Charles had not thrown himself to the floor.

By now it must have seemed to observers that the late World War had transferred to the Bessarabo household. And then, out of the blue, a letter bearing a South American postmark created further upheaval, throwing the family into panic. Extra security locks were put on doors and windows which were kept shut at all times. To those few confidants who spoke to Bessarabo during the following weeks, all he would say was: 'A man from the past is seeking my life.'

On 30 July a second letter threw the unfortunate businessman into a further panic. A couple of days after that, Charles Bessarabo disappeared.

Now a man like Bessarabo cannot be missing for long before people begin to ask uncomfortable questions, like 'Where is he?' And it seemed appropriate, in the first instance at least, to ask the person most likely to know his whereabouts – his wife.

Charles Bessarabo's mistress asked her; his chauffeur asked her. And when the chauffeur reported his master missing, the police asked her. To all, she answered that he had gone to Mexico.

In the heat of the late summer of 1920, the contents of a trunk held for collection at Nancy railway station had begun to make its presence known over a large area of the left-luggage office. So offensive did the smell become, that the local gendarmerie were called in to remove the luggage before anyone actually passed out.

The contents of the trunk, trussed up with rope and wrapped in a waterproof sheet, proved to be a man's body, naked save for a red flannel waistcoat, a bullet hole in the head through which his brains were seeping. The remains were deposited in the mortuary to await identification.

Unlike many of the celebrated trunk murders, the police were put to no trouble at all identifying the contents of the Nancy baggage. The trunk had been despatched by train from Paris by a woman giving her name as Bessarabo, whose handwriting was Paule's. That her stepfather was missing was a coincidence that the police could not ignore.

When Madame Bessarabo was invited to the morgue to view the Nancy remains she was emphatic: 'That,' she declared, 'is not my husband. He was a young man, and a handsome one. This is old and ugly.' Even so, it did beg the question why her daughter should have sent a corpse – any corpse – to Nancy packed in a trunk.

Now that was something Madame *could* explain, though it sounded as fanciful as the apocalyptic riders who had put an end to her rancher in Mexico. It involved a secret agent by the name of Becker, and a Mexican secret society who had sent the letters threatening her husband's life. Madame told the police that Bessarabo had contacted her some weeks after his disappearance and asked her to meet him at Paris's Gare du Nord at eleven in the morning, whence they would journey to Montmorency where the Bessarabos had their summer home. After loading two trunks into a taxi – one containing papers which her husband wished to go through – Madame arrived at the station. Charles Bessarabo kept the appointment, arriving by taxi with a trunk. He stopped only long enough to greet his wife and promised to return shortly. The taxi did come back, with the trunk, but without Bessarabo; only his letter directing her to send the trunk by train to Nancy, which instruction Paule later carried out. For all Madame knew of it, the body was that of the elusive enemy agent Becker who had been tracking her husband. Bessarabo, she insisted, was alive and well in America, though unable to declare himself for fear of the secret society!

It wasn't really much of a defence to present to the jury, especially as Paule had already been proved to have purchased the waterproof sheet and cord used to pack the body.

It was the prosecution's contention that Madame Bessarabo, in a fit of jealousy over her husband's infidelity, and probably aggravated by drink and drugs, had shot him, and together with her daughter disposed of the body.

In fact it was not that far from the truth. We know, because on the last day of the trial, a previously silent Paule Jacques suddenly burst out: 'The truth, the truth, I must speak the truth.'

Her version of the truth, which is about as close as we are likely to get, was that her stepfather had been making her mother's life a misery for years, and that one night she had awakened to the sound of a shot. Rushing to her mother's room she cried out: 'What have you done?'

'It was his life or mine. I cannot reveal the terrible secret of what has passed here tonight, but believe me, I did not kill him.'

Paule, who had clearly inherited many of the histrionic genes of her mother, then recalled that in the period of drowsiness just before the shot was fired, she heard two male voices, one of which was a familiar voice from long ago – it was her father, the once-deceased but now returned Monsieur Jacques! After an impassioned plea on her mother's behalf, Paule concluded: 'Although I can tell you all I heard and saw that night, I cannot tell you all I suspect – nay, what I know, for it is my secret. I understand that my father is still alive, and imagine him to be the cause of the crime.'

So what *was* the truth of the matter? Whose *was* the body in the trunk? Who killed him? And why? And what of the secret society?

The French jury decided that it was really far simpler than that; in fact they thought it was as the prosecution had contended, and returned a verdict of guilty in extenuating circumstances. Madame Bessarabo was sentenced to twenty years' imprisonment. Her daughter, unaccountably, was acquitted. But Justice is a hard mistress, and it was recounted by one senior police officer involved in the case that Paule Jacques 'an unhappy waif, lost in Paris, lives in misery'.

THE BRIGHTON TRUNK MURDERS*
(England, 1934)

Two Classic Classics

No. 1

The debate on the nature of the 'perfect murder' has stimulated people's imagination for almost as long as people have tried to commit it. The fact is that fewer murders remain unsolved than might be thought, and those that do are in the main the result of brutal flights of passion that subside as quickly and inexplicably as they rise, often between people who are comparative if not total strangers. They comprise the sordid crimes rooted in greed that get hopelessly out of hand, their very pointlessness making it easy for the attacker to creep back unnoticed into the background. By any standards, the word 'perfect' does not come to mind in such cases. Indeed, there are those who will maintain that murder is such a very imperfect manifestation of humankind that superlatives are *per se* inappropriate. The less pedantic might feel that a grudging acknowledgment might be extended to anybody who 'perfectly' achieves that which they set as a goal; for the murderer, perhaps it demands more than merely 'getting away with it', and perhaps this perfection is one of

*An abbreviated version of the 'Brighton Trunk Murders' first appeared in *The Murder Club Guide to South-East England* (Harrap, London, 1988).

those indefinable states that can only be recognised after the fact, and not compared with a blueprint. At any rate, whoever deposited the unclaimed trunk in the left-luggage office of Brighton Station on Derby Day, 6 June 1934, was aiming for perfection.

Nearly a fortnight later – Sunday, 17 June to be precise – the baggage had still not been collected. Furthermore, it was beginning to give off a decidedly anti-social smell; the kind of smell that shouted out for investigation. As none of the baggage attendants had either the temerity or the stomach to approach too closely, the trunk was removed to Brighton police station; as it transpired, exactly the right place for it.

The body in the trunk was that of a woman, minus head, arms and legs. The remainder had been wrapped round in brown paper and tied with window cord. Written on the paper in blue pencil were the letters 'ford': what had obviously been the first syllable was obliterated by blood. Not much of a clue, but since the police have been known to get a result with less, there was some degree of optimism in Brighton that night. After all, Voisin – a fellow-dismemberer – had been trapped by a faded laundry mark. The trunk itself was brand-new, clearly bought for the purpose, and yielded nothing further of significance.

With their customary thoroughness, the police circulated a general request around Great Britain's railway stations that left-luggage staff be on the look-out for other malodorous packages; they were after the rest of the Brighton body. And nor were they entirely disappointed; there was a stinking suitcase at Kings Cross station in London, and it contained four more pieces – two legs and, severed, two feet. All neatly parcelled in brown paper.

At this stage, the inspired pathologist Sir Bernard Spilsbury, the man on whose skill and experience so many murder convictions had depended, took charge of the remains. An itemised list of his findings reads:

1. Dismemberment performed by a person with some, though not expert, appreciation of anatomy.
2. No other injuries to the body apart from the points of dismemberment.
3. Age of victim: under 30 years.
4. Time of death: about three weeks prior to discovery.
5. Victim was in the fifth month of pregnancy.
6. From the state of care of the hands and feet, it was likely that the victim came from a middle class background; had not engaged in any strenuous or dirty occupation.

The King's Cross trunk also gave up two potentially useful clues in a face flannel and a quantity of inferior grade cotton-wool packed with the lower limbs.

After extensive concentrated investigations, however, the 'clues' had produced no leads whatever – either to the victim's identity or to that of her killer. The next step has always been a difficult decision for the police – to what extent is it productive to engage the help of the general public and the mass media? The advantages are obvious; within a space of hours descriptions, requests for assistance, even pictures, can be relayed to every home in the country via the powerful networks of newspapers, radio and television – though police did not have this latter to consider in 1934.

The disadvantage can be imagined; with millions of amateur detectives throughout the country, the volume of input – the reported sightings, the snippets of gossip, the fears, suspicions – could be enough to grind to a standstill any investigating team that was not thoroughly prepared and organised. It happened that in this case the police were both desperate enough, and well enough organised, to realise that asking the public's help could be their only alternative to weeks of possibly fruitless searching and questioning. And so what description could be given of the girl was broadcast; details of the crime – such as they were – published. Someone surely must have missed a well-bred young woman? Someone must have heard something suspicious, seen something suspicious . . . found something suspicious? (The police were still hopeful of finding the head for identification.)

The investigating officers were quite rightly refusing to admit the possibility of the 'perfect murder'; but they were also honest enough to admit that they were in need of a lot of luck.

The response was overwhelming, and hundreds of statements were made and checked in the first few days – missing women, found clothing, bought trunks . . . there were no fewer than 24 girls reported missing in the Brighton area alone, where police were confident that the crime originated. Investigating officers all over Britain were set to checking statements, interviewing witnesses, searching empty houses; detective agencies in Europe and the United States were checking their missing persons files. Whose was the body in the trunk?

Two hundred police officers questioned hoteliers and guest-house landladies the length of the south coast; Miss Gene Dennis, a professional medium, advised that the search should be narrowed to a man with dark brown hair and the initials 'G. A.' or 'G.

H.', aged about 36, and a resident either of London or of Southampton. Miss Dennis was even more specific on the question of the victim . . . a manicurist with blue eyes from somewhere in Lancashire . . . 'working in a white overall . . . named Dorothy Ellena Mason or something like that, and I think the crime was committed on a boat moored near Brighton. I see a toll bridge and a railway nearby. The murderer is not a murderer by type, but has been forced into this. He has worked in a wholesale seed store . . . He is a man of an artistic type, with long slim hands and bushy hair, and I believe his name is George Henricson, or Robinson . . .'

Superintendent Frederick Wensley, formerly of Scotland Yard's Murder Squad and the man who had brought trunk murderer John Robinson to justice (see page 23) was enlisted as a consultant. But with the passing of a week since the body's discovery, things were looking as hopeless as ever. By the end of the month things had advanced no further; with every erroneous sighting, every half-baked theory, every new suspicion, the dossier grew fatter. And the police really were beginning to believe in the perfect murder.

To make matters worse, Fleet Street was becoming cynical; the *Daily Express* offered £500 reward for information which, it believed, was still locked in the inner recesses of someone's mind, or still being withheld out of fear or affection. Other newspapers were getting openly critical – one had discovered the whereabouts of 25 per cent of a new list of missing girls issued by Scotland Yard before the police had started. Gene Dennis stepped into the limelight again with a whole new shoal of red herrings from the world beyond: 'This man was a savage, and killed for sheer revenge and the glory of hurting. She was killed because the man hated her. He was furiously jealous. He hit her and maltreated her shamefully. The fact that she was pregnant had no real bearing on his motives. He is a man of supreme vanity, and will boast of his crime. When you find him, he will confess and will glory in what he has done. The murder was committed in a place that is almost public. I do not think it happened in an empty bungalow. I see a nursing home with white walls. There are two people concerned in the crime, this man and a stout woman of middle age. The head will be found in a small case wrapped in adhesive paper similar to that used on the rest of the body.'

Still results were negative, and with each succeeding week the trail was growing colder; the Brighton Trunk Murder had already earned itself a place in the annals of Classic Crime; it looked set to go to the top of the list of Classic Unsolved Crime, where it remains to this day.

But on Sunday, 15 July – a month after the discovery at Brighton Station – the seaside town was in a state of unconcealed excitement. Word travelled at the speed of lightning that the police had removed a black leather trunk from a house in Kemp Street, near the station. When Sir Bernard Spilsbury was seen arriving, rumours circulated that the arms and head of Brighton's celebrated corpse had been found at last. And that would have been remarkable enough; that alone would have explained the electric charge that seemed to be sparking the town. But the truth of the discovery would have defied invention by the most ghoulish imagination; police had not found the head missing from the trunk. They had found a whole new body. Brighton had its second Trunk Murder.

No. 2

Brighton's second trunk find was, inevitably, connected in both popular and official minds with the existing enigma, and it was confidently anticipated that it would contain the hitherto missing head and arms. At the very moment that the black leather trunk was being manhandled into Brighton police station Sir Bernard Spilsbury was being driven full speed to the south coast resort. But speculation was wrong: the police, and Sir Bernard, had another mystery to unravel.

During the investigations into Trunk Murder Number One police had made extensive searches of most of the properties in Brighton; including those in Kemp Street. Number 52, however, had been split into single apartments and the several occupants were not then at home; indeed, the owner of the house had been away in London for some weeks. The police had decided to pay the house a further visit when the tenants were in residence, and in the confusion of the operation No. 52 was never searched. When the owner of the house and his wife returned they found that a number of the tenants had already left, and those that remained gradually gave up their rooms over the succeeding few weeks. This left the owners free to redecorate and take the house back into their own occupation. It was one of the house painters who first noticed the unearthly smell coming from one of the rooms.

Obviously a man with a strong sense of the dramatic as well as a strong sense of smell, he said nothing of his suspicions to the owners but went straight to the police station. After keeping watch on the house for 48 hours – heaven knows why – the police entered and were immediately assailed by the foul odour of decay; quite by coincidence – one of many to follow – the owners of the house had, literally, no sense of smell. When the offending corpse in its trunk had been removed, the police immediately issued a description of the man they wished to interview – the previous tenant of the room.

Tony Mancini, a small-time crook with a string of aliases that would have filled an address book – Antoni Pirillie, Luigi Mancini, Hyman Gold, Jack Notyre (the name in which he was later charged with murder) – aged about 26, five feet ten inches tall, sallow complexioned, and with a cast in one eye; a frequent visitor to the low dives of London's West End. Despite his Mediterranean complexion Mancini was English – in fact his real name was Cecil Lois England. It was his admiration for the Italo–American gangsters of Chicago that predisposed him to more romantic titles for himself.

Mancini had been working for some time in the Skylark café on Brighton's seafront, and he had shared his modest lodgings, then at 44 Park Crescent, with a woman he chose to refer to as his wife. She was Violette Kaye, quickly identified as the victim in the trunk. It was no surprise that police were anxious to contact him.

Ironically, they already had; for in yet another coincidence Tony Mancini had been interviewed in connection with the first trunk victim. During the search for an identity for the torso police had made up lists of missing girls on one of which Violette Kaye's name had featured. Mancini had given his full co-operation including a detailed description of Violette who, he claimed, had recently left him. The great difference in the women's ages ruled Violette Kaye out as a candidate for the mystery torso and Mancini had fled back to London.

Meanwhile the background of the second victim was being carefully pieced together. Violette Kaye; also known as Mrs Violette Saunders, though she had divorced some years previously. She was one of a family of sixteen children and from her early teens had been on the stage – dancing was what she did best, but she was also a competent singer and had enjoyed a successful career in musical revue. Although she was 42, dancing had kept her trim and she was still attractive to men. At the time she met Mancini, Violette had exchanged dancing for the arguably less exacting profession of prostitution, and their relationship had depended very much on her keeping him on her 'immoral' earnings. That said, there can be no doubt that the couple shared a deep and genuine affection for each other.

In the early morning of Tuesday, 18 July, Mancini was picked up by the police while he was trudging along the London to Maidstone arterial road where it crossed Blackheath. Later in the day the prisoner was transferred to Brighton where it seemed that the whole of the town had turned up to witness the arrival of this 'monster without parallel'. Hordes of young women in beach pyjamas and bathing costumes packed the square before the police court, hissing and booing as Mancini was hurried inside. The sight so appalled one senior police officer that he observed that it was more like a crowd at a fun-fair than at a magistrate's court, and recalled the worst excesses of the old days of public executions.

Tony Mancini came up for trial at the Lewes Winter Assizes on 10 December 1934; the judge was Mr Justice Branson. Mr J. D. (later Mr Justice) Cassels KC and Mr Quintin Hogg (later Lord Hailsham) appeared for the Crown, and Mr Norman Birkett KC led Mr John Flowers KC and Mr Eric Neve for Mancini.

Never, it must be said, was a case stronger against an accused than it was against Tony Mancini. To start with he was a known criminal – it shouldn't matter of course, not in a court of law; but it is impossible to divorce a man entirely from his past even for those with so onerous a task as a jury in a capital case. He had admitted not only that he lived with Violette Kaye – a prostitute – but lived off her as well. Furthermore, he admitted knowing that she was dead while all the time pretending to the police that she had simply left him, had 'gone abroad'. And finally he admitted to putting Violette's body into a trunk specially bought for the purpose, and of transferring it from their lodgings at Park Crescent to Kemp Street; keeping it there at the foot of the bed and eventually fleeing to London leaving his dreadful secret behind him. But at all times Mancini was emphatic that he had not been the cause of his mistress's death; it was panic, he said, that made him hide the body after coming home and just finding it there in the flat, panic, and the fear that he – a man with a police record – would never be believed if he told the truth.

But Mancini was also luckier than he could have hoped, for in the person of his leading counsel he had perhaps the most highly regarded criminal lawyer of his time, Mr Norman Birkett. And it was in great part Birkett's final address to a mesmerised jury, a speech that lasted 80 minutes, delivered entirely without notes, that turned the tables in his client's favour.

Having sown the seeds of doubt as to the strength of the prosecution case, Norman Birkett made deliberate capital out of Mancini's sordid background, emphasising his client's own submission that people like him 'never get a fair deal from the police'. Birkett told the jury:

This man lived upon her earnings, and I have no word whatever to say in extenuation or justi-fication. None. You are men of the world. Con-sider the associates of these people. We have been dealing with a class of men who pay eightpence for a shirt and women who pay one shilling and sixpence or less for a place in which to sleep. It is an underworld that makes the mind reel. It is imperative that you should have it well in mind that this is the background out of which these events have sprung.

Birkett then summed up with an appeal direct to the hearts of the jury:

Defending counsel has a most solemn duty, as I and my colleagues know only too well. We have endeavoured, doubtless with many imperfec-tions, to perform that task to the best of our ability. The ultimate responsibility – that rests upon you – and never let it be said, never let it be thought, that any word of mine should seek to deter you from doing that which you feel to be your duty. But now that the whole of the matter is before you, I think I am entitled to claim for this man a verdict of Not Guilty. And, members of the jury, in returning that verdict you will vindicate a principle of law, that people are not tried by newspapers, not tried by rumour, but tried by juries called to do justice and decide upon the evidence. I ask you for, I appeal to you for, and I claim from you, a verdict of Not Guilty.

As he paused for a brief moment, Birkett's eyes passed along the line of jurors; in the silence of the court his voice rang out: 'Stand firm.'

The jury did not disappoint him; after a retirement of almost two and a half hours the foreman rose to announce the verdict that Birkett had demanded of them: 'Not Guilty.'

Mancini was acquitted, and Norman Birkett was hero of the hour, though of the rapturous press accolades he cynically commented: 'Strangely enough it has given me very little pleasure . . . [Mancini] was a despicable and worthless creature. But the acquittal seems to have impressed the popular imagination.'

POSTSCRIPT

And Norman Birkett was quite right to have entertained his misgivings; perhaps years of involvement with the traffic of the court had given him an insight and an understanding of the human spirit not developed by the members of the jury – ordinary men like you and me. Perhaps Birkett knew; knew that he had been doing his level best to get a callous, cynical killer off the hook, off the gallows trap. If he did, then Mancini did not disappoint him.

After spending many years as a drifter, first with a fairground and later as a seaman, Tony Mancini married and settled in Liverpool. Then in November 1976, a world that had forgotten the Brighton Trunk Murder – probably had not even been born when it happened – had good cause to remember again the name of Tony Mancini. On 28 November, under a bold, black headline: 'I've Got Away With Murder', the *News of the World* printed Mancini's confession to the murder of Violette Kaye. Eighteen months later

Mancini was interviewed by journalist and author the late Stephen Knight, and before a solicitor swore an affidavit that the interview that he was about to give was the truth – Mancini was about to confess again.*

*The Knight/Mancini interview is published in *Perfect Murder*, Stephen Knight and Bernard Taylor (Grafton Books, London, 1987).

Appendix

FORENSIC PATHOLOGY

A Definition

The chief responsibility of the forensic pathologist is to undertake the post-mortem examination of bodies discovered in what are termed 'suspicious circumstances', that is to say where there is a suspicion of murder, manslaughter or infanticide. The object of the primary examination is to determine, as far as possible, the cause of death.

The next stage of the investigative procedure then frequently rests on the pathologist's professional judgement whether the case is dealt with by a coroner at inquest, as in the finding of suicide, accident or natural causes; or by the police as a criminal investigation (though in this latter eventuality also, a coroner's preliminary, or 'opening', hearing is required).

In the usual course of events, the forensic pathologist summoned by the police will first examine the body of the victim at the scene of the crime, often in far from agreeable conditions and surroundings, before attending the body in the mortuary to conduct a detailed post-mortem and prepare a report on his findings. Once he is 'on the case', the pathologist will be an occasional, though key member of the investigation team, working in collaboration with the police and the local forensic science laboratory. Finally, it may be required that he prepare expert testimony for the Crown Prosecution Service and act as an expert witness for the prosecution in any subsequent criminal proceedings.

Forensic pathologists and murder investigations are always connected in the popular imagination, though to see this in perspective it is necessary first to look at statistics. The figures for one recent year, 1987, were as follows: 175,769 deaths were reported to coroners in England and Wales, of which 77 per cent (135,961) were the subject of post-mortem examinations. Less than one per cent of these cases, about 1500, were in the nature of 'suspicious' deaths where the pathologist was summoned by the police, and in only 630 cases was a homicide recorded. Anecdotally, one report states that July, August and Christmas are the 'busiest' times.

So much for the man in the white coat. His specialism, forensic pathology, has emerged from the wider discipline of forensic medicine. Whereas previously the subject would have incorporated toxicology, biochemistry, materials analysis, ballistics, etc., each of these now forms its own specialised department, and the pathologist, while having a broad grasp of many related disciplines, now relies on experts in other increasingly complex technical fields, such as odontology, microbiology, serology, chemistry and clinical pathology.

At present (1989) there are about four dozen recognised forensic pathologists on call to the police forces of England and Wales, partly comprising the so-called 'Home Office list' of practitioners generally associated with the provincial universities or regional Home Office forensic science laboratories. Historically, the 'list' does not include the many eminent pathologists based in the capital's medical colleges who serve the Metropolitan and City of London police forces.

The United States of America

In the United States, the investigation of deaths in 'suspicious circumstances' is undertaken either by a coroner or the department of the medical examiner, depending on the system adopted by a particular state (though until comparatively recently, the coroner was the only option).

Distinct from the position of coroner in England, the American equivalent is a purely political office, and dependent entirely on the fortunes or otherwise of the political party to which an individual candidate for the post is affiliated. This is clearly not only an unstable situation, but one that is open to abuse; for example, many of those who run for the office of coroner are undertakers seeking to improve their share of the business.

For these, and other reasons, the medical examiner option is gradually replacing the coroner. Here a fully qualified and experienced forensic pathologist is employed full-time by the state and is in charge of a custom-equipped building and a team of qualified scientific staff. In many respects the system is more reliable, and certainly more realistically funded and staffed, than its English counterpart.

The Continent

Unlike the haphazard (and rapidly declining) availability of forensic medicine facilities in England, the rest of Europe (East and West) and Scandinavia have a healthy, efficient and well-financed network of forensic science institutes, usually attached to the universities, and in the charge of a professor (there were in

1989 fewer than half a dozen forensic pathologists with the status of professor in the whole of England and Wales). These operate in many ways similarly to American medical examiners' departments, though the high level of research and refinement that they undertake puts countries like Denmark ahead of the rest of the world.

A Question of Identity

'Forensic, or legal medicine provides one of the
most fascinating of all chapters in the practice of
medicine. The study of the body, usually dead,
the quiet scientific evaluation of the evidence it
bears, and the construction of reasonable inferen-
ces based on these observations cannot fail to give
interest and satisfaction.'

(Keith Simpson, *Forensic Medicine*)

The examination of human remains in the event of
suspicious death follows a very strict sequence,
developed to reveal as much information as possible as
quickly as possible. The evidence of the pathologist
and other members of the forensic science team will be
vital to the investigating officers concerned in solving
the case.

Such basic information as probable cause of death
and estimated time of death will already have been
determined by the pathologist or medical examiner at
the scene of the crime, though speculation of this kind
can only ever be provisional on post-mortem results.

In cases where the body has suffered extensive
mutilation subsequent to death, or where putrefaction
is so advanced as to render features unrecognisable, it
is vital for the forensic scientists to make a positive
identification of the victim, often before the investiga-

tion can properly proceed. And in cases such as the murder and dismemberment by Dr Buck Ruxton of his wife and maid (see page 167), identification becomes remarkable detective work in itself.

The following notes on post-mortem identification of human remains derive from the procedure developed by Professor Francis Camps, and have become, with minor regional variations, an international standard. Indeed, it is due to the tireless dedication of Professor Camps in advancing forensic medicine throughout the world that the system has become so universally accepted.

The Identification of Dead Bodies and Skeletal Remains

A. Basic facts

   a. *Sex* Clearly the genitalia are the most reliable guide to the sex of the victim, though in cases of post-mortem decomposition, it is useful to know that the uterus is the last organ to putrefy.

      If only skeletal material remains, the skull and pelvis are almost certain indicators of sex. More recently, a method of sexing body cells (nuclear chromatin) has been developed. This is a specific test for female tissue developed in 1949 by Barr and Bertram. The scientists observed that the nuclei of most female cells contain a nodule (known as a Barr body) which though present in all cell types is best seen in white blood cells, the lining of the mouth, and the skin. Tests require the skill of an expert technician.

b. *age* a criterion fraught with problems once maturity has been reached, but below the age of about 25 years the development of the teeth follows a remarkably consistent pattern.

Pathological changes, such as arthritis and arterial degeneration, together with other anatomical indicators are customarily the province of the specialist.

Skulls can be useful for broadly determining age, in that around the age of 40 the sutures of the skull vault begin to close at a fairly standard rate.

c. *Height* When a corpse is intact, measurement presents little difficulty; but in cases of dismemberment, where a body or skeleton is incomplete, estimates based on the measurement of the long bones can be calculated from anthropological tables.

d. *Race* While there is no problem identifying general racial groups in a fresh, intact, body, recourse must be made to the anatomical structure of the head and face, teeth and long bones in the case of skeletal remains.

e. *Fingerprints* (including foot and palm prints) Even where putrefaction is extensive, it has been possible to obtain a print. When, in August 1975, a badly decomposed body was found in the rubbish bay of a block of flats in Rochdale, the uncommon expertise of Detective Chief Inspector Tony Fletcher of Manchester's fingerprint squad was put to identifying the corpse. The skin had deteriorated beyond any hope of fingerprinting, with the barely possible exception of the right middle finger. Using a technique that he had developed in collaboration with experts at the Manchester Museum's department of Egyptology for the purpose of fingerprinting fragile mummies, Fletcher applied a special quick-drying, fine-grain dental putty to the tip of the finger and left it a few moments to set. The 'mould' was then peeled off and the inside treated with several coats of acrylic paint; when the paint was dry, and had been removed from the mould, it reproduced an accurate cast of the fingerprint which could be printed by the usual ink-and-roll method.

f. *Blood group* Apart from the possibility of helping to identify a victim through his or her blood group – or at least to eliminate those who do not share it – blood from the remains will be compared with staining on possible murder weapons and on the clothing of a suspect.

The fact that blood falls into several identifiable 'types' was first discovered by the Viennese-born biologist Karl Landsteiner in 1901. Knowing that red blood cells contain a number of antigens substances responsible for production of the antibodies that combat infection and disease – Landsteiner found that the presence or absence of two of these antigens (called A and B) in human blood formed four distinct groups:

A – antigen A and antibody B present
    antigen B and antibody A absent
B – antigen B and antibody A present
    antigen A and antibody B absent
O – antigens A and B absent
    antibodies A and B present
AB – antigens A and B present
    antibodies A and B absent

Subsequent refinements have led to the discovery of still further groups given indicators like PGM, Rh (Rhesus), AK, and MN.

In November 1987 rapist Robert Mellas became the first person to be convicted as a result of so-called 'genetic fingerprinting' evidence. The technique was discovered by Dr Alex Jeffries of Leicester University in 1983, and compares the pattern of DNA molecules found in every cell of the human body, a pattern which is different for every person.

B. Topographical features

In general, note should be taken of such topographical details as facial features – colour of eyes, shape of ears, etc.; hair and general shape of head; build of body and any deformities of limbs, etc. As identification is commonly the purpose of this minute examination, advantage must be taken of all the clues that a corpse might silently offer – such as tattoos and scars.

1. *Head and Face*
    i Eyes (shape, colour, etc.).
    ii Nose (shape – broken, etc.).

    iii Mouth and teeth (the separate specialist field
       of odontology is noted below).
    iv Ears.
     v Hair (colour, texture, etc.).
    vi Shape of head.
   vii Scars and other special peculiarities.

2. *Trunk*
     i General shape.
    ii Clothing (name tags, laundry marks, etc.).
   iii Tattoos, scars, other special peculiarities.
   iv Circumcision.

3. *Limbs*
     i Size.
    ii Occupational marks and deformities
      (callouses, staining, etc.).
   iii Tattoos, scars, amputations, other special
      peculiarities.
   iv Social status based on observation of care of
      hands, feet, etc.

C. Pathological information

This information will be revealed during post-mortem
opening of the body, which may show evidence of
previous surgical treatment, or current medical conditions – gallstones, cardiac disease, ulcers, etc., for
which records of treatment may be matched.

1. Specific already-known conditions – gallstones,
   ulcers, fibroids, skin disease.
2. Prior surgical treatment – scars, absence of
   organs, etc.
3. Evidence of previous accidents – scars, mended
   fractures, etc.

4. Changes that may help establish age – arthritic condition, cardiovascular disease, etc.
5. Specific pathological changes – malaria, sickle cell anaemia, etc.

D. Special procedures

1. X-ray studies of bones.
2. Special serological studies of tissues.
3. Odontology: One of the most vital aspects of forensic identification in cases of severe mutilation, the teeth are often the *only* clue remaining to a victim's identity. It is rare for a person to go through life without ever visiting a dentist, and every time a visit is made, the dentist is obliged to complete (or update) a chart of the patient's teeth, marking extractions, fillings, bridge-work, etc. Thus, with the virtual impossibility of two mouths having the same sequence and type of treatment, the dental chart becomes a veritable 'fingerprint'.
4. Photography: Special photographic techniques have been developed to aid identification of badly mutilated or decomposed bodies; notable is the process of overlaying a transparency of a known portrait of the supposed victim on a photograph of the skull that has been found. First developed in the Ruxton case, the technique was subsequently used successfully in the Dobkin case (see page 230).
5. Other procedures.

Stages of Post-mortem Body Changes ★

For obvious reasons it is vital to any inquiry into a suspicious death to establish as a priority the cause of death, means of death, and time of death. Many physical and chemical changes occur in the human organism after death, and these, if sufficiently accurately observed, can act as guides to the time of death.

Period	Change to body	Change if immersed in water
HOURS	*Cooling of body*	
0–12	1½–2°F (approx) per hour	3°F (average) per hour
12–24	¾–1°F (approx) per hour	1½°F (average) per hour [5–6 hours – body feels cold 8–10 hours – body is cold]
10–12	Body feels cold	
20–24	Body is cold	
	*Lividity**	
3–5	Begins to develop	Cutis anserina ('goose flesh') and whitening of the skin
	Rigor mortis	
5–7	Begins in face, jaw and neck muscles	Variable development
7–9	Arms and trunk, then legs	
12–18	Full rigor mortis	
24–36	Rigor mortis leaves body in the same order	Rigor mortis often still present [2–4 days] Rigor disappears
DAYS	*Putrefaction*	
2	Green staining on flanks of abdomen	
2–3	Green and purple staining of abdomen, body begins to distend	
3–4	'Marbling' of veins; staining spreads to neck and limbs	Root of neck discolours
5–6	Body swells with gases. Skin blisters	Face and neck swollen and discoloured
6–10		Body floats. Decomposition of trunk
WEEKS		
2	Abdomen tightly distended. Organs disrupted by gases	Dermis beginning to peel and hair easily pulled out
3	Blisters burst; tissue softens. Eyes start to bulge; organs and cavities bursting	Face further bloated and discoloured
4	Disruption and liquefaction of soft tissues	Body greatly bloated with gases; organs crepitant; hair so loose as to be wiped from scalp; finger and toe nails easily removed

Period	Change to body	Change if immersed in water
MONTHS	*Formation of adipocere**** (if conditions are damp)	
4–5	Established on face and head	Develops less quickly as tem-
5–6	Established on trunk	perature is lower

*All these are average times; the process is accelerated by hot weather and retarded by cold.

**Also called hypostasis, this is a condition of the body caused by the coagulation of the blood producing livid patches on the body. Where a body has been lying or sitting, the contact of the parts of the body against a firm surface will retard lividity causing white patches. Although this is an unreliable estimate of time of death, it is useful in determining whether, for example, a body has been moved from one position to another some hours after death – whether it died at the location it was found.

***A condition arising when a body has been immersed in water or inter-red in damp soil for a long period of time. Human fat, which is normally in a semi-liquid state, becomes hard and 'suety'. The process takes a long time, but is irreversible.

Some Case-files

SPILSBURY, Bernard Henry (1877–1947)

Sometimes called 'the greatest medical detective of the century', and indisputably the most widely known and influential individual in an elite tradition of forensic pathology, Spilsbury was involved in most of the famous murder cases of his generation. For decades his expert testimony in court, delivered with exceptional clarity and great confidence, was considered almost beyond question, and his post-mortems (of which he performed some 25,000 during his lifetime) were held to be the very model of forensic examination.

CELEBRATED CASES

1910. *Hawley Harvey Crippen*. Working with Dr Pepper, Spilsbury, now a senior pathologist at St Mary's, identified the remains recovered from the cellar at Hilldrop Crescent as those of Mrs Cora Crippen, professionally known as Belle Elmore (see page 227).

1911. *Frederick and Margaret Seddon*. Spilsbury and Dr William Willcox examined the exhumed body of Eliza Barrow and were able to confirm cause of death as acute arsenical poisoning.

1915. *George Joseph Smith*; the 'Brides in the Bath' case. With Willcox, Spilsbury worked out the

method used by Smith to drown his 'wives' –
putting his left arm under their knees and
pushing the head downwards and under the
water with the right hand. While attempting to
demonstrate his technique in court, Spilsbury
nearly drowned the nurse on loan from St
Mary's for the occasion.

1917. *Louis Voisin.* (See page 156.)

1918. *David Greenwood*; the 'Button and Badge
Murder'.

1922. *Frederick Bywaters and Edith Thompson.*
Herbert Rowse Armstrong. Spilsbury examined
the exhumed body of Armstrong's wife to provide incontrovertible proof of arsenic
poisoning.

1924. *Patrick Mahon.* Spilsbury was responsible for
piecing together what was left after the butcher-
ing and burning of Miss Emily Kaye's body, at
Eastbourne, Sussex.
Norman Thorne. Tried for the murder of his
fiancée, Thorne maintained that she had hanged
herself. In court, Spilsbury's evidence was seriously challenged (effectively for the first time)
by Dr Robert Bronte giving evidence for the
defence. The judge, however, considered
Spilsbury's opinion 'undoubtedly the very best
that can be obtained'. Thorne was hanged.
Jean-Pierre Vaquier. Poisoned his lover's husband with a strychnine hangover 'cure'.

1926. *John Donald Merrett.* Greatly swayed by what
turned out to be misleading evidence by Spilsbury and ballistics expert Robert Churchill, a
jury acquitted Merrett of murdering his mother.
In 1954, now using the name Chesney, Merrett
killed twice more before committing suicide.

1927. *John Robinson*; 'The Charing Cross Trunk Murder' (see page 23).

1929. *William Henry Podmore*. Bludgeoned to death Vivian Messiter in a garage in Southampton.
Sidney Harry Fox. Tried in 1930 for the murder of his mother in a Margate hotel room. Spilsbury conducted the post-mortem, during the course of which he found a bruise on the larynx consistent with strangulation. The subsequent natural disappearance of the bruise led to the pathologist's evidence being seriously opposed by Professor Sydney Smith who had been retained by the defence.

1930. *Alfred Arthur Rouse*; the 'Blazing Car Murder' (see page 97).

1931. *Oliver Newman and William Shelley*. Two itinerant labourers who murdered a fellow vagrant, Herbert Ayres.

1934. *The Brighton Trunk Murders*. (See page 274.)

1937. *Leslie Stone*. Remarkable forensic detective work, leading to the identification of Stone as Ruby Keen's murderer by matching soil and fibre particles from the scene of the crime with those embedded in Stone's trousers.

1938. *William Butler*.

1942. *Gordon Cummins*; the 'Wartime Jack the Ripper'.

1943. *Harold Loughans*. In a rare appearance on behalf of the defence, Spilsbury's evidence was instrumental in Loughans's acquittal of the murder of Portsmouth publican Rose Robinson. Twenty years later, when Loughans emerged from a term of imprisonment on a quite separate charge, he confessed to the Portsmouth murder.

1947. *Jenkins, Geraghty and Rolt.* The last appearance in court for Spilsbury (and, coincidentally, for firearms expert Robert Churchill). Two months after Geraghty and Jenkins were hanged, Spilsbury committed suicide.

SMITH, Sydney Alfred (1883–1969)

One of the celebrated products of the Edinburgh University Medical College, Smith was the equal, though in a more self-effacing manner, of his contemporary, Bernard Spilsbury. An all-rounder in the field of forensic science, Smith contributed a great deal to toxicology, microscopy and ballistics, as well as casting his brilliance on to pathology. A great champion of the comparison microscope, which he had used to such startling effect in Cairo in the case of Sir Lee Stack, it was largely through Smith's influence that the instrument achieved recognition in Britain. Arguably, Sydney Smith's greatest contributions were in the fields of firearms and gunshot wounds, on which his textbooks became standard references.

CELEBRATED CASES

1913. *Patrick Higgins.* Despite their almost complete transformation to adipocere, Smith managed to identify the two small corpses taken from the Hopetoun Quarry, near Winchburgh, Scotland, as Higgins's sons. Smith later kept the two adipocerous bodies for study, and they are still used to demonstrate the condition at Edinburgh's Forensic Medicine Department. In his autobiography, Sir Sydney revealed that it was Harvey Littlejohn who suffered for the 'body-snatching' in this piece of undergraduate doggerel:

> Two bodies found in a lonely mere,
> Converted into adipocere.
> Harvey, when called in to see 'em,
> Said: 'Just what I need for my museum.'

1931. *Sarah Ann Hearn*. Smith was retained by the defence to oppose the evidence of Dr Roche Lynch for the Crown that Mrs Hearn had poisoned her friend and neighbour, Alice Thomas, with sandwiches laced with arsenic. Mrs Hearn was acquitted.

1934. *Jeannie Donald*. Accused of murdering eight-year-old Helen Priestley in Aberdeen. Smith and fellow-Scot John Glaister matched hairs and fibres found in the sack in which the victim was found with Mrs Donald's by use of Smith's comparison microscope. 1935. *The Shark-Arm Case*. (See page 243.)

GLAISTER, John (1892–1971)

Son of Glasgow University's Regius Professor of Forensic Medicine, John Glaister became his heir, and between them the Glaisters held the chair for 65 years. John Glaister junior was among the first to set the general table of times for the development of decomposition of the human body, and to suggest a formula for the estimation of time of death; he was also a pioneer in the identification of hairs and fibres using the comparison microscope.

CELEBRATED CASES

1934. *Jeannie Donald*. A combination of Glaister's special knowledge of hairs and fibres and Sydney Smith's expertise with the comparison microscope sent Mrs Donald to prison for life.

1935. *Dr Buck Ruxton*. One of the most remarkable achievements in the history of forensic pathology brought together the three Scottish medico-legal giants: Glaister, Smith, and James Couper Brash. (See page 167.)

1947. *Stanislaw Myszka*. Using his expert knowledge in the classification and identification of animal hairs, Glaister was able to match hairs taken from Myszka's razor blade, used while in custody, with those found on a blade in the hide-out associated with the killer of Mrs Catherine McIntyre.

SIMPSON, Cedric Keith (1907–1985)

One of the greatest medico-legal pathologists of the century, Keith Simpson entered the field at a time when it was completely dominated by the personality of Bernard Spilsbury, and within a short time had established himself at the head of his profession and as a brilliant teacher. Simpson was the great pioneer of forensic dentistry (or odontology), writing in the *Medico–Legal Review* in 1951: 'Dental data, it is now realised, has come to provide detail of a kind comparable with the infinitesimal detail that was previously thought likely to be provided only by fingerprints.' A prolific lecturer and writer, Simpson adopted the pen name Guy Bailey for his more popular published offerings.

CELEBRATED CASES

1942. *Harry Dobkin.* Pioneering work by Simpson in forensic odontology (see page 230).
August Sangret; 'The Wigwam Murder'.

1946. *Harold Hagger.*
Neville Heath.

1948. *Goringe Case.* Killer identified by the teeth marks left on his victim's breast.

1949. *John George Haigh;* 'The Acid Bath Killer'. One of the most celebrated crimes of the century, in which Simpson was responsible for the remarkable identification of Haigh's victim (see page 31).
Frederick Radford. Murdered his wife with arsenic-laced fruit pie.

1964. *William Brittle.* Accused of the murder of Peter Thomas, whose decaying body was found in a wood near Bracknell, Berkshire. Brittle's alibi was destroyed when Simpson testified that maggots of the common bluebottle found on the remains had not pupated which, given the life cycle of the insect, established time of death.

1967. *Stephen Truscott.* Tried and convicted in Canada of the murder of twelve-year-old Lynn Harper in 1959, fourteen-year-old Truscott was sentenced to life imprisonment. In 1967, the controversy raised by a re-examination of the evidence resulted in a retrial at the Ottawa Supreme Court. The array of internationally famous forensic experts was unprecedented; Francis Camps, Keith Simpson and Milton Helpern of New York among them. The testimony centred around the rate of digestion and stomach emptying in the human body, and

whether or not it could be reliably used to estimate time of death. Although doubt continues
to hover over the outcome, the evidence of
Simpson and Helpern was preferred to that of
Camps and Dr Charles Petty for the defence,
and Truscott was returned to prison.

Select Bibliography

BESSARABO, Hera
The Underworld of Paris, Alfred Morain. Jarrold, London, 1928.
BRIGHTON TRUNK MURDER No. 1
Sir Bernard Spilsbury: His Life and Cases, Douglas G. Browne and E. V. Tullett. Harrap, London, 1951.
BRIGHTON TRUNK MURDER No. 2
Sir Bernard Spilsbury: His Life and Cases, Douglas G. Browne and E. V. Tullett. Harrap, London, 1951.
Criminal Files, John Rowland. Arco, London, 1957.
CAMB, James
Notable British Trials, ed. Geoffrey Clark. Hodge, London, 1949.
Too Late for Tears, Benjamin Bennett. Howard Timmins, Cape Town, 1948.
A Reasonable Doubt, Julian Symons. Cresset Press, London, 1960.
CRIPPEN, Dr Hawley Harvey
Notable British Trials, ed. Filson Young. Hodge, London, 1950.
Sir Bernard Spilsbury: His Life and Cases, Douglas G. Browne and E. V. Tullett. Harrap, London, 1951.
I Caught Crippen, Walter Dew. Blackie, London, 1938.
The Crippen File, Jonathan Goodman. Allison and Busby, London, 1985.

Some Famous Medical Trials, Leonard A. Parry. J. & A. Churchill, London, 1927.

DOBKIN, Harry

Old Bailey Trials, ed. C. E. Bechhofer Roberts. Jarrold, London, 1944.

Forty Years of Murder, Professor Keith Simpson. Harrap, London, 1978.

The Crime Doctors, Robert Jackson. Frederick Muller, London, 1966.

Evidence for the Crown, Molly Lefebure. Heinemann, London, 1975.

DUDLEY, Reginald, and MAYNARD, Robert

Clues to Murder, Tom Tullett. Bodley Head, London, 1986.

FISH, Albert Howard

The Cannibal, Mel Heimer. Xanadu, London, 1988.

The Show of Violence, Fredric Wertham. Gollancz, London, 1949.

GEIN, Edward

Edward Gein, Robert H. Gollmar. Delavan, Wisconsin, 1982.

GROSSMANN, Georg Karl

Auf der Spur des Verbrechn, H. Soderman. Berlin, 1957.

GUNNESS, Belle

The Truth About Belle Gunness, Lillian de la Torre. Frederick Muller, London, 1960.

Such Women are Deadly, Leonard Gribble. John Long, London, 1965.

The Best Laid Schemes . . ., H. W. Twyman. Harold Shaylor, London, 1931.

HAARMANN, Fritz

Murder for Profit, William Bolitho. Jonathan Cape, London, 1926.

Murder by Numbers, Grierson Dickson. Hale, London, 1958.

HAIGH, John George

Notable British Trials, ed. Lord Dunboyne. Hodge, London, 1953.

John George Haigh: Acid Bath Killer, Gerald Byrne. Headline Publications, London, [1950].

The Reluctant Cop, Gerald Fairlie. Hodder and Stoughton, London, 1958.

John George Haigh, Stanley Jackson. Odhams (Famous Criminal Trials), London, 1953.

Haigh: The Mind of a Murderer, Arthur La Bern. W.H. Allen, London, 1973.

Forty Years of Murder, Professor Keith Simpson. Harrap, London, 1978.

HAYES, Catherine.

More Famous Trials, Earl of Birkenhead. Hutchinson, London, 1928.

The Newgate Calendar; or, Malefactors Register. J. Wenman, London, 1776.

HOSEIN, Arthur and Nizamodeen

Shall We Ever Know?, William Cooper. Hutchinson, London, 1971.

The Murder of Muriel McKay, Norman Lucas. London, 1971.

Have You Seen This Woman?, M. O'Flaherty. Corgi Books, London, 1971.

HUME, Brian Donald

Inside the CID, Peter Beveridge. Evans Bros., London, 1957.

The Sound of Murder, Percy Hoskins. Long, London, 1973.

Francis Camps, Robert Jackson. Hart-Davis McGibbon, London, 1975.

A Train of Powder, Rebecca West. Macmillan, London, 1955.

Hume: Portrait of a Double Murderer, John Williams. Heinemann, London, 1960.

KISS, Bela
The World's Most Infamous Murders, Roger Boar and Nigel Blundell. Octopus, London, 1983.
Unsolved!, Richard Glyn Jones. Xanadu, London, 1987.

LANDRU, Henri Désire
Famous Trials, ed. F. A. Mackenzie. Geoffrey Bles, London, 1928.
The Ladykiller: The Life of Landru, the French Bluebeard, Dennis Bardens. Peter Davies, London, 1972.
Landru, H. Russell Wakefield. Duckworth, London, 1936.

MAHON, Patrick
Famous Trials: Patrick Mahon, ed. George Dilnot. Geoffrey Bles, London, [1928].
Bernard Spilsbury: His Life and Cases, Douglas G. Browne and E. V. Tullett. Harrap, London, 1951.
Death Under the Microscope, Harold Dearden. Hutchinson, London, 1934.
Savage of Scotland Yard, Percy Savage. Hutchinson, London, 1934.
Detective Days, Frederick Porter Wensley. Cassell, London, 1931.

NILSEN, Dennis Andrew
The Nilsen File, Brian McConnell and Douglas Bence. Futura, London, 1983.
Killing For Company, Brian Masters. Jonathan Cape, London, 1985.

PETIOT, Dr Marcel
Doctors of Murder, Simon Dewes. Long, London, 1962.
The Great Liquidator, John V. Grombach. Garden City, New York, 1980.
The Unspeakable Crimes of Dr Petiot, Thomas Maeder. Little-Brown, Boston, 1980.

Petiot, Ronald Seth. Hutchinson, London, 1963.

ROUSE, Alfred Arthur

Notable British Trials, ed. Helena Normanton. Hodge, London, 1931.

New Light on the Rouse Case, J. C. Cannell. Long, London, 1932.

RUXTON, Dr Buck

Notable British Trials, eds R. H. Blundell and G. H. Wilson. Hodge, London, 1937.

Medico-Legal Aspects of the Ruxton Case, John Glaister and James Brash. E. & S. Livingstone, Edinburgh, 1937.

SHARK-ARM CASE

The Shark-Arm Case, Vince Kelly. Angus and Robertson, Sydney, 1963.

Mostly Murder, Sir Sydney Smith. Harrap, London, 1959.

TETZNER, Kurt Erich

Dead Men Tell Tales, Jurgen Thorwald. Thames and Hudson, London, 1966.

VOIRBO, Pierre

My First Crime, Gustave Macé. Hutchinson, London, 1941.

Corpus Delicti, David Whitelaw. Geoffrey Bles, London, 1936.

VOISIN, Louis

Sir Bernard Spilsbury: His Life and Cases, Douglas G. Browne and E. V. Tullett. Harrap, London, 1951.

Detective Days, Frederick Porter Wensley. Cassell, London, 1931.

WEBSTER, John White

Some Famous Medical Trials, Leonard A. Parry. J. & A. Churchill, London, 1927.

The Disappearance of Dr Parkman, Robert Sullivan. Little, Brown, New York, 1971.

General Works on Forensic Medicine

Camps, Francis *The Investigation of Murder* Michael Joseph, London, 1966.

Camps, Francis *Medical and Scientific Investigations in the Christie Case* Medical Publications, London, 1953.

Camps, Francis *Practical Forensic Medicine* Hutchinsons Medical Publications, London, 1956.

Gaute, J. H. H., and Odell, Robin *Murder Whatdunit* Harrap, London, 1982.

Glaister, John *Final Diagnosis* Hutchinson, London, 1964.

Glaister, John *The Power of Poison* Christopher Johnson, London, 1954.

Glaister, John *A Study of Hairs* University of Egypt, Cairo, 1931.

Gresham, G. Austin *Forensic Pathology: A Colour Atlas* London, 1975.

Jackson, Robert *Francis Camps* Hart-Davis Mac-Gibbon, London, 1975.

Knight, Bernard *Forensic Medicine* Gower Medical, London, 1985.

Lucas, Alfred *Forensic Chemistry* Edward Arnold, London, 1945.

Lucas, Alfred *Legal Chemistry* Edward Arnold, London, 1920.

Norwood East, Sir William *Medical Aspects of Crime* J. & A. Churchill, London, 1936.

Picton, Bernard (Bernard Knight) *Murder, Accident or Suicide* Hale, London, 1971.

Simpson, Keith *Forensic Medicine* Edward Arnold, London, 1964.

Simpson, Keith *Forty Years of Murder* Harrap, London, 1978.

Simpson, Keith *Police: The Investigation of Violence* Macdonald and Evans, 1978.

Smith, Sir Sydney *Mostly Murder* Harrap, London, 1959.

Smyth, Frank *Cause of Death* Orbis, London, 1980.

Stockdale, R. E. (ed.) *Science Against Crime* Marshall Cavendish, London, 1982.

Willcox, Philip *The Detective Physician* Heinemann Medical, London, 1970.

Index

Names of murderers appear in italics